POPULAR PUBLICATIONS — FACSIMILE EDITIONS

Dime Detective Magazine #11 (September 1932)

Dime Detective magazine was the flagship detective pulp in the Popular Publications stable, running for almost 300 issues over twenty years. The September 1932 issue contains stories by T.T. Flynn, Frederick Nebel, Westmoreland Gray, J. Paul Suter, and Paul Ellsworth Triem, and includes installments in the Cardigan, Horatio Humberton, and Collin Windsor series.

Authors:

T.T. Flynn, Frederick Nebel, Westmoreland Gray, J. Paul Suter, Paul Ellsworth Triem

Illustrators:

William Reusswig, John Fleming Gould

EVERY STORY COMPLETE   EVERY STORY NEW

Vol. 3   CONTENTS for SEPTEMBER, 1932   No. 3

Watch for the October Issue   On the Newsstands September 20th

---

Published every month by Popular Publications, Inc., 2256 Grove Street, Chicago Illinois. Editorial and executive offices 205 East Forty-second Street, New York City. Harry Steeger, President and Secretary. Harold S. Goldsmith, Vice President and Treasurer. Entered as second class matter Feb. 26, 1932, at the Post Office at Chicago, Ill., under the Act of March 3, 1879. Title registration pending at U. S. Patent Office. Copyrited 1932 by Popular Publications, Inc. Single copy price 10c. Yearly subscriptions in U. S. A. $1.00. For advertising rates address Sam J. Perry, 205 E. 42nd St., New York, N. Y. When submitting manuscripts, kindly enclose sufficient postage for their return if found unavailable. The publishers cannot accept responsibility for return of unsolicited manuscripts, although all care will be exercised in handling them.

Yes Sir! We absolutely GUARANTEE to REDUCE your WAIST 3 INCHES in 10 DAYS
... or it won't cost you a penny!

YOU will appear much slimmer at once, and in 10 short days your waistline will actually be 3 inches smaller—three inches of fat gone—or it won't cost you one cent.

For 12 years the Weil Belt has been accepted as ideal for reducing by men in all walks of life...from business men and office workers who find that it removes cumbersome fat with every movement...to active outdoor men who like the feeling of protection it gives.

IT IS THE MASSAGE-LIKE ACTION THAT DOES IT!

Now there is an easy way to reduce without exercise, diet or drugs. The Weil Health Belt exerts a massage-like action that removes fat with every move you make.

> NO Drugs
> NO Diets
> NO Exercises

It supports the sagging muscles of the abdomen and quickly gives you an erect, athletic carriage. Many enthusiastic wearers write that it not only reduces fat but it also supports the abdominal walls and keeps the digestive organs in place—that they are no longer fatigued—and that it greatly increases their endurance. You will be more than delighted with the great improvement in your appearance.

DON'T WAIT—FAT IS DANGEROUS!

Fat is not only unbecoming, but it also endangers your health. Insurance companies know the danger of fat accummulations. The best medical authorities warn against obesity, so don't wait any longer.

You Can't Lose—Either you take off 3 inches of fat in 10 days or it won't cost one penny! Even the postage you pay to return the package will be refunded!

Send TO-DAY for details of TEN DAY TRIAL OFFER

THE WEIL COMPANY, 1029 HILL STREET, NEW HAVEN, CONN.

Gentlemen: Send me FREE, your illustrated folder describing The Weil Belt and full details of your 10 day FREE trial offer.

Name_____ Address_____

City_____ State_____

3

Give me your measure and I'll **PROVE** You Can Have a Body like Mine !

I'LL give you PROOF in 7 DAYS that I can turn you, too, into a man of might and muscle. Let me prove that I can put layers of smooth, supple, powerful muscles all over your body.

If you are underweight I'll add the pounds where they are needed and, if you are fat in any spots, I'll show you how to pare down to fighting trim.

And with the big muscles and powerful, evenly-developed body that my method so quickly gives you, I'll also give you through-and-through health—health that digs down into your system and banishes such things as constipation, pimples, skin blotches and the hundred-and-one like conditions that rob you of the good times and the good things of life.

Here's All You Do!

Just jot down your name and address on the coupon below, mail it to me—and I'll send you, absolutely free, a copy of my new book, "Everlasting Health and Strength." It reveals the secrets that changed me from a 97-pound, flat-chested weakling into a husky fellow who won the title of "The World's Most Perfectly Developed Man" against all comers! And it shows how I can build you into an "Atlas Champion" the same easy way.

I haven't any use for apparatus; I don't dose you or doctor you. Dynamic-Tension is all I need. It's the natural, tested method for developing real men inside and out. It distributes added pounds of powerful muscles over your body, gets rid of surplus fat, and gives you the vitality, strength and pep that win you the admiration of every woman and the respect of any man.

> **NOTE: No other Physical Instructor in the World has ever DARED make such an offer!**
>
> *Charles Atlas*
>
> *Holder of the title:*
> *"The World's Most Perfectly Developed Man"—won in international contest against ALL strong men willing to compete with him.*

Charles Atlas As He Is Today.

Gamble a 2c Stamp—To Prove I Can Make YOU a New Man!

Gamble a 2c stamp today by mailing the coupon for a free copy of my book, "Everlasting Health and Strength." It tells you all about my special Dynamic-Tension method, and what it has done to make big-muscled men out of run-down specimens. It shows you, from actual photos, how I have developed my pupils to the same perfectly balanced proportions of my own physique, by my own secret methods. What my system did for me, and these hundred of others it can do for you too. Don't keep on being only 25 or 50 percent of the man you can be! Find out what I can do for you.

Where shall I send your copy of "Everlasting Health and Strength"? Jot your name and address down on the coupon, and mail it today, CHARLES ATLAS, Dept. 83-Y, 133 East 23rd Street, New York City.

THE RED VENOM

by
T. T. Flynn

Author of "Dead Man's Lottery," etc.

From Old Ghost Swamp fanged horrors had come to Bill Hyde, hideous tokens tipped with the deadly venom of the moccasin. And now, as the sullen rumble of the murder drums rolls out, he meets their challenge—fights to learn the dread secret held in the coils of the cottonmouth.

Its great coils flew through the
air, writhing and twisting.

CHAPTER ONE

The Golden Circlet

PROFESSOR AMOS HYDE leaned forward in the bed, his bright old eyes shining excitedly from under craggy eyebrows.

"Come in, my boy!" he called. "Demmit, I'm glad you're here! Been watching for you all afternoon. I even had Pinkney call New York on long distance, but they said you had taken the train already. You young rascal, you would have a fling at the bright lights the first thing. Ouch —oh, demmit! I'll strangle that fool doctor if he doesn't do something for this sciatica!"

There are professors—and professors. Some of them spend their lives in books and musty classrooms, despairing with restless students, examination papers, routine lectures. And excellent lives many of them turn out to be. On the other hand there are professors like Amos Hyde.

At seventy Amos Hyde was tall, rugged as a wind-gnarled forest oak. His face was seamed, lined, tanned to the texture of old leather by hot suns and scourging winds. For forty-odd years of a busy life he had poked into far and near corners of the world, seeking the secrets of the past. He had tramped the cordilleras of South America, burrowed in the deserts of the West. North Africa, inner China, Tibet, Alaska, and the depths of the sea had given their secrets to his sharp scrutiny. Now back in Washington, he was directing the great institution with which he had been connected all these years.

Bill Hyde grinned as he towered by the bed, and engulfed his uncle's lean hand in a big brown paw. He was an inch taller than the old professor had ever been, and fully as broad. There was a string of degrees after his name twice as long as any young man of thirty-one had a right to possess. And already his face had the same leather texture as the old man's; his hands were calloused, his body lean, hard. He had just now returned from a summer of toil among the pueblo ruins of the New Mexican desert.

"No bright lights for me," Bill chuckled. "You set all-time records for that sort of thing thirty-five years ago when you came back from the north Australian expedition. Old Sam Blount was speaking of it this summer. I'll swear there was still awe in his voice. He said you threw five bartenders out their own doors, and chased—"

"Demmit! Let the past be!" Professor Amos snorted. "Sam Blount's in his dotage! Doesn't know what he's saying any more! It was only two bartenders. And anyway what do you mean by raking up scandal on an old man's good name? Pinkney, close that door!"

Bill sat down on the edge of the bed and watched Pinkney slip mouselike to the door and close it. His sun-bleached eyebrows raised inquiringly, for Pinkney was pale, slender, delicate and shadowy— almost ethereal.

"Pinkney came highly recommended," said Professor Amos drily. "Harvard and Oxford, *cum laude ad valorem ad nauseam*. He's been cataloguing specimens at the museum this summer, and when this demmed sciatica drove me into bed I had him transferred over here to handle my paper work and look after me. He's a very good secretary; aren't you, Pinkney, my boy?"

Pinkney blinked owlishly behind shell-rimmed nose glasses, said solemnly: "I trust my efforts are satisfactory, professor."

"Eminently so," Professor Amos mimicked gravely. "Now then, Pinkney, where's that demmed letter?"

PINKNEY turned to a table against the wall, picked several sheets of paper and brought them to the bed.

"He always knows where everything is," Professor Amos complained, snatching them. "I'd have looked an hour, and found 'em in my own pocket. Here, read this."

> Magnolia Plantation,
> Near Charleston,
> South Carolina.

The Smithfield Institution,
Washington, D. C.
Gentlemen:

I am writing to apprise you of an interesting discovery that has been made on the plantation I have recently bought. Part of my holdings includes the major portion of Old Ghost Swamp, a large and worthless tract of swampland. With prospects for cotton growing thin, I sent two of my niggers scouting the swamp for cypress timber. One of them came back with a wild tale about dead men's bones and gold, guarded by ghosts. He claimed that when they started picking gold out of the bones a ghost screamed at him and his companion, and came flying through the underbrush. They ran and got separated. The other man never did come back. I took a gun and some of my men and went into the swamp, disregarding their advice to stay at home.

We found the place, a large hummock of dry land, containing large mounds that look artificial to me. A recent hurricane had blown down a big gum tree which struck the edge of one of the mounds and caused its collapse, uncovering bones and ornaments of gold. We found our man dead nearby. He died of snake bite, if I know the symptoms. I could not keep my niggers near the place after they found the dead body. Two of them finally offered to stay that day and clear one of the mounds. They didn't return.

Next morning we went out to see what was the matter. The tools were lying by the brush they had cut down, and that was all we could find. Now I can't get a nigger to go within a mile of the place. After thinking the matter over I have decided that this is case for your institution. I could drive my niggers in there and stand over them with a gun, but we would probably ruin evidence that must be of great interest to archaeologists, and of greater value to me. If you will send a man down here I will go into the matter more fully with him. I am sending you a piece of gold I brought out.

Very truly yours,
Martin Jasper.

Bill looked up. "Sounds like a fairy story," he grinned. "We know there aren't any mounds in that part of the country containing gold."

"We thought we knew," Professor Amos corrected. "Pinkney, hand me that arm band."

Pinkney brought a small cigar box from a drawer in the table. Professor Amos opened it eagerly, took out an arm band full two inches wide. Hieroglyphics were stamped in the metal. It had been bent, rebent; was battered, worn. At one time it had been a complete circlet. A knife had hacked through the soft metal, allowing it to be spread out and removed. Despite the ravages of time and wear, the unknown centuries it had lain underground, the virgin gold gleamed yellow, alive.

Bill whistled softly as he turned it be-

tween his fingers. "Gold, all right," he agreed.

"Gold?" Professor Amos snorted. "Certainly it's gold! But that's not all. D'you get what this means?"

Bill frowned thoughtfully. "Aren't these Aztec hieroglyphics?"

"Undoubtedly," Professor Amos agreed. "Pinkney, here, has made some study of Aztec and Toltec civilizations. He thinks the same thing."

"Never heard of any Axtecs that far north or east," Bill muttered.

"That's the beautiful thing about it!" Professor Amos said feverishly. "We've got a discovery here that may rock the whole scientific world. And I'm laid up with sciatica and can't go down and look into it! Ouch! Demmit! I'll make that doctor miserable when he comes. That's why I've been trying to get hold of you. The field force is all out. You'll have to go I had Pinkney wire Jasper yesterday that you'll leave tomorrow."

"I've made arrangements to run up into Newfoundland for a little salmon fishing next week."

"Dem your salmon fishing!" old Amos snorted. "Since when has a salmon been as important as anything like this? You'll pack your bag and get to the bottom of this. Pinkney will go as your assistant. He's the only man we've got in town who knows anything about Aztec civilization."

An alarmed expression came over Pinkney's thin face. "Er—perhaps I'd better stay here, professor," he suggested weakly. "I have a slight touch of cold. Swamp work will be very bad for it. And my family has always been subject to malaria."

"Flapadoodle!" said Professor Amos testily. "The swamp air will do your cold good. If you catch malaria it's your own fault. Bill, your field outfit is at the station, I suppose. You can buy supplies down there."

"All right," Bill sighed. "We'll beard the ghost in the swamp, eh, Pinkney?"

"Ghosts!" said Pinkney hollowly. "My goodness!"

WHEN the telephone rang outside in the hall two hours later, Bill started to get up from the bed and answer it. His uncle waved him down.

"Pinkney'll take it," he said tersely. "That's what he's here for. Go on and tell me how the three rings in the timbers of the north kiva matched up with your index."

So Bill went on talking until the door opened and Pinkney's pale puzzled face looked in.

"What is it?" the professor barked.

Pinkney said apologetically: "The call seemed to be for Mr. William, sir. A man asked if he lived here. When I said that he did, he asked me if Mr. Hyde were here tonight. I told him Mr. Hyde arrived about two hours ago, and he hung up without asking anything more."

"Did you get who it was?" Bill questioned.

Pinkney blinked behind his nose glasses. "I'm sorry," he confessed. "That really didn't occur to me until it was too late."

"Nothing ever occurs to Pinkney," said Professor Amos ironically. "It was probably someone from the papers wanting a story."

Bill frowned as he rolled a cigarette slowly between his palms and lighted it. "Newspapers couldn't know I'm here. Didn't tell anyone in New York I was barging off. Haven't seen anyone since I arrived. A newspaper man wouldn't have hung up, anyway. He'd have called me to the telephone and started asking questions."

"Something in that," Professor Amos admitted. "Well, then it might have been a subpoena server, or a bill collector."

"I don't owe any bills, and I haven't done anything to be subpoenaed for," said Bill, still frowning.

"Forget it," his uncle advised.

"I'm curious. Sounds as though someone were trying to check up on me."

"Some girl probably wanted to find out if you were back so she could send you an invitation."

"Rats!" said Bill.

Pinkney withdrew and the matter was dropped. Bill had been talking for two hours. A few moments later he looked at his wrist watch and got up. "Bedtime," he said cheerfully. "I'll see you in the morning."

"And take the morning train," reminded Professor Hyde.

"And take the morning train," Bill agreed. "I suppose I sleep in my old room tonight?"

Professor Amos shook his head apologetically. "I forgot to tell you. Doctor Donaldson, an old friend of mine, is here in town for several weeks, doing research work. I let him occupy your room. You'll have to take the end guest room tonight. Your things are all in the trunk and dresser as you left them. You can get to them now. Donaldson doesn't come in until late."

The house was a sprawling old colonial mansion, set in a two-acre tract of land out near Chevy Chase, in Washington, D. C. Bill's bedroom was in the north wing, on the ground floor. The guest rooms were in the same wing. He met Pinkney in the hall as he went toward it, asked the serious young man in.

"Got a gun?" Bill asked conversationally as he unlocked his trunk.

Pinkney gulped. "Gun? Why, no. I've never held a gun in my hand. I don't approve of them. They're—they're dangerous."

"Mighty handy sometimes," Bill grinned.

Pinkney blinked uneasily as he lingered

inside the doorway. "I don't approve of them," he repeated sternly.

"Might be a good idea to have one this trip," Bill chuckled.

"I don't think I shall need one," Pinkney said firmly.

"Haven't forgotten the ghosts, have you?"

"That is a hoax," Pinkney insisted. "I'm sure you don't believe it. Science has proved beyond doubt that there are no such things as ghosts."

"I've seen 'em," said Bill gravely, tossing a stack of shirts onto the bed.

"You're joking," Pinkney said uneasily.

"Never more serious in my life," Bill said solemnly. "As a matter of fact, science doesn't know anything about ghosts, Pinkney. They're nothing you can classify and catalogue. Can't break them down into their component parts, or get a line on them by a series of skeletons. Ghosts there are, and ghosts there always will be. And it looks as though we're going to tangle with them this trip."

PINKNEY drew a deep breath. "It is my duty to stay here with Professor Hyde," he said bravely. "He has quite a bit of work to do, and—"

Bill waved aside the objection, speared Pinkney with a severe glance. "Not a chance of it. Amos has got his teeth into something that interests him. He'll make any sacrifice to have it investigated at once. If you have your career at heart, Pinkney, my boy, I'd advise you to pack tonight and get ready to trot in the morning."

Pinkney sighed. "I suppose so," he agreed morosely. And then suddenly Pinkney's eyes went wide and his mouth dropped. He raised a shaking hand and pointed at the window. "Th-there!" he stuttered. "L-look!"

Bill whirled to the window, saw nothing. Pinkney stammered out in a shaking voice: "There was a f-face there at the window! A h-horrible looking thing, staring in at us!" Pinkney's face was chalk-white. His eyes were staring fixedly. It was plain that something had shocked him into a state of absolute terror.

Bill sprang to the window. The curtain was up; there was no screen outside. And nothing was visible out there.

"It disappeared when I pointed!" Pinkney bleated.

The window was unlocked. Bill shoved it up, leaned out. The night was moonless, dark. The few stars overhead diffused little light. He listened, heard no sound.

"Sure you didn't imagine it?" he asked over his shoulder.

"I saw it!" Pinkney insisted excitedly. "It was big and white, with a bristly short beard and—and big staring eyes. It looked like—like a dead man's face!"

"Like a ghost," Bill supplied.

Pinkney nodded tremulously. "Like a ghost," he agreed in an awed whisper.

Pinkney was an excitable, easily overwrought type. It was more than possible his imagination had conjured up some grisly picture beyond the glass. Perhaps a turning headlight in the street over beyond the hedge had thrown a curious shadow against the pane.

"I s-saw it!" Pinkney quavered insistently after a moment.

Bill's gun was in his field kit at the express office. He had no weapon handy. Disregarding that fact he climbed out the window, walked swiftly to the back of the house.

Nothing there. He continued on around the house, zigzagging to the various clumps of shrubbery nearby; went all around the house, and found nothing. As he popped head and shoulders in the window again Pinkney flinched.

"It's all right," Bill said, climbing

back in. "Nothing out there. I looked all over the grounds."

Pinkney mopped his forehead with a silk handkerchief, polished his glasses nervously, fitted them on his nose with fingers still shaking slightly. "I'm sure I saw something," he insisted weakly.

"It was your imagination," Bill assured him as he closed the window.

"Perhaps, Pinkney agreed, dubiously. "I know I shall dream of it tonight." He shuddered visibly, slipped out of the room shaking his head.

Bill collected what articles he needed, pulled down the shade, turned out the light and left the room. In his own room he repacked his two kitbags, slipped into pajamas, into bed; was soon asleep.

CHAPTER TWO

"Snakes Is Pizen"

BILL never knew what brought him sharply awake. He found himself sitting bolt upright in bed, every nerve tense as he peered about in the darkness.

The house was still, quiet. No reason for it, yet the feel of near danger gripped him. So vivid, insistent was that feeling that Bill did not thrust it aside. In the back of his mind was dim recollection of a wild cry of fright which had reached his ears just as he awakened.

The other guest room was next to his. An uneasy stirring sounded in there. Feet shuffled hurriedly to the locked connecting door. Knuckles rapped. Pinkney's agitated voice called: "Mr. Hyde! Are you awake?"

"Yes," said Bill, throwing back the covers and sliding his feet into slippers.

"Did you hear that scream?" Pinkney quavered nervously.

"Something woke me up."

"I was awake! I heard it. It was terrible! A ghastly scream, and then a groan."

"Where?"

"In Doctor Donaldson's room on the other side of mine. Something terrible must have happened!"

"I'll meet you out in the hall," said Bill. But Pinkney did not open his door until Bill stopped outside of it.

"What do you think it was?" Pinkney gasped.

From the front hall an explosive, "Ouch! Demmit! I'll have that doctor's scalp! I'll take the hide off him!" marked the approach of Professor Amos and his sciatica. The professor hobbled into the wing hall, groaning, swearing at the twinges of pain. "What's the matter down here?" he called at sight of Bill.

"Just going to look into Donaldson's room," said Bill. "Something wrong in there."

He stepped to the doctor's door, found it unlocked, pushed it in. The room was dark. The ceiling light flashed on as his fingers found the switch. Bill swore under his breath. For grim tragedy met him with all the force of a physical blow.

The covers of the bed against the wall had been dragged to the floor in a twisted heap. Face down near the door, which he had evidently been trying to reach, lay a crumpled, contorted figure.

One look at the grizzled gray head made plain that this was Doctor Donaldson. The man did not move as Bill dropped to a knee beside him. The arm Bill lifted was flaccid, limp; no pulse stirred in the wrist. Bill turned him over, felt for the heart. Donaldson was dead!

The face confirmed it. Doctor Donaldson had died in horrible fear and agony. It was stamped plain on his set, contorted face. The eyes were wide, bulging. The teeth were clamped tightly on the lower lip, as if pain unbearable had racked the body after that first loud cry.

"What is it?" Professor Amos rasped in the doorway.

"He's dead," said Bill harshly, standing up.

"Good heavens! Dead? What killed him? What happened in here anyway?"

"God knows," said Bill, shaking his head. "The window's open. Something must have entered the room."

"He always sleeps with his window open."

"All the easier for someone to enter."

And as Bill went hurriedly to the window he remembered what had happened earlier in the evening. That face at the window! And he suddenly believed that Pinkney had really seen something.

His uncle was carrying a revolver in one hand, flashlight in the other.

"Give me that gun and light!" Bill ordered.

HE SLID through the window again, flashing the light about the lawn. The street was lighted wanly beyond the hedge. The neighborhood was silent. A dog barked in the distance; an automobile horn sounded faintly still further away. But here at this spot of death there was silence—sinister silence.

With the flashlight Bill searched every corner of the yard, found it and the outbuildings empty of any alien presence. Back at the open window he examined the ground beneath. Grass grew clear up to the foundation. It held no footprints, no trace of any intruder. Some of the grass blades seemed bent down, but he might have done that himself. He re-entered the room.

Professor Hyde had seated himself in a chair against the wall, was staring sadly at the body. "I told Pinkney to call the police," he said dully. "He was babbling something about seeing a face at this window earlier in the evening."

"Right. He did," Bill agreed curtly. "I thought it was his imagination. Was sure of it after I looked around the yard and found nothing. But he must have been right. A nasty sight too, by the effect it had on him."

"I made a quick examination," Professor Hyde said heavily. "I see no wounds. His heart was perfect. He was telling me several days ago that he had been examined and pronounced fit as a fiddle."

Bill wrinkled his forehead in perplexity, nodded at the bed. "Something happened. Look at those covers. He dragged them off. Didn't even stop to throw them back. Even a sick man would do that."

"But what could have happened?" Professor Hyde burst out in perplexity.

"Something pretty terrible," Bill said soberly. "Something that made him cry out at the top of his voice, and then groan. It woke us all up. What's the matter with that left hand of his? It's red, swollen."

"So it is," said Professor Hyde in surprise. "I hadn't noticed it."

Bill stooped, pulled the sleeve up. The whole arm clear to the shoulder was an angry purple, swollen by congested blood. Bill looked close, pointed to a spot on the biceps muscle. Two little red dots were visible there.

"It looks like a snake bite," Bill exclaimed without thinking.

Pinkney reached the doorway as he said that. "Snake bite?" Pinkney uttered thinly. "That's what happened to those colored men down in the swamp! Don't you remember what the letter said? They saw a ghost, and then they were found dead. As if—as if a snake had bitten them, and tonight I saw something at the window that looked like a ghost. And now he's dead from—from—"

"Nonsense!" said Professor Hyde sharply. "Those other things happened a thousand miles from here. There is no connection."

But Pinkney was not to be denied. "It happened. You can't deny it happened!" he chattered nervously.

PINKNEY was an unhappy young man as the train thundered south. Professor Hyde had insisted they leave as planned. Due to the professor's reputation they had not found it necessary to remain in Washington as witnesses. Excitement had gripped the house for hours after the discovery of Doctor Donaldson's dead body. Detectives from the homicide squad had arrived; a coroner's assistant had followed. There had been many questions, pointed, searching, after Pinkney had burted out his story of the apparition beyond the window.

The scene he described was so grisly, incoherent, unreasonable, that the detectives had frankly been skeptical. Bill's failure to see it, his fruitless search of the yard immediately after, Pinkney's uncertain personality, had influenced them against crediting the story. They had searched the yard and house, examined the window, gone over the room inch by inch, and found nothing.

The coroner's assistant had examined the swollen left arm, minutely investigated the two red dots on the biceps, already fading away. Offhand he had guessed that it might be a spider bite, a snake bite. The symptoms indicated it. The dead man's actions in leaping wildly from the bed, and lapsing into the coma of death before he could reach the doorway, had indicated that. He had felt or seen something that had shocked him into terror. And death had come quickly—in a matter of seconds.

On the other hand there was the fact that no trace of a spider, a snake, or anything else that could have caused death, had been found. It was a complete mystery. Doctor Donaldson had no known enemies. There was no reason why he should have been killed.

But since getting on the train Bill had done a lot of thinking. Certain facts had shaped in his mind. First, that telephone call inquiring for him—a mystery there. Second, that face at the window—another mystery. That room was his. Anyone looking in would have concluded that he was getting ready to spend the night in it. Had Doctor Donaldson been mistaken for him? The wrong man been killed unintentionally?

But who would want to kill him? Why? There was no real proof that Doctor Donaldson had been murdered. The more Bill pondered it, the more inexplicable, mysterious, unreasonable the whole thing seemed. He immersed himself in a book on Toltec and Aztec civilizations. It touched another mystery.

It was well known that the Aztecs flourished principally in the Valley of Mexico, up and down the coastal plain. After Cortez, with the tacit approval and help of part of the Aztecs, had overthrown Montezuma, Spanish civilization had blanketed the old Aztec empire. The Aztecs had never reached the territory where South Carolina now was. It had been a land of vast forests, of Indians; a savage wilderness without wealth and the trappings of more advanced lands.

Yet there was no doubt that the golden arm band which had been sent to Washington was of Aztec origin. What was it doing among dead bones in South Carolina? In the heart of a swamp where ghosts screamed and men died of snake bite—as the old doctor had in Washington?

Bill found the mystery of the thing gripping him, making him keen to find the answer. Pinkney's growing fears only whetted that feeling.

He had wired Martin Jasper from Washington, giving the time of the train's arrival. Now as it came to a jolting stop in the Charleston station and he and Pinkney climbed down beside their baggage, Bill looked around expectantly.

THE other passengers claimed their luggage and departed. The porter looked curiously at them. A redcap stood poised. Finally Bill signed him to take their bags. As they followed, he said to Pinkney: "Seems as if Jasper would have met the train, after the trouble he took to get us down here. He didn't give directions how to get out to his plantation."

Pinkney sniffed lugubriously. "I suggest we take the next train back. The whole matter may be a hoax."

"We'll find him," said Bill. In the waiting room he spoke to their redcap. "Do you know of a place around here called Magnolia Plantation?"

"No suh," the redcap grinned. "Cain't say I evah heerd of it. Maybe Mistuh Simmons ovah at de ticket window know."

But the man at the ticket window shook his head also. "Never heard of it," he said. "Lots of plantations around here. Some of them have names and some don't. The Chamber of Commerce might be able to tell you."

As Bill turned away from the ticket window Pinkney came hurrying over to him, followed by a stranger. "This man asked if I was Professor Hyde," Pinkney said coldly. "I judge he is the one we are looking for."

Bill had only a moment for swift appraisal of the stranger before he was asked in a surly tone, "You the p'fessor from Washington?"

The speaker was short, slight, round-shouldered, with a week's growth of stubble on his face. He wore old overalls and heavy mud-stained shoes. A hitch at his overalls disclosed bare ankles. A slouch hat was pulled down over his forehead. His skin was darkly pigmented. And there was a curious slurring to his words vaguely reminiscent of a foreign tongue. But he looked like a southerner, bore himself like one. In his surly manner there was no welcome.

"I'm Professor Hyde," Bill told him. "Did Jasper send you to meet me?"

The stranger hooked his thumbs under the straps of his overalls, showed tobacco-stained teeth in a mirthless grin. His bleached right eyebrow raised insolently. "How d'you know I ain't Jasper?" he asked with a trace of a sneer.

A thin thread of displeasure creased Bill's forehead. This was a strange welcome. "I spoke without thinking," he said. "Are you Jasper?"

"Naw, I ain't him," the other denied. "I'm his plantation foreman. Ben Keely's my name. He hied me in to meet you." Keely spoke with a soft, slurring southern accent, in the manner of an illiterate. He was an unprepossessing, ill-favored fellow. After volunteering that, he lapsed into sullenness again.

"I'm glad you showed up," Bill told him. "I was wondering how we were going to find the place. That redcap has our bags."

Keely drew a dirty box of snuff from the pocket of his coat and fingered some back of his lip. He spat on the floor, replaced the box, scowled. "I guess he can put 'em back on the train," he grunted. "Jasper sent me in to tell you he can't be bothered with you-all now. He wants you to go back."

Bill heard that statement with amazement. "What's the matter?" he asked.

Keely shrugged. "He took sick. Got him a fever that might' nigh killed him. It took all the starch out of him. He ain't up to botherin' with strange folks now."

"Is he at the plantation?" Bill asked in perplexity.

"Yep."

"I'll go out and have a talk with him," Bill decided.

"Naw, you don't," Keely said sullenly.

"He give me my orders an' I ain't the man to go back on 'em."

"We won't be any trouble," Bill said sharply.

"That ain't got nothin' to do with hit."

"Sad, but true!" Bill snapped. "I'm sorry to hear Jasper has been sick. But we've made the effort to come down here in answer to his letter, and I'll be damned if I'm going to turn around and go back without talking to him. Let's get started."

"Nope," Keely refused in a surly growl.

"Maybe he is right," Pinkney put in nervously. "We can get a train back without trouble."

"We'll take no train until I've looked into this," Bill said curtly. "If this man won't take us out to the plantation, I'll hire someone else to do it."

KEELY shuffled his feet, scowled, spat on the floor again. He shrugged. And suddenly his manner changed. A fawning smile broke through his scowl. He became friendly. "I reckon if that's the way you feel about it, you better go out an' have a talk with the boss," he said agreeably. "I'll take you in my boat. I left her down at the water front."

"Can't you get to your place by road?" Bill queried.

"No," said Keely promptly. "Leastwise, not on any kind of a road you'd want to travel now. She's kinda off the track, up there by Old Ghost Swamp."

Pinkney coughed, adjusted his nose glasses, looked at the plantation foreman almost pleadingly. "I say," he said, "there isn't any truth in all the tales you hear about that—er—place, is there?"

Keely eyed him from unblinking, half-lidded eyes. The smile came back on his grimy face. "That depends on what you've heard," he said. And slowly one lid drooped in an unfathomable wink.

"I mean," explained Pinkney uncom-

fortably, "these stories about ghosts and snakes and all that."

Bill chuckled, good-humored again. "Forget about 'em till you run up against 'em," he broke in. "I think I'll check our bags here until we know more about our plans."

Keely turned to him quickly. "You better bring 'em along," he suggested. "Like as not you'll stay, once you get out there."

Bill looked at the man sharply. It seemed to him there was an undercurrent of meaning in the words—biting, sarcastic, almost threatening—an undercurrent he did not like. But Keely met his gaze blandly, innocently. Bill noticed that his eyes rarely ever blinked.

"All right," Bill decided. "We'll take them along."

Keely stood by while they got their bags; and as Pinkney reached him again, walking toward the entrance, Keely gave him another slow wink. "About that question of yours," he drawled. "Ghosts is where you find 'em. And snakes is pizen."

CHAPTER THREE

Old Ghost Swamp

A TAXI took them to the water front. As they rolled through Charleston streets Bill wondered about the reception they had received.

The lack of welcome was puzzling, in view of the efforts this unknown Martin Jasper had made to get them down here. Queer he had not wired that he was sick, asked them to postpone the trip. He could have reached them on the train with a telegram. He wondered too at the quick change of attitude on the part of their guide. Was Keely afraid of his employer's displeasure?

A rickety landing stage ran out into the water at the point where the taxi brought them. They got out. Bill paid the driver.

Keely pointed with a soiled left hand. Bill was to remember that hand in a few minutes. He saw it clearly now.

"That 'un out at the end," Keely directed. He made no effort to help carry the bags out there. Shuffled after them with his grimy hands in his pockets. Stood by in silence while they got down in the boat.

It was a metal skiff propelled by an outboard motor. Keely untied the mooring line, stepped into the boat, started the motor. They *put-putted* away from the landing.

Pinkney plucked at Bill's coat sleeve some minutes later. Leaned over close. His thin face was worried. "Did you see that ring on his finger?" Pinkney husked.

"No."

"It is a snake!" Pinkney hissed. "A gold snake!"

The full implication of Pinkney's statement struck Bill at once. Every turn in this amazing series of events was marked by reference to a snake. It had been too frequent, too pertinent to disregard. He turned quickly on the seat.

Keely was sitting behind them in a half slouch, his right hand on the tiller. But he was steering by instinct. His eyes were glaring at their backs. Bill got a quick glimpse of the unshaven face before it changed. And there was such utter malignancy, such blazing hatred on the man's face, that Bill could not believe at first he had read it right.

That vanished as he looked. Keely's lips curled back over his tobacco-stained teeth in a sneering smile. His sullenness was gone. But he was crouched there like a poised reptile—like a snake!

On the third finger of Keely's left hand was the ring. It was gold, shaped like the body of a snake, coiling three or four times around Keely's finger, with a fat, wide, malignant head resting almost on the middle finger joint.

Bill had seen that hand clearly at the dock. The ring had not been there then. Keely had slipped it on since.

Keely saw the direction of his glance. He shoved his hand in his pocket. Bill swung clear around on the seat.

"Queer ring you're wearing," he commented casually.

"Lots of things is queer," Keely grunted.

"Where did you get it?"

"Found it."

"Let me see it."

Keely shook his head in surly refusal. "I ain't showin' my things 'round."

"Where did you find it?" Bill persisted.

"Out in the swamp."

That could be possible. There were gold ornaments in the swamp. Martin Jasper had said nothing about his foreman in the letter. It was possible the fellow had gone out in the swamp, found the ring, secreted it, did not want his employer to know about it.

But Keely's sudden change of attitude was startling. Puzzling because of his quick friendliness in the station. That had been a mask over his real feelings. It shouldn't matter one way or the other to him what they did. Bill eyed him thoughtfully.

"How long will it take us to get there?" he asked.

Keely shrugged. " 'Bout three hours." He was good-natured again, amiable. If Bill hadn't caught his face off guard, he might have believed the man's manner now.

"That's a long trip," Bill said.

"We got a ways to go."

"You've got a good boat."

"Have to have," Keely answered briefly. And did not amplify the remark.

IT WAS late afternoon now. The sun was already dropping toward the horizon. Bill eyed it speculatively. Dark was not far off. No matter what reception they received, they would have to stay all night. He turned his back to Keely again, resolved to ask a few questions about the man when he met his employer.

Charleston was dropping back. The toll bridge and Drum Island lay behind. They plowed on up Cooper River. Tall buildings, smoke stacks, the rush and bustle of city environs faded away. The boat held well out from shore, angling gradually off into the wide expanse of water that stretched before them. Keely said nothing more. Pinkney crouched disconsolately on the hard seat. Bill sat thoughtfully.

An hour passed. Then another hour. The sun set. Dusk began to close down about them as the boat abruptly left the open water, rushing through banks of reeds and canebrakes into a still, winding stream of black water that came without perceptible current out of a wilderness of vegetation.

In the space of minutes they were surrounded by towering cypress trees, live oaks, gums, leafy thickets, heavy underbrush. Long streamers of gray moss hung in thick motionless veils from branches stretching over the water like gaunt reaching arms. The world was suddenly far removed. The still loneliness, broken only by the fast *put-put-put* of the motor, seemed to close down about them like a darkening curtain. Bill caught himself feeling that anything might be possible in here.

The motor's speed slackened. They swung into a narrower branch of the bayou-like creek; into a wilderness of water, of shallow mud banks, of gaunt cypress trees rising black and threatening out of inky water. Now and then they had to duck as branches brushed close. The boat seemed to wind and wriggle into the fastness which looked impregnable at first glance.

This was a queer way to approach a plantation of any kind. Bill swung around to Keely. "This the way you get to the plantation?" he demanded.

Keely nodded. "Got to get there, ain't we?"

Now and then the bottom scraped over shallow mud. They went more slowly. A great loglike form ahead of them came to life and torpedoed off into the dusk, thrashing water madly with a long scaly tail—a huge 'gator. A dozen times sinuous cottonmouth moccasins slipped from mud banks or rotting snags and slithered out of sight. The number of snakes was amazing; they seemed everywhere. The cypress trees grew larger, the wilderness more tangled and lonely as they progressed.

Bill shot a quick look at Keely again, surprised a grin on his face. And sudden conviction gripped him that all was not right. "You're not taking us to the plantation!" he charged angrily.

Keely laughed. "Just you sit tight," he advised.

"Stop the boat!"

"I'm handlin' it," Keely retorted venomously. And as he spoke his hand slipped inside his overalls, came out with a revolver.

Pinkney had turned to watch. A gasp came from him at sight of the gun. Bill leaned forward slightly, his eyes narrowing. "What's the idea?" he asked sharply.

Keely did not answer. He steered with one hand, held the gun with the other. All pretense was gone from his manner now. His crouch seemed threatening, vindictive. And suddenly Bill knew he'd have to act quickly, before it was too late.

"Get down quick when I move!" he said through motionless lips to Pinkney. And a moment later Bill waved his arm off at the rear and shouted: "Tell Martin Jasper!"

It was a hoary old ruse. But the man at the tiller fell for it. He flashed a look around to see who Bill was calling to. And as he did that Bill dove toward the stern.

KEELY realized in an instant that he had been tricked. The rock of the boat jerked him back. He shot at first sight of Bill coming toward him. But he shot quickly, hastily. Bill felt a hot slash across his left arm—and then he was on the man.

He knocked the gun arm aside, clamped both hands on the wrist as the weight of his body knocked Keely back over the motor. For all his ill-favored vindictiveness, Keely was not a large man, not a strong one. He screamed suddenly as his wrist bent back. The gun flew from his pain-racked fingers, splashed out of sight in the black water alongside.

The boat yawed crazily, swung off its course, threatened to tip over as Keely writhed on top of the hot motor, beating Bill's face with his free fist. He straightened up with an effort. Bill knocked him back again with a chopping blow to the face.

Keely screamed a slurring oath at him, barely understandable. And Bill almost let him go in amazement at hearing it. For Keely had sworn at him in the bastard French of Haiti, used the argot of the black republic as if it was his mother tongue.

Keely was fighting in a frenzy, scratching, clawing, kicking. Panting oaths dribbled from his lips—Haitian French, all of them. Bill had spent months on the island and recognized them all.

All that took place in the space of moments. The boat tipped, lurched from the swift surges of their weight, swung here and there as they knocked the rudder back and forth.

"Look out!" Pinkney cried in alarm.

The next instant they struck a clump of cypress knees a hard glancing blow. The bow reared over a root and the craft tipped. All three of them were flung out into the water. The boat turned over, slithered past. Its engine died with a few last convulsive *pops*.

Bill went down deep, releasing his hold on Keely as the water closed over him. His feet and hands struck deep oozy swamp mud. He oriented himself, shot to the surface, found that the water came just to his shoulders.

The stern of the skiff was going under the surface twenty feet beyond. Pinkney broke water nearby, gave a strangled, choking cry and went down again, arms thrashing wildly. Evidently he could not swim. And water that came to Bill's neck was over Pinkney's head. Bill forgot everything else as he reached the spot with several powerful strokes.

Pinkney came up again, coughing, choking. Bill caught him, held his head above water. Pinkney fought him a moment, then realized Bill was supporting him and turned his efforts to coughing the water out of his lungs. That took a full moment.

Then in a rapidly closing darkness, Pinkney turned a pallid face to Bill and gulped: "I can't swim!"

"I judged that," Bill agreed drily.

He had been edging over as he held Pinkney. And near the cypress knees that had wrecked them the water grew shallower. They had evidently tipped off into the deeper channel that Keely had been following.

Keely—where was he?

Bill had heard a few faint splashes behind him, but had been unable to investigate them. Now with Pinkney once more on his feet he looked around. Keely was not in sight.

"Did he drown?" Pinkney asked thinly.

A faint splash some distance away answered that. A distant oath drifted back. Then all was still.

"Keely!" Bill shouted.

THE swamp seemed to swallow his voice, smother it—and them. The cypress trees loomed about them like gaunt, menacing sentinels. The boat had sunk out of sight. Bill waded a few yards in the direction of the sounds, saw nothing, heard nothing, turned back.

"He's gone," he said; and his jaw set grimly as he added: "Good thing for him. I guess. I've got a lot to settle with him."

Pinkney shivered. He looked forlorn, crushed as he stood there in water to his waist, peering uncertainly about. "I—I don't understand all this," Pinkney stammered.

"Neither do I," Bill retorted. "But I'm going to find out."

"Why did he bring us here?"

"He knows."

A booming, rolling cry came echoing through the still trees. A horrible, ghastly, eery bellowing that swept across the surface of the black water like a basso echo from the tombs of the dead.

"What was that?" Pinkney bleated, shifting nervously.

"Bull alligator," Bill replied briefly. "Get a grip on yourself. We're in no danger."

Pinkney threw back his thin shoulders and combed a lock of damp hair out of his eyes with dignity. "I am not afraid," he said firmly. "But I am hungry, and I do not like swamps. My family is subject to malaria, and I knew all along we should have stayed in Washington. G-ghost Swamp!" There was loathing in Pinkney's voice.

"We seem to have found it anyway," Bill chuckled.

"How are we going to get out of here?"

"Search me," Bill said drily.

In the silence following, they both stiffened, listened. Far away, faintly, had sounded the double blast of an automobile horn. There was no mistaking it.

"I guess that settles it," Bill said cheerfully. "There's a road where that auto is. We'll wade over there and get our bearings. Friend Keely evidently was lying when he said cars couldn't reach the plantation."

"I don't like that man," Pinkney said coldly.

"What I think of him is searing," said Bill. "But," he added thoughtfully, "I'm curious about him. We've stumbled into something that's mighty queer, Pinkney."

"I don't like queer things," Pinkney said flatly.

"Wait here," Bill ordered. He waded toward where he had last seen the boat, dived under the surface. He was up long moments later with one of their bags in his hand. He waded back, gave it to Pinkney, and repeated the process. In ten minutes they had all their luggage together again.

"Now then," said Bill cheerfully, "all we need is a fire to dry out and we'll be all right again. Let's go."

They started off, wading cautiously through the inky water. Before they had gone far they were groping their way through pitch blackness as night closed down for good.

CHAPTER FOUR

The Hand of Death

OLD Ghost Swamp was noisome, fetid, lonely. Owls hooted dismally in the trees. Furtive splashings and slitherings in the darkness marked unseen, unknown life. The water for the most part was shallower than the channel into which they had been thrown. Carrying their heavy bags, they advanced slowly, slipping, sliding in the oozy mud, stumbling over rotting trees, running into branches, and the cypress knees that were everywhere.

And then without warning the water

grew shallower. The thick tangle through which they had been struggling thinned out. They walked up on dry land, under a sky ablaze with stars.

A black shape moved uncertainly in front of them. A startled voice called: "Who dar?"

"Where are we?" Bill called back.

A frightened exclamation was followed by the sudden spurt of running feet. Bill shouted for the stranger to halt, but the feet only went faster.

"Let him go," Bill said in disgust. "We're all right now."

They were at the edge of a broad cotton field. The bursting bolls of snowy fiber stretched off into the night like a ghostly blanket. On the other side, half a mile away, yellow lights winked and gleamed reassuringly. Bill led the way through rows of cotton toward them.

A thin fringe of trees bounded the other side. Beyond, to the left, was a line of low flimsy cabins. Small wood fires were glowing and flickering over there.

Around one of the fires a number of figures were clustered—two dozen at least—plantation darkies, silhouetted against the restless glow and shadows of the fires, like ebony statues carved from the night.

"Here's where we find out where we are anyway," Bill said, turning toward them.

Silence greeted their arrival, although heads turned and watched them. Even before he reached them Bill was struck by the queer uneasy way they were all huddling together. A common desire to be close to one another seemed to animate them.

Their silence was queer too—inexplicable. No one stepped out to meet them; no one spoke a greeting. But as Bill walked up he saw white eyeballs rolling fearfully.

Men and women were in that crowd—all ages and sizes—and all drawn together and animated by the same common fear. For fear it was. It was stamped plainly in every move and attitude. Bill set his kitbags down on the ground and surveyed them in astonishment. Pinkney stopped beside him.

Uneasy glances rolled at them, but still no one spoke.

"What's the matter with them?" Pinkney asked, jarred out of his moroseness by the sight. He stood there, head cocked forward on his thin neck, staring back at them.

"What's going on here?" Bill spoke.

A low groan came from the middle of the crowd. A voice breathed: "Lawdy! Lawdy! Hit's comin'! Hit's comin'!"

A sharp sucking sigh arose from the common mass huddled there. Bill's question went unanswered.

"This—this is queer," Pinkney muttered.

Bill thought so himself. More than queer. It was startling. He had never seen darkies act this way before. The very atmosphere around the spot was different. An electric tension hovered in the air. It plucked at his drawn nerves, brought uneasiness too. It was involuntary, nothing he could help. And that irritated him.

"What the devil's wrong with all of you?" Bill snapped. And then he noticed that not one of the crowd was looking at him now. Every eye was riveted on a common point. A sobbing mass groan well out of them. The group shuffled into a compact knot, stood frozen.

Bill's eyes followed the direction of their common stare. And suddenly he found himself standing frozen too. A cold shiver drove through him. Emotions older than history gripped him for one helpless moment.

NEAR the cabins was the bulky mass of a barn. Beyond it across a stretch of lawn loomed a large mansion, surrounded on three sides by great spreading live oaks draped with streamers of moss. No trees stood at the back of the house. One lighted window gleamed downstairs. The edge of the high flat roof was dimly silhouetted against the sky beyond.

At that roof every eye in the huddled group was staring. And Bill saw a pale phosphorescent mass shimmering and weaving there—moving restlessly back and forth—rising and falling, expanding, contracting.

Fingers dug into Bill's arm convulsively. A horrified gasp burst from Pinkney. "Do you s-see what I see?" Pinkney got out.

"I seem to," Bill answered.

He wouldn't have believed this if he wasn't seeing it with his own eyes. But there in plain sight that pale shimmer of life and movement writhed against the sky. Everyone around him was seeing the same thing. It *was* there.

A moaning wail burst from one of the huddled group. "De ol' swamp ghost!"

"Hit's come fer company!"

"Gonna be death tonight!"

"De hour of blood has come! Hit's dancin' for de daid!"

With a mighty effort Bill threw off the dread feeling that gripped him. Such things didn't really happen. He knew it, despite his words to Pinkney. It couldn't be; it was an illusion. And the best way to puncture it was to get close.

"Come on, Pinkney," he whipped out. "Let's see what that is!"

And he started toward the house at a run, his kitbags slamming unheeded against his legs. Behind him he heard Pinkney running. Not one of the terrified group watched their going. They all lapsed into a moaning, groaning, trance-like state.

And never a more bewildered and mystified young scientist raced across a dark lawn at night than Bill Hyde as he made that dash. For overhead on the edge of the house that queer luminous spot of life continued to writhe and dance.

His foot crashed into a small wooden box on the ground. He stumbled, almost went down, recovered himself with an angry exclamation and went on. And as if the sound of his voice had broken the spell that gripped the night, the glowing mass up there dwindled down and vanished.

Bill stopped, staring. It did not come back. It had gone completely as if aware of his approach. Pinkney caught up with him, gasping for breath.

"Where did it go?" Pinkney burst out.

"That's what we're going to find out!" Bill rapped out. "Quick, around to the front! The windows are all lighted there!"

As they dashed around the house Bill got an idea what a majestic old ruin the house was. It must date from before the Civil War. One of the great manor houses of that opulent, slave-holding period. But the years had not treated it kindly. It crouched there in the grove of live oaks, a weathered and weary old relic of its former glory.

A wide shell drive curved before the great pillared front porch, two stories high; and standing before the front steps was a small roadster, dark, quiet. As Bill and Pinkney burst out on the drive a slender, skirted figure sprang up from the steps where she had been sitting and stared at them in startled surprise.

And as she poised there against the light of the porch windows behind her, a shrill, startled scream sounded faintly inside the house. A scream knife-sharp with terror and hysteria. A woman's scream that rose to a shrill crescendo of fright. . . .

"Help! Rhoda! C-come quick!"

BILL stopped short. Pinkney bumped into him from behind, staggered aside with a muttered apology. The girl on the steps wheeled around and ran to the front door. Bill was following her as the door slammed behind her.

No more screams had sounded after that desperate call for help. Bill dropped his bags on the front porch, jerked the door screen out, tried the solid front door. It was locked.

He rapped with the handwrought iron knocker. No one answered. Inside he could hear faint sounds of confusion.

"We've got to get in!" Pinkney insisted excitedly. "We've got to get in! Someone's being murdered in there!"

Disregarding him, Bill ran to the nearest window. The shade was up, curtains inside pulled back. Inside he could see a pair of glass doors opening on a side terrace. Bill dashed around there, found the doors still open. He stepped through into a scene of helpless confusion.

The long, high-ceilinged living room ran half the length of the house. It was a room still faintly musty from long neglect and disuse; a room full of priceless antique furniture, old rugs, old pictures, with a great white Georgian fireplace opposite the glass doors. A crowding knot of people were gathered before the fireplace, making futile, fluttery movements, as people do when shocked into panic.

The only calm one among them was the slender girl who had run in from the front steps. She said crisply: "Put Aunt Ida on the sofa, Raff. She's only fainted."

A brawny young negro servant in a white house coat lifted one of the forms off the floor—that of an elderly woman—and started toward a brocade-covered sofa with her. He caught sight of Bill, stopped short, said in a startled tone: "Someone heah!"

The girl had dropped to her knees beside the second form, was shaking its shoulder, saying sharply: "Dad! What's the matter? Can you hear me?" She threw a glance over her shoulder at Bill, ignored him. But the others didn't.

A stoutish lady of forty-odd years, dressed in a primly flowered print, asked shrilly of those around her: "Who is that awful looking person? What is he doing here?"

An equally stout and pompous little man advanced a step, demanding loudly: "Who are you, sir? What do you want?"

Bill came on into the room. He spoke calmly, for they were overwrought, keyed high. His wet muddy clothes, disheveled, bedraggled condition were not sights to reassure them. "I heard someone scream murder," he said. "Can I do anything?"

The pompous little man turned red. "Get out!" he shouted, waving his arms. "Raff, put this man out!"

The negro turned away from the couch, scowling. He was a squat, broad-shouldered, ebony-hued fellow with an egg-shaped head. He moved with feline alertness as he started toward Bill.

The girl ordered crisply over her shoulder: "Let him stay!"

Ignoring the others Bill went to her side. "What happened?" he questioned.

She looked up. Her face was pale; her hand was shaking. But otherwise iron control was holding her steady. "Dad walked in here and collapsed. My aunt was alone with him. She screamed and promptly fainted. I can't get him to answer me. Are you a doctor?"

"First aid is all," said Bill briefly. "Let's see him."

He knelt beside her, scrutinizing the tall, thin, stoop-shouldered man who lay there. He had iron-gray hair. His long-jawed face was clean-shaven; it was flushed now. He was breathing heavily, harshly. One arm was outflung, the other clenched over his middle. His eyes were open. There seemed to be a degree of recognition in them.

"How's his heart?"

"Good," she said.

On the brick of the fireplace hearth lay a fresh spatter of water, shattered fragments of glass. He had evidently *dropped a water glass before or after he fell.*

WORDLESS fright, suffering, held back by a strong effort, were in the girl's glance at him. No one seemed to know what to do. Bill's sharp scrutiny, roving over the body of her father, stopped at that clenched hand on his stomach. The forefinger was slightly swollen by congested blood.

Into Bill's mind flashed a picture of that dead body they had discovered back in Washington, its swollen arm, angry red. He picked up the hand, straightened out the clenched fist, examined that forefinger.

A tiny blot of blood stained the skin of the middle joint. Bill looked close, made out two tiny punctures in the flesh of the forefinger. They might have been made by the close-set fangs of a striking snake!

A chill of presentiment struck him. It was as if the grisly hand of death had reached out a thousand miles and struck before his eyes. It was uncanny, nerve-shattering. He was gripped by a sudden, certain conviction that this thing he had stumbled onto was part of a greater web.

From the scream that had reached him out front to this moment was a matter of a minute or more, so quick had it happened. Bill's hand shot in his pocket, brought out the keen-bladed pen-knife that he carried always.

The stout lady cried fearfully: "Henry, do something! The man is mad! He's going to stab him!"

Even the girl looked startled, frightened at sight of the knife.

"I'm not going to harm him," Bill said coolly. Holding the finger firmly, he slashed down to the bone crosswise, then again lengthwise. Red blood spurted out.

Cupping his handkerchief under the finger, Bill ordered: "A towel, quick!"

The girl sent the negro running for a towel. Bill massaged the arm, bringing down the blood to that open cut, forcing it out. For he was certain poison had gone in those punctures, was working up the arm toward the rest of the body. It had not acted fast, probably due to the small circulation through the fingers. There was a chance it could be minimized.

As the hand drained they could see the victim grew no worse. His eyes continued to watch them. He began to breathe more regularly.

"Any snake-bite antitoxin in the house?"

The girl—for the swirl of corn-colored hair close to her head and the little bunch of curls at the base of her neck made her look little older than a girl—shook her head.

"None," she said anxiously. "How is he? What—what happened to him?"

"Don't know," Bill said briefly. "Looks to me like a snake, spider, or scorpion bit his finger. I saw the punctures. Tried to clear out the poison as quick as I could." He didn't tell her about the death of his uncle's friend. Wasn't sure yet whether this man would live. No use to fan her fears.

He ripped off a strip of cloth, bound the finger. "Any whiskey?"

"Raff, get the decanter," she ordered instantly. She had taken charge of the house. The others, clustered behind them, were mute, helpless. Bill had given them no more than a glance so far.

A cut-glass decanter was brought. Bill unstoppered it, forced a little whiskey between the victim's lips. The man choked, coughed, swallowed, drank again. His head nodded weakly.

"I think he's going to be all right," Bill said briskly. "Let's get him into bed."

"Raff, help," the girl ordered, getting to her feet also. "The rest of you stay down here."

BILL and the negro carried the limp form up a great sweeping staircase to a second-floor bedroom the girl indicated. He was already stronger when they put him into bed. The girl hovered there anxiously as the negro went out.

"Let him rest quietly," said Bill, drawing her to the door. "Do him good. Give the body a chance to throw off the poison."

Her eyes were shining as they faced each other outside the door. "You saved him!" she said impulsively, laying a hand on his arm. "We couldn't have gotten a doctor here in time!"

Bill smiled her gratitude aside. "Where am I?" he asked.

A frown etched between her eyes as she remembered. "Look here, who are you?" she demanded. "Where did you come from? You look as if you had been wallowing around in the swamp. Both of you." For Pinkney had slipped from the room downstairs and stood in the background as they worked over her father.

"We have been," Bill confessed. "My name's Hyde. My friend is Professor Pinkney of the Smithfield Institute. We were looking for Magnolia Plantation."

"This is Magnolia Plantation. I am Rhoda Jasper."

Bill nodded. "I thought it must be," he agreed.

She snapped that remark up quickly, almost suspiciously, despite gratitude for what he had just done. "Why did you think so? And what were you doing back in the swamp?"

"Trying to get here. Didn't you know we were coming?"

Astonishment greeted that. Her blue eyes searched his face. "Know you were coming? Why should I know you were coming?" she asked with a shrug.

"Didn't you father tell you about us?"

"No. What was there to tell?"

"He wrote to Washington, asking the institute to send someone down here."

"Why?"

Bill saw she did not know anything about it. Her father had acted secretly for some reason. And he saw something else as he glanced down the hall. Raff, the black servant, was lingering furtively by the head of the stairs, rolling his eyes in their direction. Hearing their conversation.

"Tell your man to go downstairs," Bill requested.

Rhoda hesitated, then complied. And when Raff's soft tread had faded away toward the ground floor, Bill asked her: "Was anyone downstairs here just before it happened?"

"Not that I know of. You haven't told me why you came here," she persisted.

"Some archaeological work on the plantation your father suggested we do."

"Oh. He was always interested in such things." But her gaze became challenging again, and her voice a shade sarcastic as she said: "You weren't working in the swamp tonight, by chance?"

"We were trying to get here from Charleston," Bill explained grimly. "Has your plantation foreman shown up yet?"

"Popei?"

"Keely is the name he gave us."

Rhoda shook her head. "We have no one here by that name."

"I wired we were coming. Your manager met us at Charleston. Started to bring us here in a boat."

"We did not know you were coming," she said positively. "I'm sure father would have mentioned that, and met you himself. Besides, the road is the quickest way to get here. And our manager has not been to Charleston today."

"I see," Bill said thoughtfully.

"See what?"

"Never mind," he put her off. There was much that needed explaining. He didn't want to go into it now. She would either doubt him entirely, or face added fear tonight. Best say nothing until he knew more.

He thought of the eery sight he had seen atop this house. Recalled the groaning prophecies of the frightened negroes. The hour of blood had come, they had cried. The swamp ghost was dancing for death.

And death had followed swiftly, checkmated only by chance. It was a gruesome, baffling mystery. And Bill was gripped by the feeling that more was to come.

CHAPTER FIVE

The Pewter Pitcher

TWO figures appeared at the head of the stairs, came toward them. One was the pompous Henry. The other was tall, slightly stooped, with broad shoulders sloping under his drill coat in bulging knots of muscle. Long dangling arms ended in great weathered hands, one of them clutching an old stained hat.

"That's Popei, our manager, now," Rhoda Jasper said uneasily. And as they came up she asked sharply: "What is it, Popei?"

"He said he had to see Martin," Henry explained. "Insisted it was important, so I thought I'd better bring him up."

"You can't talk to him now," Rhoda said flatly.

Popei ducked a bullet-shaped head. His jaw was prognathous, his cheeks weatherbeaten slabs, his nose flat and broad. A receding forehead sloped back into closeclipped black hair. His eyes were big, slightly bulging. They rested without expression for an instant on Bill, and then turned to Rhoda Jasper. The man looked starkly primitive, but he spoke in mild slurring tones to her.

"Thought I'd better see him, miss. I didn't know anything was wrong till I come to the door. You see, the niggers is fixin' to light out."

"Leave? Why, they can't do that!" Rhoda said vigorously. "Cotton-picking time is here! They're in debt to us! We've carried them ever since last spring!"

"Yes'm. That's what I told 'em," Popei said with another polite duck of his head. He reminded Bill of a tamed bear. The overseer looked sad, spoke sadder. "You can't never tell what niggers'll do," he said apologetically.

"What is wrong with them? Why do they want to go?" Rhoda demanded impatiently.

"Won't none of 'em tell me," Popei confessed. "But they're powerful uneasy. Big Joe, that slate nigger in the end cabin, tried to tell me the place has got a ha'nt on it. I had to beat it out of his haid."

From the bed inside the doorway Martin Jasper spoke, weakly, but with emphasis. He was rapidly getting stronger. "Tell them not to dare leave the plantation until I talk with them, Popei. I'll have a sheriff after them so fast it'll make their heads swim. Understand?"

Popei stared through the door curiously. "Sho' glad to see you're feelin' better, sah. I'll sho'ly do that. I'm mighty sorry to hear about your trouble. Good night, sah." He turned and shambled down the hall with a final duck of his head to Rhoda, paying no attention to the two men with her.

When he was gone Rhoda remembered and introduced the pompous one. Fisher was his name. He and his wife were down from New York for a visit—old friends.

Fisher said expansively: "Sorry about my mistake when you came in, Hyde. Your friend has explained who you are and given us an idea of the trouble you've had this evening. It's a case for the sheriff, I say. When decent people are tricked away to be robbed, it's high time to take action, by Gad!"

Pinkney was improving, Bill saw. He had evidently spun a yarn to account for their disheveled appearance, without going into details. There was hope for him yet. Fisher left a moment later. Martin Jasper called weakly for them to come to his bed. He talked stronger, looked better.

"I heard what you were saying at the door," he said from the pillow. Glad to see you, Hyde. You got here just in time. I thought I was gone."

"What happened?" Bill asked bluntly.

"Don't know," Jasper confessed wryly. "I left the bridge game across the hall and started to pour myself a drink. I keep a pitcher in there on the mantel. Doctor ordered lots of water. Just as I set it down I felt a sharp pin in my finger. Next thing I was down on the floor. Couldn't move or speak. And I had not tasted the water."

Bill remembered a large pewter pitcher that had been standing on the fireplace mantel. He said quickly to Rhoda Jasper: "Go down and see that no one touches that pitcher. Not even yourself."

SHE went out without asking why. Bill stripped off his damp coat, found that the wound in his arm was only a crease, and pulled a chair to the bed. Jasper was strong enough to talk. They were not interrupted. And Bill quickly got a composite picture of affairs here at Magnolia Plantation.

Martin Jasper was a retired business man from New York, fond of a mild climate, good hunting, fishing. Finding both in this isolated spot, he had purchased the plantation at a tax sale in the spring —in time for cotton planting. Some of the negroes had already been living in the cabins, rent free. They stayed. Others came in and were hired, for the plantation was large.

But somehow things had not gone right. The negroes were slipshod, accomplished little. Often they failed to show up for work for a day or so. Property was stolen. Strange sights and sounds were occasionally heard. One day the man called Popei appeared and asked for work. He passed as white, was plainly part negro. But he displayed an astonishing ability to handle the negroes, was made manager.

Still, strange things happened. A barn burned down. Mules and chickens were found mysteriously dead. In the house at night queer sounds were heard. Jasper's sister had taken sick, cured herself by fasting, in which she was an ardent believer.

Popei had told them the negroes claimed the place was haunted, that bad luck followed everyone who lived there. The big house had been empty for years, following a strange series of deaths. Then two recently hired men had discovered gold and death in the swamp. Two more had disappeared. Now not a man would go near the swamp. They seemed gripped by a queer terror.

Jasper had kept these recent events from the rest of his household in order not to alarm them more. For a strange nervous tension had fallen over Magnolia Plantation. Fear had come among them.

Jasper knew no man named Keely, did not recognize his description. He had not received the telegram Bill had sent when he boarded the train. Jasper could give no explanation of the man who had met them, or the reason for it. And when Bill told him about the death in Washington, the sight he and Pinkney had witnessed on the roof and the strange actions of the negroes back at the cabins, Jasper was bewildered.

"I'm beginning to believe the place is cursed," he said with an effort, turning a haggard glance on Bill.

"We'll uncurse it," Bill promised cheerfully.

But as he left Jasper lying there on the bed and went downstairs, Bill wondered about that promise. How was he going to get to the bottom of these strange happenings? Where should he start first? What was behind it all?

He found the company in the living room. Jasper's sister, who had fainted, was sitting erect once more in a straight-backed chair, fanning herself with a palm-leaf fan. She was a spare, thin-faced, acidulous woman in the middle fifties. She was talking in a shrill voice when Bill entered. "I told Martin yesterday I was going to leave if he didn't do something soon! I haven't had an easy night in weeks. And now, look, tonight!"

"Aunty," Rhoda said, taking Bill to her, "this is Mr. Hyde. Miss Ida Jasper, my aunt."

Aunt Ida sniffed as she looked him over. "You seem to have had more than you share of swamp mud and water tonight, young man."

"I think so too," Bill smiled.

He met the others. Mr. and Mrs. Fisher, the stout couple from New York; Audrey, their son, a portly, vague young man, whom Bill remembered as standing by helplessly when he was needed; Miss Connors, pretty, chic, stylish, visiting also; and Waldeman and Madden, two men around fifty, who bore the unmistakable stamp of business. Pinkney was sitting off to himself, solemnly surveying the gathering through his shell glasses.

There was no talk after the introductions. They were all uneasy. Rhoda said quickly: "I know you both want to go to your room. I've had Raff take your bags up. I'll show you."

Pinkney stood up with alacrity. Bill walked over to the fireplace mantel where the water pitcher stood. It was a large old pewter tankard with a hinged lid and double sides to keep the contents cool. Bill picked it up by the top, careful not to touch the handle.

"I'd like to take this up to my room," he said to Rhoda Jasper.

"Why, certainly, if you want to," she assented. And as they left the room Bill

heard a suppressed buzz of conversation break out behind him. On the stairs Bill asked her: "Where did you get this pitcher?"

"It came with the house. What are you going to do with it?"

"Look it over," Bill said.

Their room was near the middle of the hall, a large high-ceilinged room with a brick fireplace. Rhoda Jasper told them that the bath was at the front of the hall, and left them.

WHEN the door closed behind her Pinkney collapsed in a chair and wiped his brow with a damp handkerchief. "Did you ever see such a situation?" he appealed.

Bill grinned as he set the pitcher on a table and removed his coat. "It's all for science, Pinkney, my lad. Better get into some dry things. You'll be catching cold."

Pinkney nodded at the pitcher. "Why bring that up here?"

"I'm cursed with an awful curiosity," said Bill. "I do things like this." He drew a chair to the table, sat down, scanned the handle of the pitcher closely.

An embossed scollwork design had been cast into the handle, and around the top, bottom and lid. It was obviously a very old tankard. Bill peered inside the handle, and almost at once grunted with satisfaction. The scrollwork in there had been shaped to fit the fingers. At one spot it had been carefully altered. A knife or sharp tool had cut the soft metal out into two tiny little points, razor sharp. Points that would stab deep into any flesh that pressed against them.

Jasper had said that he kept the pitcher there on the mantel all the time. His habit had been used in an attempt against his life. There was nothing ghostly about those fanglike points. Human hands had formed them. A human mind had conceived the idea. Poison had evidently been put on the points. Jasper had done the rest himself when he lifted the pitcher and filled his glass.

"Pinkney," said Bill, straightening in his chair, "if I had my hat here I'd take it off to someone."

"Who?" Pinkney queried in astonishment.

"That," said Bill dreamily, "is where the fun starts. I think I know, but it's so obvious I have my doubts. Turn around and press that brand-new bell button by the door before you go for your bath."

Raff answered the ring a few seconds after Pinkney vanished toward his bath. "Come in," said Bill. He stood up from the chair, noting that Raff's eyes rolled from him to the tankard curiously.

"Take that downstairs," Bill requested, nodding at it.

"Yes, suh." Raff walked to the table, picked the tankard up by the handle without hesitation. A soft exclamation escaped him. He put his other hand under it and looked at his right forefinger. Two little dots of blood had appeared there. "Ole thing done cut me," Raff said with annoyance. "Now, how dat come? Nevah do hit before."

"Did you put it on the mantel tonight?" Bill asked.

"Yes, suh. I keeps it full all de time," said Raff uneasily, wiping his hand on his trouser leg. "Got three of 'em, but mostly only uses one."

"Never mind. Leave it here," Bill said, watching Raff closely. He showed no ill effects from the cut. Jasper must have gotten all the poison off the points.

Raff went out, plainly puzzled by the queer behavior of the guest, and the tankard that had scratched him. Bill undressed, frowning thoughtfully. Raff had not known about those points. Who did, then? How had the filled pitcher gotten there on the mantel with its deadly poison,

when Raff confessed to putting it there himself?

The question was still unanswered after he and Pinkney ate the food that was sent up for them, and turned in for the night. It savored of black magic.

CHAPTER SIX

Fanged Warning

IN the morning Pinkney shook him awake frantically. He looked almost ill as he stood trembling there by the bed. "The door's locked!" he gulped.

"What of it?" Bill yawned, sitting up.

"That tankard is gone!" Pinkney pointed dramatically to the dresser where the tankard had been left. Bill snapped wide awake, saw Pinkney was right. The tankard had vanished.

"Look there by the side of your pillow!" Pinkney gulped. "There was one on my pillow too!"

Bill looked down, swore softly under his breath at what he saw. It was the severed head of a huge cottonmouth moccasin. Its white-lined jaws were gaping wide; and curving down from them were two long deadly poison fangs. Its lidless eyes had in death the same viciousness they had possessed in life.

On Pinkney's pillow was a second head. "I almost rolled on it!" Pinkney said with a shudder. "Suppose those fangs had gone in my cheek?"

Bill reached down gingerly, picked up the head, pressed in the back of the fangs. A thin spray of yellowish venom shot out in the air. "I'm afraid the eminent career of Professor Pinkney would have collapsed," Bill said drily. "You say the door is locked?"

"Yes. See the key."

Bill tried the door. It was exactly as he had left it the night before—locked from the inside. Their dinner tray was still on the table. But the pewter tankard had vanished from the bed room.

"Someone tried to kill us last night!" Pinkney shuddered.

"No doubt about it," Bill said, throwing the snake head out the window. "Forget these. I'd say they are warnings. Gentle little hints."

"What would anyone warn us about?" Pinkney queried helplessly.

"That it's unhealthy to stay here."

"You mean we're in danger?"

"Suppose," Bill suggested cheerfully, "those heads had been alive? Your nose would have been an awful temptation, Pinkney boy."

Pinkney rubbed his nose hastily, looked slightly ill at the thought.

The sun was shining outside. A breeze was rippling through the moss-hung live oaks near the house. The scent of flowers was in the air. A bird flashed past the window. A dog barked nearby. It was a warm, bright morning, peaceful, beautiful—and yet despite his ragging of Pinkney, Bill felt a cold chill of premonition run through him.

What kind of place was this, anyway? Where had that tankard gone? None of the servants could have removed it because the door was still locked from the inside. They would have taken the tray of dishes anyway. Who had left those grim warnings? Who did not want them around here?

While he bathed, dressed, ate breakfast downstairs and chatted with the house company, questions sapped at Bill's mind. From first to last it was all one mystery. Who had killed the man in Washington? Did that atrocity link up with this place in the far south?

Bill was inclined to think that it did. Otherwise, how that ghastly death so similar to Martin Jasper's mishap? But what in the name of reason did his uncle's learned friend have to do with this plantation?

And there was the matter of the sly, malignant fellow who had represented himself as the overseer of the plantation. How had he known they were coming in on that train? Why had he gone there to meet them? And what had been his purpose?

All mysteries! Grim mysteries, as evil as the expression he had surprised on Keely's face.

Those things only led up to the heart of the matter . . . the frightened negroes, the ghostly specter whirling on the roof as Martin Jasper walked in to face death. And lastly the mystery of the vanishing tankard, and the fanged warnings!

Was it possible that the legends about the place were true? It took some solid fact for a place to get a bad name. Negroes were psychic. They felt things, sensed things other people did not notice. How right were they in saying the place was haunted?

AT the breakfast table Bill said nothing about the missing tankard or the objects he and Pinkney had found on their pillows. The rest of the company were obviously ill at ease. Rhoda Jasper looked as if she had slept little through the night. She walked out on the front porch with him after the meal.

"What did you do with dad's pitcher last night?" she asked bluntly. "Raff tells me he can't find it."

"Gone this morning when I woke up," Bill told her, omitting mention of the rest of the story.

Rhoda looked stunned. "Gone?"

"Yes."

"But where did it go?"

"I'd give a lot to know," Bill assured her. "The door was locked. We both slept soundly. Didn't hear a thing."

Rhoda Jasper looked more mature today than she had last night. She came only to Bill's shoulder, but there was a line to her chin, a firmness about her mouth one didn't find often in a girl so pretty. Bill judged she was about twenty-three. Her mother had died when she was a small girl. With her aunt she had managed her father's domestic affairs since then. Responsibility like that tended to make a girl grow up quickly. And she had evidently been bearing her share of the worry lately. Dark circles were under her eyes. The lines of strain in her face had evidently been there before last night.

"I talked to dad after you left him last night," she said slowly. "He told me everything. What did you find on that pitcher, Mr. Hyde?"

Bill told her. And her eyes went startled, apprehensive. "I think I'll tell our guests they'd better go home," she decided instantly.

"I don't know that I'd do that," Bill remonstrated.

Rhoda Jasper faced him, her blue eyes flashing. "Do you know what this means, Mr. Hyde?" she asked, and answered the question herself. "It means that something terrible is happening to us! It means that none of us are safe! We don't know anything about it. We don't know what to do! We can't stop it. Any one of us might be the next! I won't let our guests risk it."

Bill shrugged. "You're probably right at that. Are you going to report the matter to the authorities?"

"Why—why—"

"I wouldn't just now," Bill suggested. "No one's been killed here at the house. I'd rather let my part in it lie doggo until I see what I can do. Your father is all right now. We haven't any evidence. Raff put the pitcher on the mantel, and I'm convinced it was all right then. He picked it up in my room without hesitation and was mighty surprised when it cut his finger. Anyone else in the house you suspect?"

"Why—no," Rhoda admitted. "The servants are all right, I'm sure."

"There you are," Bill pointed out. "Get the law here now and they'll turn everything topsy-turvy, and probably not find out anything more than we know now."

"But what are we to do?" Rhoda asked tensely. "It's—it's ghastly to go on like this, never knowing what to expect, or what is going to happen next. Everything we touch and eat may be fatal! If that pitcher could disappear from your locked room, we may be killed while we sleep."

"I know," Bill agreed. "I've thought of all that. You might all go into Charleston and stay."

"And you?"

Bill's jaw hardened. "I came down here to do something," he said flatly. "I'll do that, and look into the rest of this while I'm doing it."

Rhoda Jasper smiled, and it was like the sun breaking through a bank of clouds. "I thought you'd say that," she commented. "Dad and I will stay here, of course. And that means Aunt Ida. She won't leave him. But the rest will have to go. I shall insist on it." And by the set of her jaw as she said that, Bill knew the others would soon be departing.

"I'd like to see your father," he suggested.

"He's still sleeping. I looked in his room before I came to the table. Last night he said I was to do anything for you I could."

"First, I want to get out in the swamp and have a look at the place he described. Where's the man who came back with the report?"

"He should be back at the cabins. Popei can get him for you. Dad told me he hadn't reported any of that because he didn't want the thing to be made public right now. The first man died from snake bite; and there's no evidence that anything happened to the others. They were both unmarried men, and might have got frightened and wandered off."

"Might have," Bill agreed, but privately he felt different. He doubted that first accidental death from snake bite, too—in the light of what had happened since then.

MAGNOLIA PLANTATION was a curious backwater of life. Bill got the feel of it after he had walked around half an hour. The big house was old, old brick, probably brought over as ballast in long-vanished ships. The slave quarters were of cypress logs, peeled of bark by age. The big trees on the place had seen generations live and die. Time had passed this place by in its steady march. Even the negroes were half-wild, aboriginal primitives, with none of the boldness, the ease of their more modern brothers.

It flashed over Bill that they looked even more primitive than the half-savage hill people of Haiti he had known. It was easy to see how their superstitions were excited, their credulity ready to believe haunts and strange sights they could not explain. Popei the overseer, had evidently prevailed on them to remain, but they were not working and they drew off half timidly, half suspiciously when Bill walked near them. Little black pickaninies played naked in the sun, dashed for cover when he came in sight.

A walk further afield showed the country around to be little better. It was a region of wild pine woods, of deserted fields, of a tumbledown house here and there that looked like the crouching ghost of long-forgotten life.

He talked to Popei when he got back. The overseer shook his head, rubbed a great hand through his close-clipped thatch. "Mighty certain I can't get none of the niggers to go in the swamp," he said in his mild slurring tones. "Fact is, sah, that nigger that came back with the story is gone. Lit out last night, I guess."

"What's the matter with them?" Bill asked with irritation.

Popei shook his head doubtfully. "They been livin' out here so long I reckon they ain't any better than their gran'daddies from Guinea. They got an idea unhealthy things is in the air, an' they've balked. Took all I could do to get 'em to stay heah, sah."

"Can you guide me there?"

"No, sah," said Popei hastily. "You see, I never was back there. Don't know just where 'tis."

Feeling that Popei was as craven as the rest, Bill made him point out one of the men who had gone into the swamp with Jasper. But the fellow, a slim, gangling young man in ragged trousers and sleeveless shirt, shook his head, rolled his eyes, disclaimed knowledge of how to get to the hummock. He refused to try, too, even when tempted with money. And as they left him, Bill saw him hastily cutting back of the cabins to get out of the way.

Bill smoldered inside. He couldn't believe these people could spend their lives here and not know the interior of the swamp fairly well. But seemingly he was up against a stone wall of terror and superstition.

The guests left, driving off in two cars piled with luggage, and looking relieved to be going.

Martin Jasper appeared at lunch, still a little weak from his experience the night before. "I'll make those fellows jump!" he promised. And a little later failed at what he had promised. For not a man would stir to find the hummock and help dig there. Nor would they give any explanations.

"I don't know what to make of it," Jasper fumed. "I'll take you out there tomorrow myself. Don't feel up to it today."

THE matter of the missing tankard had been plaguing Bill. He went to the kitchen, found only one there. Two were gone. The fat negress cook and the gangling young black girl who helped her, volubly disclaimed any knowledge of the second missing tankard. They showed him the top shelf in the big pantry where it had been placed. Using only one, they had paid no attention to the other two.

The peculiar feeling of helplessness grew on Bill. The place was still, lonely, with the guests gone. Across the cotton field he and Pinkney had traversed, the cypresses at the edge of the swamp stood like an opaque screen hiding unwholesome secrets.

Careful, watchful for suspicious actions about the place he caught furtive conversations that stopped instantly when his attention was noted. In the air was the feeling of dread waiting.

Martin Jasper brought out a handful of gold objects he had brought from the hummock. Rings, bracelets, arm bands and beads. Some of them were crude, showing evidences of having been worked over from other objects. But they sent Pinkney into a fever of excitement. He declared they were undoubtedly of Aztec origin.

Bill felt his curiosity rising also. He asked Jasper to draw him a map from memory, showing the way into the swamp.

"You don't want to go in there alone," Jasper protested.

Bill grinned. "We were in once and got out. I've an automatic in my luggage. I don't feel like waiting around and doing nothing. Draw me a map and we'll go in and have a look this afternoon."

"You'll have to take a boat," Jasper warned. "The water gets pretty deep in spots. I went in a dugout canoe belonging to one of the men."

"I've paddled them," Bill assured him.

So Jasper drew a map, as well as memory would permit. Bill unpacked his automatic. A pick and shovel brought from the plantation stores made them ready. Rhoda Jasper joined her father in protesting.

"You might get lost," she argued. "And you don't know what trouble you'll find in the swamp."

"That's partly why I want to go," Bill chuckled. "Can't stand wondering about it any longer. If there's anything back in there, I want to find it. Pinkney does too, eh, Pinkney?"

"If you go, I shall have to go too," Pinkney said weakly. His eyes behind his shell glasses were distinctly uneasy. But he followed manfully at Bill's side as they left the plantation house.

Beyond the point where they had come out of the swamp, hidden in a swampside thicket, they found the short dugout canoe Martin Jasper had said to look for. It had been hollowed skilfully from a solid log, was narrow, tricky.

"These darkies aren't very far from the old days in Africa," Bill commented as they dumped the tools in and seated themselves gingerly. "This is pure jungle craftsmanship."

"It appears unsafe to me," Pinkney declared as the small craft rocked alarmingly when he sat down in the bow, legs outstretched before him.

"Don't move," Bill warned. "I'll do the paddling. Learned how to handle one of these in Venezuela four years ago."

CHAPTER SEVEN

Voodoo

THE swamp swallowed them and in half an hour they were far in its depths, following narrow waterways that abruptly opened into still, sun-drenched pools of black water, that skirted banks of water reeds, cut through dark shadowy stretches of cypress like damp vaulted tombs.

Now and then they found little hummocks of dry land, but for the most part the swamp was a wilderness of still water and lush growth. Bright water flowers and blood-red parasite plants on the tree trunks made vivid blobs of color. In the shallow open spaces long-legged water birds rose and flapped ponderously away. Butterflies sailed silently down the swamp aisles. Now and then fish leaped and splashed back.

The soft paddle dips startled one big alligator from its sleep on a mud bank. It vanished in a geyser of water. Several times they saw the twin knobs of gators' eyes staring with evil fixedness from the surface, only to sink silently as they drew nearer. Snakes were plentiful as ever, mostly ugly cottonmouth moccasins that wriggled away, or flowed into the water at their approach.

Jasper's directions were necessarily vague. They lost their way, paddled haphazardly, cutting back and forth as chanels presented themselves. More than once they got out and dragged the canoe through shallow mud and water that barred the way. It was pure luck that sent them across a small pool to a higher bank that held no cypresses. It proved to be dry land. Leaving the canoe on the bank, they pushed into a tangle of palmetto, moss-draped live oak, scrub pine and chinquapin brush.

Little brown swamp rabbits scuttled away from their noisy push through the thick growth. A wood duck flew out of a hollow tree overhead. Here and there were the fallen trunks of great trees, ripped out of the soft soil by high winds that crashed them down to death and rot.

"Looks like we're close," Bill said over his shoulder. "The hurricane hit this spot pretty hard just as Jasper described."

Pinkney, scuffling along in wet shoes, panted: "I hope so."

The dry hummock was perhaps a quarter of a mile long. They had landed at the lower end. At the other end Bill stopped short. "There you are," he said calmly.

Several large mounds rose from the level soil, covering the space of an acre. One was long, slender, not more than four feet high, built in the sinuous form of a traveling serpent. The others were shaped like loaves of bread, some as high as eight feet. All were covered with thick growth, including large trees. On the outer mound a great live oak had been growing for a century or more; a giant tree that had thrust its roots deep into the soft soil. The recent hurricane had struck it squarely, swept it over, tearing out roots and half the side of the mound.

The bushes and swamp grass had been trampled down all about the spot. Human bones and skulls lay in the sunshine where they had been carelessly tossed. Some were stained dark from contact with the soil. Others were gleaming white as they had been protected in their long rest. Two picks and shovels lay on the ground where they had been dropped hastily. A great deal of dirt had been dug out and thrown aside.

"Someone has been working here!" Bill exclaimed, eyeing the spot.

"Jasper said he had two men here," Pinkney reminded, scrambling into the excavation. "Look! This is a burial mound!"

Pinkney was right. The unknown dead had been buried in layers, wrapped in bark and skins; buried with the implements and ornaments they had prized most highly in life. Shreds of bark and skin had survived. In the debris that had been tossed out by the diggers were arrow heads and bone fishhooks, stone axe heads, necklaces of teeth and carved bone, remains of feathers—but no gold.

"They've robbed it!" Pinkney cried angrily. "It was the two men Jasper left!"

"Looks that way," Bill agreed. "But

they haven't gotten clear down in the mound. Grab a shovel and we'll see what we can uncover."

Both lost themselves in the absorbing task of hard dirty digging. They uncovered more skeletons. Found one wearing a gold arm band around fleshless bone. Aztec gold!

LOST in work they did not count time. Bill's shovel struck hard metal. By the side of a disjointed skeleton he carefully uncovered a rust-encrusted sword with a large basket hilt of gold. Wiping away the dirt with his handkerchief he was able to decipher the letters: *"Con Dios, 1603."*

"With God, 1603," Bill translated. And looked at Pinkney with a quizzical smile. "There's your answer. It's Aztec gold, all right, but it never came overland with the Aztecs. This is a Spanish sword. That gold went out of Mexico after the Spanish conquest and got here sometime after 1603. Might have been a shipwreck on the coast, or a raiding party of Indians may have gobbled a troop of Spanish explorers who carried gold with them. The Indians prized the ornaments and were buried with them. Some they evidently worked over to suit their taste."

Pinkney wiped his perspiring brow with the back of his hand. "That must be it," he agreed. "Shall we keep on digging?"

"These mounds should be excavated," Bill decided. "But that can wait. It'll be dark in a short time. Let's start back. I'll wire Amos and see what he wants to do."

Using Bill's coat for a basket, they gathered the ornaments that were in sight, dumped in two grinning skulls for type checks and started back to the dugout. And it was gone!

"Where the devil did it go?" Bill exclaimed. He stepped to the water's edge,

looked around. There was no sign of the canoe.

"Could it have drifted off?" Pinkney asked uneasily.

"Not unless it had legs. We left it clear up on land."

"I—I don't like this," Pinkney decided, staring about nervously.

The sable cloak of night was closing down fast. The deep booming chorus of swamp frogs was rising in waves of sound all about, backed by the shriller whine and rasp of insects. Already they were slapping at mosquitoes. And the gaunt trees draped with moss, the still black water, the noises rolling in from every side were bringing the swamp eeriness that had vanished as they worked.

"It looks like we've found trouble," Bill remarked. "Don't know what it means."

"Can't we wade out as we did before?"

"Not this time," Bill decided. "Too much deep water. We had to keep going then. Don't now. We can light a smudge fire back there where we were working, and spend the night here. Jasper will show up in the morning."

It was dark when they returned to the mounds. Bill shot a swamp rabbit on the way. The fire he quickly lighted from dead branches did not entirely drive away the effect of bleached bones and grinning skulls about them.

Bill cleaned the rabbit, washed it in swamp water, speared it on a sharpened green stick and broiled it over the fire. Pinkney refused food. Bill ate the whole rabbit, washed his greasy hands, lighted a cigarette and sat by the fire, smoking thoughtfully.

Something was due to happen. The dugout had not been stolen without purpose. Half an hour later a cracking stick nearby brought him to his feet, peering at the spot.

Pinkney did the same, and suddenly

chattered: "Look at that! Do you see it?"

Bill did see it. And his hand streaked to his pocket and jerked out his automatic. For just beyond the reach of their firelight a ghostly swirling patch of luminosity was rising, falling, expanding, contracting against the black background of the night.

PEOPLE react in different ways. Pinkney gave one frightened gasp, and then calmed down. Bill stood there, gun in hand, watching the sight. And in spite of himself a sensation like trickling ice water ran down his spine.

The swamp ghost! The dance of death! Precisely as they had seen it atop Martin Jasper's house! Only here in the depths of the swamp, with the frogs booming and strange harsh cries coming out of the unfathomable night it was doubly awful.

It seemed to be poising there before it swooped down on them. It made not a sound. No part of it touched the ground. Suspended in the air it jiggled and writhed, making sinuous darts back and forth, little advances and retreats as if getting ready to leap at them.

Sliding the safety off his gun, Bill started forward a step at a time. And Pinkney caught up a pick and advanced with him.

"I'll handle it," Bill said through his teeth. "Stay back!"

And right there Pinkney won Bill's respect. For the pale, slender man of the laboratories and books said fiercely: "I'll help! No g-ghost can sc-care me!"

It had not been an optical illusion before. It was not now. Its soft, glowing bulk was plain enough. It retreated a little before them, swept back instantly, poised.

Bill's voice sounded harsh against the silence. "I'm going to shoot!"

The words had no effect. He raised the automatic, pulled the trigger. A tongue of flame streaked from the muzzle. The roar of the shot echoed far and wide through the swamp. Then sudden silence fell. The frogs stopped their chanting. The swamp seemed to hold its breath.

The swirling emanation jerked back, writhed violently, gathered itself together, swept slowly toward them again. Bill watched it with something like horror. He had hit it squarely. And yet no harm had been done. He advanced toward it with steady strides, jaw set, body taut. And every few feet as he went the automatic thundered in his hand.

Shot after shot, carefully aimed. Every one ripping, tearing square into the middle of the macabre splotch of luminosity. And the shots went right on through it, did no harm. All were futile, useless against that awful formless presence.

The last shot spat out. Bill clubbed the pistol and continued on. Walked into a vague cloud that brushed across his face and swooped down about him. Walked into a thing that had no body and no form.

And as he struck viciously with the clubbed gun the night seemed to explode with a mighty crash. Everything went black as his knees buckled.

BOOM-BOOM . . . *boom-boom* . . . *boom-boom* . . . *boom-boom-boom* . . . That was the throb of drums beating in low, blood stirring rhythm. It came into Bill's ears dimly; then more clearly as his senses cleared.

He was lying on his face. The decaying smell of the swamp was strong in his nostrils. And the drums throbbed and throbbed. Bill lay there quietly trying to collect his thoughts. What had happened to him?

His head ached infernally, felt like the top had been battered in. His face was swathed in coarse cloth that barely admitted enough air to breathe. He heard the soft steady splash of water, placed it in a moment—paddles dipping into water. He was lying in the bottom of a small boat that was slipping through the swamp maze. He could see no light through the cloth. The frogs were singing close.

Bill tried to move and found that his hands were tied behind him. Tied so tightly that the cord seemed to bite into the swollen flesh. His arms were half numb.

There was nothing he could do at the moment, so he lay there listening to the drums come closer and closer. The bow of the craft grated on land. Feet splashed in the water alongside. He was hauled to his feet. Through the cloth mesh over his head he made out the red flare of a fire, heard the nearby hum of voices.

He was hauled out of the boat so roughly that he stumbled to his knees, was jerked up again and urged forward. The drums were close now, filling the night with their fast steady rhythm, quickening the blood, stirring vague unknown feelings at the back of the mind; stripping away the veneer of civilization, weaving the stark savage jungle into body and soul.

So the Voodoo drums had throbbed back in the mountain fastnesses of black Haiti. The three Rada drums, *maman, papa, cata*—mother, father and baby. Beaten with horny black palms, calling the devotees to the weird ceremonies of the Congo, and Guinea rites where strange gods were worshiped. Ayida-Wedo, goddess of the rainbow, Papa Legba, Zo, the god of fire, Lisa, the moon god, and the great Damballa-Ouedda, the serpent god, mightiest of all the gods.

Back in the trackless forests of Africa, that these blacks called Guinea, they had worshiped these gods, and the gods had come to the new world with them. Law, civilization—Christianity had not been enough to stamp out of mind the gods that had lived with them for countless generations. They brought their gods and their jungle magic, and in Haiti both flowered mightily. Nor did they vanish from other places to which their devotees were sold. Spotted over the entire Southland fragments of the old rites flourished in secret, under the unseeing eyes of the modern world. Witchcraft, Voodoo, Obeah, Ju-Ju. And what more perfect spot to find them than in this aged backwater of the South around Old Ghost Swamp?

So Bill knew in a measure what to expect as he was jerked to a stop and the hood taken off his face. They were standing in a clearing on a swamp hummock, lit by four leaping bonfires. At one end, under a frame of poles and swamp grass was a small three-sided shelter, containing a crude altar covered with offerings of food in plates, bottles and packages, small charms and necklaces of snake vertebrae, and lighted candles. And in a screen-wire cage in the back center of the altar was the largest cottonmouth moccasin Bill had ever seen. It must have been six feet long, and as thick as his arm. Its great scaly triangular head weaving restlessly around inside the wire was like an evil spear point.

Damballa-Ouedda, the great snake god, personified here by this monster reptile of the swamp.

Bill looked around swiftly. They were at one corner of the building. Before it was a huddled group of full thirty darkies. The same half-wild, half-savage types that he had noticed around Magnolia Plantation. But now they had come into their own. Their bodies were swaying, their eyes were fixed and glowing at the jungle rhythms coming from the Rada drums opposite. Three drums of unequal size, beaten by the palms of three half-naked drummers squatting on their heels.

STANDING beside Bill in the grip of two brawny blacks was Pinkney blinking in astonishment as his head was uncovered too. Pinkney's glasses were askew, his face was dirty, and his wrists were tied behind him also. Their heads had been covered by burlap sacks which were now on the ground.

Pinkney's eyes were bulging as he looked around and he edged a step nearer Bill as if seeking company. "What is this?" he gulped.

"Voodoo," said Bill briefly.

"In this country?"

"What does it look like?"

"What are they going to do with us?"

Bill shook his head. He wasn't sure himself. But a vague premonition was stirring in him. On the blood-spattered ground in front of the altar was a dead goat, its throat cut. Half-empty bowls of blood were on the ground beside it. A living sacrifice to the snake god, Damballa-Ouedda, its blood drunk by the emotion-crazed worshippers. That bloody cane-knife leaning against a corner of the altar was the sacrificial knife.

Many disjointed facts were swiftly arranging themselves in Bill's mind. The deaths by fang bite, the golden snake ring on their guide's finger; each of those traced to this cult of the snake god, with its Voodoo poisons and strange deaths.

But why should it have reached out for Pinkney and himself? Where did Martin Jasper come in, with the attempt on his life, the strange happenings that had taken place at Magnolia Plantation since he had come there to live? How had death reached out from this lonely swamp to Washington? And why?

Half-naked bodies were swaying and dancing mechanically. Glistening black faces were moaning strange chants. And the great snake in the frail cage swayed its wedge-shaped head back and forth, eyeing the company with lidless unwinking eyes. Bill looked around and saw Keely standing behind him with the golden snake ring on his finger, a blood-red cloth wound around his head, and a shirt to match, half open.

"You're mixed up in a queer business," Bill said coldly, raising his voice above the sound of the drums.

Keely swore at him in Haitian French.

"*Qui,*" Bill nodded. "What are you, a *papaloi*—a priest of Voodoo?"

A startled look flashed over Keely's face. He asked in the island speech: "You know Voodoo?"

"Yes," said Bill drily. "This is Damballa-Ouedda, isn't it?"

Keely dropped all pretense and sneered: "And tonight they'll sacrifice goats without horns."

"What does he mean?" Pinkney asked nervously.

"Human sacrifice," said Bill briefly. "It's done sometimes. And it looks as though we're elected."

Keely sneered in good English: "I tried to turn you back."

"Why?"

"We didn't want you two here."

"Who is 'we'?" Bill jerked his head at the chanting blacks, who were paying no attention to them. "They aren't interested in us."

"They will be in a few minutes," Keely promised ominously.

"Look here," said Bill, "do you believe in this?"

Keely shrugged carelessly, enough to show it didn't matter. From the pocket of his overalls protruded the butt of Bill's automatic.

"What happened to us tonight?" Bill questioned.

Keely grinned crookedly, cunningly, said nothing. He walked away a moment later, around to the back of the pole shelter. Bill started to follow and was stopped by the two blacks who had hustled him and Pinkney from the water's edge.

One of them Bill was certain he had

seen at Magnolia Plantation, but when he spoke to the fellow he got no answer. Both were gripped by the spell-binding rhythm of the drums, the mad emotion that was flowing through everyone there but themselves and Keely.

"Look here—this is preposterous, ridiculous," Pinkney protested to Bill. "People aren't sacrificed in this country. They wouldn't dare try anything like that. They'll—they'll try to frighten us, and then turn us loose, won't they?"

"Wish I thought so," Bill said bluntly. "These people are living back in Africa right now. Look at them. They don't know what they're doing. We're out in some secret hiding place in the swamp. The Petro sacrifice where blood is shed is a part of their ceremonies. White blood probably ranks higher. It's up to Keely, and he looks like a snake to me. He knows what he's doing, too. He's in this with his eyes wide open."

"But it's against the law!"

"There's no law here in the swamp."

"What can we do?"

Bill had been wondering that himself. He had seen enough, heard enough in black Haiti to know that this was not a matter of mumbo-jumbo that one could laugh at. These people were in dead earnest. Their lack of caution about sound showed that they felt themselves safe. He and Pinkney were bound; they were guarded. If they died here tonight, and the swamp claimed them, no man outside would be the wiser.

He strained at the cords around his wrists, and they only bit more deeply into the flesh. They didn't have a chance. Keely came back, spoke sharply to the two guards. Pinkney and Bill were shoved in before the altar, their backs to it, the dead goat at their feet. The tempo of the drums dropped to a low steady thump. The chanting dropped lower, and Bill was conscious of many unseeing eyes fixed on them.

CHAPTER EIGHT

Cult of the Cottonmouth

FROM the other side of the shelter a blood-chilling sight shuffled in. It was a man, clad in an all-enveloping robe of red cloth, his face concealed by a hideous mask with boar's tusks protruding from the mouth, his head crowned by a red turban like Keely was wearing. And his hands were stained with the blood of the goat.

He shuffled to them silently, picked a bottle of oil from the altar and shook drops over their heads. Setting that down he took cornmeal from a plate and tossed it in their faces.

This must be the *hougan*, or Voodoo high priest, although Bill had never heard of one masking in Haiti. Not that it mattered now. A guard stood on each side of them watchfully in case they tried to run away. It wouldn't be any use. Bound this way, they were helpless.

It seemed like a nightmare as they stood there, each moment bringing them nearer the grim ending of this business. One of the lighted candles threw its feeble heat on Bill's hands.

And the idea he had been racking his mind for flashed on him.

Bill leaned against the altar, pushed his hands farther back. His fingers touched the candle. He raised them, held his wrists over the flame. No one noticed that casual movement. His body hid the candle. The masked priest picked up a gourd rattle wound with snake vertebrae, and turned to the crowd, shaking it in time with the drums.

The hot flame of the candle seared against Bill's wrists as it ate into the cords stretched tautly between. He clenched his jaw as the pain grew, held them there steadily. The odor of burning hemp drifted out. No one else noticed it. The cords gave a little—then a little more . . . suddenly snapped apart.

"Run!" Bill snapped to Pinkney.

The masked priest heard the words, wheeled around. And Bill crouched, smashed his fist square into one of the eyeholes of the mask, driving the other staggering back.

The drums faltered, stopped as Bill whirled, grabbed a bottle off the altar and slammed it in the face of the guard who jumped at him. The black fellow went down like a poled ox.

Pandemonium broke loose.

The drummers leaped to their feet. The audience surged forward, shouting wildly. Bill swung to the altar for another weapon. The screen-wire cage caught his eye. Its top was held by a sliver of wood through a hasp. He snatched out that sliver, caught the cage, swung around. With a mighty heave he hurled the big reptile out.

Its great coils flew through the air, writhing and twisting. Screams of alarm rose as it fell in the midst of the crowd. They broke, scattered in wild fear.

Bill lunged and grabbed the long blood-stained knife.

"Watch out!" Pinkney screamed in warning. He had refused to run and leave Bill there.

Bill ducked, just as a shot roared out across the shelter. He felt a flick past his ear, knew that death had brushed him close. Keely was standing there with the automatic in his hands. He had found cartridges for it.

To run meant a shot in the back. To wait meant as bad. Sheer stark murder was writhing across Keely's face. As he straightened, Bill whirled the cane-knife and launched it point forward. It struck Keely's breast just as his finger pressed the trigger again. The shot went wild. And Keely reeled back and down with the knife half through him.

The impact of a heavy form drove Bill against the altar front. Powerful fingers clamped about his throat. He caught a glimpse of the ugly mask pressed close to his face. The fingers dug into his throat like steep clamps. He tried to tear them away, found it impossible. Pinkney was struggling with the second guard.

It had all happened in split seconds. And as those mighty fingers sank in Bill's throat everything began to swim. In a few more moments he would be helpless —and all this gone for nothing.

BILL'S outflung hand struck a bottle on the altar, closed about its neck. A blind blow shattered the bottle against the edge of the altar, spilling the contents. And Bill shoved the jagged end of the bottle neck against the back of a hand throttling him; shoved it, and twisted.

A howl of pain followed. The lacerated hand jerked away. Bill swiped with the bottle neck again and his assailant stumbled back, dodged aside and leaped away to safety. Bill didn't waste time in following him. As he whirled around with the bottle neck, Pinkney's attacker released him and jumped back too, from the menace of that jagged glass.

"Come on!" Bill shouted to Pinkney. He ran out of the shelter, catching up the automatic from where Keely had dropped it. Keely was lying there on the ground in a huddled heap, the cane-knife sticking out of his breast.

And then they were out in the darkness with the firelight, the milling confusion of the Voodoo gathering behind them. Bill fished in his pocket as he ran and found his knife. He opened the blade, stopped long enough to slash the cords from Pinkney's wrists.

A glance back showed figures heading after them. Bill shot once at them. They stopped, scattered. Bill and Pinkney plunged down off land into water, waded through it to their waists. They lost themselves in a black tangle of cypress, then found shallower going. They struggled through a thicket of reeds, more cypress, more mud and water and reeds. And half an hour of that brought them to dry land, soaked, mud-covered and alone.

They dropped down for a few moments' rest, got up then and headed away from the swamp. There was starlight out here over old uncultivated fields. Two miles further on they found the little-used road that ran near Magnolia Plantation. Twenty minutes of hard walking brought them to the plantation itself.

There were lights in the house, none around the cabins in back. Rhoda Jasper opened the door, and showed clearly the strain she had been under as she exclaimed: "Thank heavens! We thought something had happened to you! Dad tried to get a party out after you, but most of the darkies were gone and those that were here refused to stir. We were going to wait until morning and then notify the sheriff."

Jasper hurried into the front hall, gave one look at their condition and demanded: "What happened? Did you fall out of your boat?"

"Is your man Raff here?" Bill questioned quickly.

"Yes."

"All your house servants?"

"They don't stay in the house," Jasper stated. "Most of the darkies have gone to a dance."

"They may call it that," Bill said grimly, and told the two of them what had happened.

Jasper's face grew grim and strained. "So that's what we've been living around," he growled. "I'll get word to the county sheriff and start a posse out to round them up."

"Later," Bill begged. "No one is out there in the swamp now. If Keely is dead he can wait. If he's alive he won't be there now. I doubt if I'll be able to rec-ognize many of them. I've got a better idea."

"What?"

"Got a gun?"

"Several of them. Want me to go back there with you?"

"Hardly," Bill grinned. "I've got a hunch. Think it may work out. He outlined what was in his mind.

Jasper looked doubtful. "It may work out," he said grudgingly, "but I doubt it."

"I think it's worth a trial," Bill urged.

"All right. D'you think Rhoda had better go to her room?"

"No. She can stay with you. Probably be safer there. We'll go on up now."

Bill and Pinkney went up to their room.

"I wish I had a gun too," Pinkney said. He was a changed man. His shoulders were straighter. His eyes were shining. He looked as if he might welcome trouble now.

"Changed your mind about them being dangerous?" Bill grinned as he closed and locked the door.

"I've changed my mind about a great many things," Pinkney said recklessly. "I—I don't care what happens now. I believe I should enjoy a fight."

"You're liable to get it," said Bill drily.

HE rumpled the beds, slipped the pillows under the covers so at a casual look each bed would seem occupied. He pushed the window up and, standing silhouetted before it in the light, removed his damp coat and shirt.

Pinkney watched with growing impatience, finally exploded: "You're not going to bed, are you?"

Bill chuckled as he turned away from the window and tossed his shirt over the foot of his bed. "Publicly, I'm thinking of sleep, Pinkney, old horse. And so are you."

"I most certainly am not!" Pinkney insisted emphatically. "This is a time for action! Decisive action! It is ridiculous to come up here to this room and remove our clothes!"

"If you ever took your clothes off for decisive action, do it now," Bill ordered with a grin. "The coat and shirt only, professor. Right there in front of the window, too. And try to look sleepy while you do it. That's right—now a great big yawn."

"Er — uh — flapadoodle!" Pinkney snorted as he gave a prodigious yawn and removed his shirt. He turned away from the window with a glare. "I have yawned!" he said stiffly. "Now what?"

"Sit down there in the corner and take a nap," said Bill. He snapped the light switch by the door and plunged the room into darkness. Then he pulled a chair to the foot of his bed, retrieved his gun from his coat pocket and sat down.

From the corner Pinkney protested plaintively: "The floor is hard and my back will not fit in the corner. This smacks of the ridiculous to me!"

"Doesn't it just," Bill agreed. "But you sit there just the same. Pretend you're a cigar-store Indian. And you might snore a little."

"Cigar store Indians do not snore," Pinkney stated with dignity.

"Snore anyway."

"That is a thing I never do!"

"Then sit there and think," Bill sighed. "And if you never think, just sit there."

Silence fell.

Half an hour dragged by. Downstairs the house was dark and silent, too. A second half hour went its tedious way. Pinkney groaned once or twice from the corner, and subsided when Bill hissed warningly.

It was uncomfortable sitting there in damp clothes. Bill began to wonder if his hunch was wrong after all. Through the open windows night insects shrilled monotonously. An owl's hoot drifted through the blackness in mournful protest. Outside the house a dog barked, yelped, fell silent. Bill thought he heard a sound near the house but couldn't be sure. But it brought him tense and wary with his eyes fastened on the window.

Ten minutes of that and he began to believe the he was wrong after all.

Then without warning the merest scrape sounded in the room. It might have been a mouse. It came again. Bill's eyes glued on the open window, watching for a darkening bulk against the starlight outside.

But the open window remained empty. *"Sssssssst . . ."*

That was breath sucking sharply through Pinkney's lips. A sharp gasp of startled fright that he had been unable to control. Bill peered at the corner where Pinkney was. Then a movement at the side of the room whipped his glance over there and Bill almost gasped aloud himself.

At the side of the fireplace a white luminous cloud was taking form in the darkness. A shimmering ghostly blotch of light was seeping out of the solid wall.

Out of the solid wall!

It was so startling, so unexpected from that quarter, so against all rules of reason, coming out of the blank wall, that Bill leaped to his feet involuntarily. The chair clattered noisily to the floor behind him.

Mindful of the terrific blow that had struck him senseless when he rushed to close quarters before, Bill stayed where he was. His finger pulled the automatic trigger hard. The gun emptied with a tearing burst of shots.

CHAPTER NINE

The Red Venom

THE crashing reverberations of the shots were deafening. The sharp stinging bite of powder smoke bit into

Bill's nostrils as he swung around and groped for the light switch.

The room flooded with light.

And Bill swore under his breath. For the room held only himself and Pinkney, standing bolt upright in the corner. Where his target had been now there was nothing.

"Did you k-kill it?" Pinkney gasped.

"I don't know what I did!" Bill flung at him as he strode across the room. The fireplace extended several feet into the room, a massive old-fashioned piece· of work with paneled sides and a heavy wooden mantel. It was at the side of the fireplace that the luminous blotch of light had appeared. It was there Bill had shot.

The wood paneling in the side showed two bullet holes.

It took an ·instant for the significance of that to sink in. He had shot in one direction. The bullets had entered the paneling from another. And the splinters around the holes showed that the bullets had come out from *behind the paneling.*

There was only one way that could have happened. The paneling had been swung out when he shot! It was hollow behind! Bill tore at it with his fingers. The paneling seemed solid, would not budge. He stepped back and eyed it.

"Get it, Pinkney?" Bill suddenly demanded. "We're over the living room! The same master chimney must serve both fireplaces!"

"Uh—yes. But what of it?" Pinkney countered weakly.

"Quick! Downstairs!"

Bill jumped to the door, unlocked it, raced for the stairs, whirled down them. He met Jasper coming up, shotgun in hand. The lower floor was lighted.

"What happened?" Jasper cried.

"Did you see or hear anything?" Bill rapped out.

"Nothing. Except those shots."

"Does the big fireplace chimney go down in the cellar?"

"Yes."

"How do you get down there?"

"Through a door in the kitchen," Jasper answered, staring at Bill as if he thought his guest suddenly unbalanced.

"Take me there quick!"

But as they reached the bottom of the stairs Rhoda Jasper cried out in the living room.

"Dad! Quick! The fireplace! Look at it!"

Bill lunged past her into the big room. And stopped abruptly at what he saw. The paneling in the side of the big fireplace had swung out. And creeping through it was a hulking figure clad in a blood red robe. Its face was covered by a horrible mask that had gleaming boar's teeth thrusting from the mouth.

One bloody bandaged hand clutched a wad of cheesecloth. The other was pressed to the side of the red robe where a great spotch of blood was spreading fast.

Harsh rasping breaths filled the room as the figure straightened up to full height and staggered forward a step. The eyeholes of the mask glared with a burning insane light.

"Cover him with that shotgun!" Bill ordered Jasper, who had stopped behind him. "Blow a hole through him if he tries anything!"

IT WAS a strange and terrible sight as they all stood frozen—Bill wary, Jasper holding the shotgun ready. Pinkney and Rhoda Jasper in the doorway. The red-masked figure glared at them, shuddering with the effort to get breath. He had been wounded grievously. The spreading blood was over his heart.

One lurching, staggering step the masked horror took toward Bill, and then pitched to the floor. Bill stepped to him as he rolled over on his back. The hand pressing his side suddenly lashed out. Bill leaped back. So narrow was the escape that two sharp points in the big golden snake ring on one finger ripped through the cloth of Bill's trouser leg.

With a lunge Bill grabbed the wrist, saw from the flat venomous head of the golden snake two fanglike points projecting, held out by a finger pressing the back of the head. The finger lifted as he looked. The fangs slid back in their golden case.

From behind the mask rattling oaths in Haitian French rasped in weak fury. Bill snatched the mask off with one hand. Grabbed the bundle of cheesecloth with the same hand, and leaped back.

"Popei!" Martin Jasper gasped.

It was Popei, the big, hulking, apelike overseer of the plantation; lying there with a froth of blood on his lips and a murderous glare in his eyes.

"I wasn't sure," said Bill with satisfaction. "I thought I recognized his hands tonight when they went around my throat, but it wasn't proof!"

Popei rolled over, tried to reach him with an outstretched hand. Bill stepped back out of his reach.

"Sweet little killing tool on his finger," Bill said to Jasper. "One stab with those points is probably enough. They're poisoned. Sort of symbolic death from Damballa-Ouedda, the Voodoo snake god."

Bill lifted the cheesecloth, sniffed at it. A grim smile came over his face. "And here's the swamp ghost. The thing that dances for death. Cheesecloth covered with phosphorous. I'll hand it to you, Popei. It makes one of the sweetest ghosts I've ever heard of. No wonder I couldn't shoot it down. Holding it on a stick out there in the swamp, weren't you? And when I rushed it you cracked me on the head."

Popei lay there breathing painfully. A venomous grin twisted his bloody lips. He spoke in English. "If it'd been me, sah, I would have busted your haid!"

"I don't doubt it," Bill agreed. "It was Keely, I suppose?"

Popei rolled his head in a nod of assent.

Bill looked at the open panel at the side of the fireplace. "And one of you slipped through here and planted the doctored pitcher for Jasper to pick up?"

Again Popei nodded his head in agreement. Bill spoke fast, for there was no doubt that the man was fatally wounded. It would take a long time to get him to a doctor.

"You're going to die, Popei," Bill said.

"Yes!" Popei whispered harshly. "Damn you, sah! You did it!"

"And if I hadn't, there would have been a couple of dead ones in their beds in the morning," Bill said. "Weren't running any chances of me rounding you up after tonight, were you?"

"That's it," Popei agreed weakly.

"I thought that would be the next move," Bill said to Jasper. "Pinkney and I had seen too much. We were warned away last night. And when that didn't take, and we ran into the midst of things and still got away, a final visit to shut us up was in order. Only I thought it would be through the window. I didn't see any other way to get into the room. Never dreamed there would be anything like a well up one side of the chimney. How did you discover it, Popei?"

A look of cunning pride flashed over the man's twisted face. "I lived in this house for years while it was standing empty and boarded up," Popei wrenched out. "There was an old man whose grandfather had helped build this house. He had heard of the passages. One started in the cellar at the bottom of the chimney and went up to the attic. And I looked and found them."

"You could get in the cellar and go right up. Make ghosts walk in the attic and dance on the roof?"

"I am a very smart man," said Popei.

"I believe you are," Bill agreed. "Traveled some, haven't you?"

Popei nodded.

"Lived in Haiti?"

"Fifteen years," Popei whispered.

"Mixed in Voodoo?"

"I know its secrets," Popei muttered as a spasm of pain wrenched him.

"So you brought Voodoo here. What was the idea?"

"I'm dying," Popei whispered.

"You are," Bill agreed bluntly. "Better get it off your mind."

"It was murder," Popei gasped. "Keely and I left Haiti together. He was born there. Was in the gendarmes until they put him in prison. We went to New York. Killed a man and left. Came down here. It was a good place to hide. We couldn't go back to Haiti. I started Voodoo and ran the district. Lived here at the house until it was sold. I wanted to buy it and settle down when I got the money. Could have got rich with them working for me."

"And that's why everything went wrong for Jasper. You were trying to drive him out," Bill guessed.

"Yes," Popei groaned. "And then Keely found the gold the same day Jasper's men hit it. It was our gold. Enough to give us everything we wanted. I tried to stop Jasper from getting it. Made the two men he left to dig come away. Then I saw the telegram that said a man was coming from Washington in a few days to dig it out. I sent Keely there on the next train to stop him."

"And he got the wrong man."

"Yes," Popei admitted hoarsely. "He came back half a day before you and told

me it was all right. And I showed him a telegram I had gotten from the mail box at the road that said you were coming. So he went to the station to turn you back."

"And when I wouldn't turn he tried to take us into the swamp and stop us there?"

"Yes," Popei rattled in his throat.

"And while he was doing that, you tried to kill me!" Jasper charged angrily.

"Yes, sah. While you-all were eating I changed the pitchers of water."

"And perhaps let the darkies know the ghost of death would be around," said Bill, "and showed it to them on the roof about the time Jasper was due to die."

"Yes, sah," Popei writhed, clutching his chest.

"You're a smart man," Bill sighed, and meant it. "Murder on all sides, and no explanation for it. Take that ring off, and we'll rush you to a doctor."

But his words were ignored. With a mighty effort Popei rose to a sitting posture on the floor. The dew of death was on his face. His life's blood was staining the red robe he wore. His whole body was racked with the effort to breathe. But a thick-lipped grin of pride twisted Popei's mouth. His voice came strong and firm.

"I am a smart man, sah!" Popei cried thickly. "I got the gold! It's in my house!" A shudder ran through him. He suddenly slumped back on the floor. twitched and lay still.

Cautiously Bill knelt beside him, felt his pulse.

"How is he?" Jasper asked anxiously, grounding his gun on the floor.

Bill stood up again, slowly lighted a cigarette. "He was a smart man," he said slowly. "But he overreached himself, as a lot of them do. Magnolia Plantation will be peaceful now. You'd better notify the sheriff. Popei's dead."

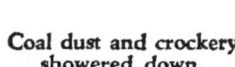

Coal dust and crockery
showered down.

Lead
Pearls

A Cardigan Story

by
Frederick Nebel

Author of "Rogues' Ransom," etc.

It all started with murder—nothing new to that big dick Cardigan. The motive was what mattered. That and the bloodstained string of pearls which belonged around the Kemmerich woman's throat.

CHAPTER ONE

"—as a Hounds Tooth"

LILY KEMMERICH moved onto the tiled terrace twenty stories above the East River. The drone of voices was behind her, in the big living room. She was in evening clothes—pale ice-blue against the creamy whiteness of her skin. Her hair was blond, parted in the middle and drawn tight to a doughnut over each ear. She leaned over the railing and looked down. She shuddered, turned away and pressed hot, moist palms together. A pulse in her throat throbbed.

The butler lay face upward on the living-room carpet. He had lain face downward until the arrival of Sayer, the medical-office man. The carpet was mouse-colored, and there was a large blotch of darker color near the butler's head.

A couple of uniformed cops stood near the corridor entry. Detective Dirago stood with hands on hips trying to make sense out of a futuristic water color on the wall. Lieutenant McCartney came down the short corridor from the bedrooms. Behind him came fat Leopold Kemmerich.

"This is a lulu," said McCartney, irritably.

Dirago turned a swart, handsome face. "Hahn?"

"Nix," McCartney growled. "The place is all busted up and nothing's been h'isted. This guy's been beaned to death and there ain't even a penny missing. Tie that!"

Kemmerich sat down heavily and said, "*Ach, du lieber,*" wearily.

Sayer, the medical-office man, looked at his hat. "Well, I'm all set, lieutenant. I'll breeze. Got a date. This is murder."

"You're telling me?" McCartney said. He looked at his watch. "Ain't that guy come yet?"

He was an angular man, with one shoulder higher than the other and a warped, sour face.

Sayer went to the door and had his hand on the knob when a knock sounded. He opened the door and Cardigan stood there hat in hand, his shaggy mop of hair shadowing his forehead. He nodded to Sayer and came in.

Sayer said: "Well, be seeing you," to McCartney, and went out, closing the door softly.

"Hello, Cardigan," McCartney said.

Cardigan stared at the body on the floor. "What's this?"

"What's it look like?"

Cardigan tossed his hat to a divan, crossed to the body, stood over it and after a moment lifted his eyes to McCartney. "Brained, huh?"

His eyes left McCartney and settled on Lily Kemmerich who stood now in the terrace entry, one hand held against her throat. She dropped her glance sidewise, entered quietly and took a chair in the shadows. He swung his eyes back to McCartney.

"Where do I come in?"

McCartney raked a short laugh between his teeth. "I understand your agency's working for the indemnity company that handled Mrs. Kemmerich's necklace—the one that was stolen a week ago."

"Sure."

McCartney poked a finger toward the body. "I just thought you might be interested in this. Mr. and Mrs. Kemmerich came in here half an hour ago and found the butler conked out. He was socked on the dome with a blunt instrument and rubbed out. Sayer said about two hours ago. Find any dope about that necklace yet?"

"No."

"You wouldn't by any chance ever take it into your nut to crash this apartment to see if the necklace was really stolen, would you?"

Cardigan narrowed one eye. "Clear that up, Mac."

"I mean, suppose you figgered that the necklace might still be here."

"Nonsense!" cried Leopold Kemmerich.

McCartney raised a hand toward him, said to Cardigan: "How about it?"

Cardigan sighed. "I thought it'd be something screwy like this. I was in bed, Mac. Where'd you birth that idea, anyhow?"

"Nothing's been taken," McCartney said. "Mrs. Kemmerich's bedroom was turned upside down but there wasn't a thing h'isted. Not a thing. Jewels are layin' around, dough, lots of things. It wasn't an ordinary house break. There's a fluke somewhere. That room was dressed down by a guy who knew his groceries, but there wasn't a thing—not a thing— lifted. I ask you, now."

Cardigan was looking at the shadowed Lily Kemmerich. "You're sure of that, Mrs. Kemmerich?"

"I'm sure," she said in a throaty whisper.

Fat Leopold Kemmerich was annoyed. "My wife has said she is sure. I am sure. That is finished. Find the killer, lieutenant!"

SITTING in the shadows, Lily Kemmerich kept her hands pressed tightly together, her chin up, her breath bated. She moved her eyes from one to another of the men in the room; she did not drop them to the dead man on the floor.

Irritable, whiny-voiced, McCartney came up close to Cardigan. "I'm trying to think that this here murder's got something to do with that stolen necklace. That necklace was worth thirty thousand bucks. It was stolen from Mrs. Kemmerich last Wednesday night in the theatre crowd in front of the Dorado on Forty-fourth Street. That's her story. It's possible, ain't it, that you might have doubted it was stolen?"

"Don't be an egg, Mac."

Kemmerich was on his feet. "You're calling my wife a liar?"

"Now, now," McCartney whined, shaking his hands, "don't get me wrong, Mr. Kemmerich. I've got a job to do. I'm just wondering about Cardigan here."

Lily got up and left the room, swiftly, quietly.

Cardigan was glowering at McCartney. "You don't have to wonder about me, Mac. I'd sure be a sap to crash this apartment. Give me a little credit, anyhow."

"All right, then. What ideas have you got on the stolen necklace?"

"Just that—it was stolen, fat-head. We're working on it and we've got a good chance of getting it back."

McCartney's eyes widened. "Oh, you have! Good! Been getting some good leads, eh? Well, I'm glad to hear that!"

"Yes, you are!"

Cardigan turned on his heel, crossed the room and scooped his hat up from the divan.

McCartney looked worried. He flopped his arms up and down in a nettled, jointless fashion and yammered: "Don't get all steamed up now, Cardigan. You don't have to get all steamed up now, do you?"

Cardigan turned on him. "Oh, I don't, don't I? I should maybe thank you for getting me out of bed and over here on some half-baked idea! Goom-by, sweetheart!"

He yanked open the door. Looking beyond McCartney, he saw that Lily had returned to the living-room entry. She was tall and beautiful against the low light of the inner corridor and her hand was against her throat again; her face was unnaturally white.

Kemmerich began complaining gutturally: "All these stupid questions about the necklace, when what you police should be doing is sending out alarms for the murderer!"

"On what?" moaned McCartney, shaking his arms. "On what? When nobody saw the guy. When not even the elevator boy saw the guy. On what, I ask you?"

Cardigan was saying to one of the cops: "If you think hard, it might occur to you that I want to get through this door."

"Should I, lieutenant?"

McCartney came over wearing a pained expression. "I don't want to hold you, Cardigan. I'm a white man. I had no idea of holding you. I—"

"You just want me to sit down and tell you how I know about that necklace job. Christmas is five months away, Mac, and you don't notice me wearing a white beard."

McCartney looked crestfallen. He waved his hand loosely. "Let him go, Abel—let him go or he'll get nasty."

Cardigan went out.

PAT SEAWARD was small, trim, neat. She had a one-room suite on West End Avenue, high enough to overlook the Riverside Drive houses and catch a glimpse of the river and the Jersey shore. It was late. She wore black pajamas and a mandarin coat and she sat curled up on a divan buffing her nails when the buzzer sounded.

She got up and opened the door and Cardigan squinted at her. "At this hour," she said.

"Detectiving is the curse of the leisure classes, little home girl."

She shrugged, kicked the door shut when he had entered and stood with her back to it, buffing her nails industriously. He scaled his hat across the room into a chair, dropped to the divan and smacked his knees, stared hard across the room at nothing.

"The Kemmerich butler got it," he said.

"Got what?"

"A look at back of beyond." He sighed. "Croaked. Bumped off. Finished."

"Oh!" she said, softly, and stared at him for a full minute.

He nodded. "McCartney woke me up and got me over to the Kemmerich casa. Crime in the stronghold of the élite always seems out of place."

Worry masked her eyes. "Oh, chief, you didn't—"

"Now you're going to start that," he growled; shook his head, saying: "No, I had nothing to do with it. McCartney thought he had an idea that this murder was in connection with that necklace job —a house break. The butler must have poked in and the guy took a haul at him. You should see him."

"Thanks, no." She shuddered.

He said: "Pat, there's something on the low-and-low about the necklace business. When I hit that apartment tonight Lily Kemmerich looked like a ghost. Like a very beautiful ghost. I heard her speak once. Her voice sounded—you know— clogged. She's worried about something."

"What do you think?"

"I don't know."

"Do you think it was really stolen?"

He looked at her. "Yes, I'm sure it was stolen. It was lifted in the street, on the sidewalk. It was on her neck when she walked through the lobby. Her coat was open and six people saw it. She lost it between the lobby and the curb—in the crowd."

"What did they get tonight?"

"Nothing That's the funny part about it. The apartment was crashed; McCartney said Lily's room was knocked apart— but nothing was taken. She said nothing was taken."

"Then why was she frightened?"

He stood up. "Listen, little wonderful. Get out bright and early tomorrow morning. Get on her tail. No matter where she goes, tail her. See what kind of people she meets. Stick with her till she gets back home. That clear?"

"Perfectly. What's on your mind?"

"I'd like to know why she looked so white tonight."

Pat sighed. "Listen, chief. Why get mixed up in this killing? Leave it to the cops. You've got a pretty good steer on who snatched that necklace. You've got two men tailing 'Packy' Daskas and if they tail him long enough—"

"I know, I know," he broke in. "Packy was in Forty-fourth Street that night and we know snatching necklaces is his business. But do as I tell you. Tail Lily Kemmerich."

She shrugged. "O. K., iron man."

He went to the door, opened it and turned to smile at her. "You look nice in black, Pat."

She was back at her nails. "You should see my grandmother," she said.

H E WENT downstairs and grabbed a cab. West End Avenue was dead as a country lane and he leaned back, crammed an old briar and lit up. He'd got the tip about Packy Daskas from a barman in a Forty-fourth Street walk-up speakeasy. The barman was a cop hater but on the other hand he had no use for Packy Daskas. He liked Cardigan, and when Cardigan had dropped in a few nights after the robbery the barman had told him about Packy.

"See that front window?" he had said. "Well, Packy was in here for an hour before the show let out. And three or four times he went to that window and looked across at the Dorado. He left here about ten minutes before the show was out."

Two agency men, working through stoolies, had landed on Packy's tail. They'd frisked his room on Seventh Avenue, found nothing. He wouldn't be fool enough to carry thirty thousand dollars worth of pearls in his pocket. The natural assumption was that he had fenced them, and the agency had the two men still on

his tail in hopes of finding Packy's connections.

The cabman was taking corners rapidly. "What's the hurry?" Cardigan asked.

The driver said: "I don't know for sure, buddy, but I got an idea you're bein' followed. There's been a checker takin' all these turns with me. I'm headin' for the bright lights and then you give a guy a break and get out. I got a wife and kids and I ain't figgerin' on gettin' me or the buggy shot up."

Cardigan looked around. Then he turned front and said: "Thanks. Here's half a buck. I'll take the next corner on the hop."

"Am I relieved!"

Cardigan opened the door, and when the driver slowed for a southbound turn he swung off and went bounding to the shelter of the corner building. He crowded it and watched the checkered cab take the turn. The tonneau was dark, but he had a feeling that a face inside was turned toward him. He shrank back. The checker loafed south, stopped at the next block. Cardigan, standing now on the curb, saw a figure leave it and duck down a side street. He knocked out his pipe, walked east as far as the park and boarded another cab.

When he reached his apartment hotel on Lexington Avenue he went straight to the telephone and called Pat.

"I was tailed," he said, "from your hotel. So watch your step. . . . I don't know who it was. May be one of McCartney's men trying to be bright or it might be somebody else. But keep your ears pulled in, little girl."

He hung up and then called his boss, George Hammerhorn. He said: "Listen, George. The Kemmerich butler was killed tonight during a house break. McCartney's on it. Thinks it has some connection with the necklace. The police department may be camped in your office when you get down in the morning, so act innocent.

. . . I'm clean as a hound's tooth. . . . That's all."

He pronged the receiver, jacked a chair against the door, undressed and piled into bed. He drank a stiff nightcap straight from the neck of a flask he kept in the bed-table drawer. Elevated trains slammed up and down on Third Avenue, but he went to sleep in a few minutes.

CHAPTER TWO

Sol Feitelberg Entertains

IT WAS nine-thirty when Cardigan entered the outer office of the agency on Madison Avenue. Miss Goff, the stenographer, had a handkerchief to her face and above it Cardigan saw that her eyes were wet. He closed the door softly.

"Man trouble?" he said.

She shook her head, made a face, started to say something and then began crying harder. He shrugged, crossed the little office and pushed in the glass-paneled door that led to the sanctum of his boss.

George Hammerhorn sat at his big flat-topped desk. His hands were palms-down on it, the arms at full length. His bulk was motionless. His big face was a mask and his eyes stared out through an open window. In an instant he was aware of Cardigan's presence, and he made a sound in his throat, blinked his eyes, and began moving things aimlessly around on his desk.

"Well, Jack. . . ."

Cardigan was scowling.

Hammerhorn looked up at him. "Fogarty got it."

"What!"

"Two A. M. this ack emma."

"Fogarty!"

"Fogarty was killed at two this morning in West Tenth Street, near Sheridan Square. Two shots—both in the back of the neck. He wasn't carrying any identi-fication, so they didn't find out who he was until an hour ago."

Cardigan ripped out, "Packy Daskas—"

But Hammerhorn raised a hand. "Don't get hot. Sit down a minute. Don't go off half cocked."

Cardigan looked brown and ugly. "If that Greek so-and-so—"

"Sit down, sit down, sit down."

"If that Greek so-and-so gave Fogarty the heat I'll bust more than his schnozzle!"

Hammerhorn slammed the desk. "Sit down! I tell you, sit down, Irish!"

Cardigan rolled to an iced cooler and drew a glass of water. He slopped half of it on the floor, downed the rest. He planked the glass back in the metal container, gave all indications of an impending explosion, then suddenly relaxed and walked quietly to a chair, sat down, put chin in palm.

"Poor old Fogarty," he sighed, heavily.

Hammerhorn blinked wistfully. "He was my first operative."

"Where was Goehrig?"

"Goehrig covered the tail till midnight. Fogarty picked it up then and Goehrig lammed home to get some shut-eye."

"Who found Fogarty?"

"A cook in an all-night restaurant—on his way home."

"I mean the cops."

"A patrolman—Ferraro. He busted over from Sheridan Square and found poor old Fogarty in the gutter. He got nervous and took a swing at the cook with the locust. So the cook passed out for two hours and everything was balled up. The cop called an ambulance and the ambulance hit a drunken driver in Hudson Street and that tied things up too."

Cardigan made a jaw. "O. K. I'll go out and find me this yap Daskas. Or have the cops got him?"

Hammerhorn passed a cold palm across his forehead. "No. I didn't tell the cops. You know how I feel about Fogarty. I know how you feel. That's all very jake.

But you've got a job to do. We've got to recover that necklace. If we stick the cops on Daskas that'll end things. If Daskas did lift that necklace, we'll never get it if the cops slap him in jail. There'll be a big commission for us if we get it—and a nice slice for poor old Fogarty's wife. We've got to think of that too. Fogarty—you know—didn't carry any insurance. We've got to—well—look out for his wife." He made a few awkward gestures. "It's the only right—kind of—thing. You know?"

"I get you, boss." Cardigan stood up, made a fist with his right hand and eyed it; then snapped the fingers open toward Hammerhorn and sighted down along them. "But I'm going to make contact with this Greek."

Hammerhorn hardened. "I don't want you clowning around just for the sake of a grudge."

"I know what I'm doing."

Still hard, Hammerhorn said: "Remember, it was on your say-so that we put the tail on Daskas. You haven't got a thing on him. You don't know that he lifted that necklace. After all, I'm running a detective agency here, not a crap table. And I'll be damned if I'm going to have you run this Greek punk against the wall and load his belly with lead! Not while I'm in these pants! If you want to play the rôle of avenger, we're quits. You may be Irish, but I'm Dutch."

Cardigan let the echoes die, meanwhile regarding the ceiling. Then he lowered his gaze and said in a tranquil voice: "I stuck Pat on the Kemmerich woman."

"Why?"

Cardigan told him, then added: "Pat'll be glue on that lady's heels and we may find something. Lily Kemmerich's got something up her pretty sleeve and I don't mean her shapely arm."

Hammerhorn stood up and got his hat, cleared his throat. "Well—I'm going to run up and see what I can do for Fogarty's wife."

CARDIGAN was marking time in the office when Pat rang in a little before noon.

He said: "O. K., sugar. I'll run right over."

He hung up and was reaching for his hat when McCartney came in chewing the stub of a cigar to shreds. Everything about the bony lieutenant was shapeless—his hat, his coat, his shoulders, his worried, irritable face. When he took his hat off his slabby hair was partless and ragged. He took it off to scratch his head. He was not a bad man; he was a fair cop but he had a reputation for a busybody and by some he was called "Old Woman McCartney."

"Sorry," Cardigan said. "I was just about to leave."

"Cardigan, Cardigan...." McCartney's head shook like the head of a loose-jointed marionette. He yanked at his loose pants and ran the back of his hand across his sour, worried lips. "Look at this now, Cardigan. Here your man Fogarty is bumped off only a few hours after the Kemmerich butler gets slammed out. Cardigan, now listen—"

"Mac, I've got a lunch date."

McCartney wobbled his loose arms and stamped one foot like a child being deprived of candy. Half embarrassed, half petulant, he also seemed on the verge of tears.

"Honest, Cardigan, I can't help believing this kill of the butler has some connection with the necklace. You say it's your job to get that necklace. O. K., and luck to you. But it's my job to get the guy who knocked over the butler. You must have a suspicion. Give me a break."

Cardigan slapped on his hat, nodded toward the door. "Going down?" He did not wait for an answer but headed out, reached the corridor and drifted to the elevator bank.

McCartney was at his heels, plucking at his elbow. "Here I am a good guy, always giving other guys breaks, living a straight home life and taking no more graft than I need—and everybody takes advantage of me."

"Going down!" sang out the elevator boy.

Cardigan bowed. "Before me, Mac."

McCartney stamped into the car, jerked at his tie, made irritable sounds in his throat until they reached the lobby. Out in the street, Cardigan turned and gripped the lieutenant's arm.

"You made a few cracks about me last night I didn't like, Mac," he said, then shook his head, adding, "but I'm not holding that against you. Fogarty was the best-liked man in this agency. I liked him especially. The old boy broke me in. Seven years ago he took a bullet in the gut to save me. Now I'll tell you—and it's on the up-and-up, strictly kosher— that I don't know who bumped him off. I don't know if there's any connection between that and the rubbing out of the Kemmerich butler. I don't know anything that would be worth a damn to you. I have suspicions, but I learned long ago that they're worse than dynamite to handle. Now for crying out loud, don't hang to my tail. Scram."

He turned sharply on his heel and strode down Madison Avenue. A little farther on, he hopped a cab and sat back while it tussled with traffic down and across town to Grand Central. He got off at the Forty-second Street entrance and found Pat waiting for him inside, near the bootblack stand. She had never looked more trim. They walked down to the oyster bar and climbed onto high stools, ordered Blue Points on the half-shell.

"So what?" Cardigan said.

"She came out of the apartment at nine-thirty. She didn't ride in the family chariot. Took a cab at Third Avenue and I, therefore, into a second cab. No, I don't use Tabasco."

"McCartney turned up. Good old Mc-Cartney. He said—"

"I thought you wanted to hear my story."

"I do, keed."

"So I followed her, with the old female eagle eyes. Directly to a pawnshop on Eighth Avenue. Here's the address. I popped into a drug store across the street and ordered a milk shake. I don't like milk shakes, so I was able to make it last longer than any other drink I could think of. She was in there half an hour. When she came out she walked a block and got into another taxi. I followed her to a hairdresser on Fifth Avenue. Probably she stopped in for an appointment, because she came right out and then I followed her to a modiste in Fifty-seventh Street, east. She was in there half an hour. When she came out she took another cab and so to home. I spoke with Miss Goff before. What's poor Fogarty's wife going to do?"

"George'll find a way." He laid down the oyster fork and looked Pat square in the eye. "Fogarty must have got pretty close. So close that the heel let him have it. There might be something doing down around Sheridan Square."

"I don't like the way you say that."

"Why?"

"The tone seems to indicate that you might revert to the sod and do something crazy."

He picked up the oyster fork. "What do you suppose Lily was doing in that pawnshop?"

"Buying a doohickey, maybe"

They both looked at each other and then Cardigan said, "I can imagine. S. Feitel-berg, *huhn?* Pawnshop—Eighth Avenue. All right, Pat—back you go to watch Lily. Watch every move she makes."

Pat said, "Swell," and slid a morning paper across the counter. "That item I checked off there. It probably means nothing, but just the same everything concerning Kemmerich ought to interest you. Heinrich Van Damm, the Holland gem expert, is arriving on the S. S. Oberstadt today and is to be entertained by Leopold Kemmerich, his boyhood friend. With butlers being killed, cops, private and city, horseplaying around the Kemmerich bailiwick, I imagine Mynheer Van Damm will find the entertainment gorgeous. No, thanks; no dessert. The old waistline, governor!"

"Watch Lily, little wonderful."

"I'd stare my eyes out even if I didn't know her. She knows how to wear clothes."

HE STOOD for a while outside, in front of the sporting-goods store, getting a cigar started after Pat had walked east. He had watched the smart, rhythmic swing of her bright, trim heels. He had given a bum a quarter.

Presently he walked down the broad sidewalk and pushed into a taxicab. It hauled him westward across town through a stubborn honeycomb of traffic and deposited him on Eighth Avenue. By this time the cigar was half smoked. He walked south. He had the lunging walk of a big man.

Sol Feitelberg's pawnshop was bigger than most, but fundamentally it was the same inside—so dark that Cardigan, coming in from the harsh sunlight, stood for a moment blinking his eyes. Then he was aware of a head bent toward him over a small counter between a high brass mesh and a high showcase.

"Feitelberg?"

"No, I'm the clerk."

"Where's Feitelberg?"

The temporary blind-staggers left Cardigan. Out of the mist came the face of the clerk, clear now in its pale thinness. And the too-large glasses, the black alpaca coat with elbows out, the cuffs ragged.

"You want to see Mr. Feitelberg?"

"Of course," Cardigan said.

The clerk disappeared behind the counter. When a door in the rear opened, Cardigan heard voices, but they stopped immediately—and then the door closed behind the clerk. But in a moment it opened, and there weren't any voices.

The clerk and a small, chubby man came out. The chubby man was bald and very white. There was not a hair on face or head. He had owlish eyes that attempted to be so frank that you got the opposite impression.

"Yes?"

"I want to talk to you alone a minute," Cardigan said.

"Me?"

"Mr. Feitelberg."

"Who are you, please?"

"Just now I'm representing the Odegard Indemnity Company."

"Come around back."

The office behind the store was small, dusty, cluttered, and had another door in the rear. There was an ash tray on the desk with a cigarette still smoldering. Cardigan took out his leather cigarette case.

"Smoke?"

"I don't smoke, thanks," the chubby man said.

Cardigan crushed out the smoldering cigarette and Feitelberg made a nervous gesture with his hands. Cardigan saw the gesture, but did not let on. He sat down.

He said: "You do a good business, don't you?"

"Good—yes, sometimes."

"High-class trade?"

Feitelberg shrugged. "I never ask. A man comes in. He buys something or he pawns something, but I never ask."

"Or a woman."

"Eh?"

"Or a woman comes in."

"Yes, yes, sometimes a woman."

Cardigan looked at his hands, said toward the floor: "What was the biggest loan you ever made?"

Feitelberg knew his rights. He was polite, saying: "That of course is something I am not obliged to give out. Just what do you want here, mister?"

"I'm looking for the lost Kemmerich pearls—a necklace valued at thirty thousand bucks."

IT WAS a blunt statement, and it sent the chubby man back a few paces. But he straightened against the wall. He laughed, nervously. "That is simple. I can tell you I know nothing about it. It was stolen last week, wasn't it, was it not? Ah, yes—now I remember. It was in the papers. Yes, I read all about it." He seemed suddenly cheerful, his owlish eyes sparkling. "It was a big piece in the papers about it—"

"Know Mrs. Kemmerich?"

"I have not the pleasure."

"What name does the lady go under who spent half an hour in here this morning?"

"There were a number of ladies in here this morning."

"One about ten o'clock."

Feitelberg bent his hairless brows studiously. "I do not seem to remember. I mean I do not associate any particular lady with any particular time."

Cardigan stood up. "You're a liar."

Feitelberg recoiled against the wall. "I hope I am not going to be insulted in my own place of business."

"I said you're a liar!"

Feitelberg leveled an arm. "Get out! Get out of my place of business!"

"Mrs. Kemmerich was in here this morning. She spent half an hour here. Her butler was killed last night. One of our agency men was killed shortly after

midnight. There's a hook-up somewhere."

Feitelberg got excited and knocked over a chair. He cried out in astonishment. The door leading to the store opened and the big-spectacled clerk stood there with a gun in his hand. He was young and scrawny but he was also cool.

"Trouble, Mr. Feitelberg?"

The chubby man was panicky. He picked up the chair and promptly stumbled over it again. But he reached the phone, and though his chin had the shakes there was a white grimness about it.

He panted: "Now get out, get out or I call the police! This is my place of business and I will not be insulted in it!"

The hand of the clerk was very steady and that made the gun he held doubly menacing. Cardigan scowled at it, scowled at the clerk, scowled at Feitelberg. He said nothing. He turned and walked into the store, out into the street.

He doubled around the block, scaled a board fence and worked his way into an alley that terminated in a small yard behind the pawnshop. He made his way to the door. Looking down, he saw three cigarette butts on the cement apron in front of the door. One was still smoldering.

Cardigan began backing away. He returned into the maw of the alley between two brick buildings, found another way to the street without scaling the board fence. There he slowed down, took up a position in the recessed doorway of a store placarded with *For Rent* signs.

Ten minutes later he saw a man come down the alley. The man walked rapidly, with head down. He was neatly dressed though his pants looked too tight and he wore patent-leather shoes. He appeared wiry, quick, and there was something definitely hard and sleek about the way the short-brimmed gray fedora was yanked down over one eyebrow.

The man was Packy Daskas.

CHAPTER THREE

P. & O. Punk

CARDIGAN lined out after him, taking his time, taking it easy. Packy flagged a cab on Seventh Avenue and it headed south. Cardigan caught one and passed a two-dollar bill through the window with brief instructions. At Fourteenth Street the cabs shot west and then south on Hudson Street. The tail wound up at Sheridan Square. Packy stood on the corner of West Fourth and Grove long enough to light a cigarette. Cardigan stood on Christopher near the subway entrance and let Packy get a start.

Packy went down Grove Street and slipped down into an areaway speak short of Bedford. Cardigan walked as far as Bedford, turned, killed a couple of minutes watching the areaway, then went toward it, down into it and pushed open an iron gate.

The bar was long with a lot of colored lights behind it. A couple of heavy afternoon drinkers stood at one end of the bar; a looking-glass drinker stood alone in the center hiccuping, and Packy stood at the other end nursing a drink between his hands and looking absorbed in thought. Cardigan went to the opposite end where there wasn't much light and ordered a gin rickey. A cop came in, got a pint, shoved it under his coat and went out whistling. Between mixing drinks, the barman read an account of a love-nest murder and made clicking, disapproving sounds with his tongue. It looked like a clean, orderly and law-abiding place.

After a while a man came in, looked around and then went slowly to a place at the bar beside Packy. Their elbows almost touched. Their heads went down, eyes shaded by hat brims, and the barman mixed two drinks. The man who had just come in looked older than Packy. He had a brown face, lined, and a black

mustache and broad shoulders. He wore a Homburg and looked like an actor or a gambler or like a good imitation of either. His air was one of faded elegance and he looked dissipated. He also looked haggard and he addressed Packy with a nervous, sidewise twitching of his mouth which he half concealed by a restless hand.

The two drank up; the older man paid and both went out. Cardigan planked a half-dollar piece on the bar and went out a minute later. He saw them walking toward Sheridan Square and followed them to West Tenth Street. They entered a narrow red brick house and when Cardigan slipped in he heard them walking frontward in the hallway above. Then he heard them mounting a second flight of stairs and he was up on the first landing by the time they reached the second. He heard keys jangling and catfooted up the second flight. His head came level with the hall floor and he saw through the railing that they entered a door at the rear of the hall.

He went downstairs, into the street and started walking east. He stood on the corner and watched the red brick house. An hour later the two men came out and headed west. When they had disappeared Cardigan strode to the house, entered the hall door and climbed to the second floor.

It took him three minutes to work his way through the lock. There was dirty chintz on two rear windows of a square, old-fashioned room. In the center stood a large brass bed. There was a cheap bureau. Under the bed was a battered steamer trunk which Cardigan dragged out. It was locked. He went through the bureau drawers and through the single closet, found nothing except indications that only one person occupied the room. It took him ten minutes to get the trunk open.

He found a couple of Luger automatics.

There were cord breeches and boots, flannel shirts, canvas coats, and lots of white duck. In the bottom he found a large photograph of a woman. On the back was inscribed "To my husband, forever. Lily." He whipped the photograph into better light.

It was Lily Kemmerich—Lily Kemmerich maybe ten, twelve years before. In the lower right hand corner were the name and address of the photographer—Lundmann, Cape Town.

Cardigan repacked the trunk, relocked it. But he did not replace the photograph of Lily Kemmerich. He had to fold it to get it into his inside coat pocket. He searched the room again, replacing meanwhile everything as he had found it. Then he stood in the center of the room, his back to the foot of the bed, and looked around.

Finally, satisfied, he moved toward the door, but before his hand settled on the knob a light knock on the oaken panel stopped him in his tracks. His shaggy brows bent—all his body went into quick, steel tension. Pivoting quietly, he went to the rear windows. There was no fire-escape, no way out. He swung around and then moved so that he would not be in silhouette and at the same time his hand slid beneath his left lapel, came out gripping a flat black automatic.

HE saw the knob turn. Saw the door open, slowly at first, then more rapidly. And because the room was dim due to the thick, dirty chintz on the windows, Lily Kemmerich did not see him at first. He lowered his gun. He saw she was alone, plainly dressed in something dark blue and tailored with an oval-shaped hat of dark straw quite concealing her blond hair.

Then she said, "Oh!" in a soft, strangled whisper.

"Quiet," his low voice warned.

"You!"

"Quiet!"

She swayed once, a little forward. He crossed the room, closed the door and stood with his back to it. She was a tall woman, but Cardigan dwarfed her. The top of his hat was on a level with the top of the door. His face was brown, lined heavily, almost malignant now because, perhaps, he was thinking of poor Fogarty who had been killed only half a block up the street.

Sarcasm touched his words— "From the swank east side to the dumps of the west side, Mrs. Kemmerich. This is not so sweet and lovely."

She moved backward, not smoothly, but with wooden-kneed steps, until she touched the brass rail of the bed. She leaned against this, and in the dimness her pale face was beautiful, almost exotic.

He growled: "Why did you come here?"

Her lips opened, but a visible pounding in her throat seemed to gag her. She made a short, inarticulate sound, and then suddenly tears made bright-shining pools of her eyes.

"Oh," she murmured. "Oh, God."

"Talk to me. Not God."

"Oh, please—please!" she sobbed. She staggered sidewise.

He took a quick step. He was Irish, with the quick moods, good or bad, of the Irish.

This time he said: "Take it easy, Mrs. Kemmerich. Steady does it. For crying out loud, don't pass out."

She sat down on the edge of the bed and stared white-faced at the soiled chintz curtains. Her lips quivered and there were little sounds fighting one another in her throat.

Cardigan growled: "Say something."

"What shall I say?"

"Who lives here?"

"A man."

He chided with—"Honest?"

"Don't—don't ridicule me."

"What did you come here for?"

"I can't tell you." She said it desperately, her hands clenched, her jaw firm.

"What were you doing at Sol Feitelberg's this morning?"

She was on her feet. The move was so abrupt and accompanied such a look of terror that the momentum carried her to the wall and she flattened against it, her eyes wide.

"No—no!" she cried.

His voice hardened. "A man of mine was killed in this street early this morning. He was following a man named Packy Daskas. Packy Daskas was in this room a short while ago with a man you know—the man who lives here, the man you came in to see. Our man was murdered because he was too close to something. He was murdered by either Daskas or the man you came to see. Where are the pearls?"

"I don't know."

"You lie. It was a frame-up on the insurance company. You pretended they were stolen so that you'd get dough from the insurance company and also dough from a fence. Those pearls were turned over to Feitelberg."

She shook her head, cried passionately, "No—no! You're wrong! Oh God, you're so, so wrong! Please—" She straightened and started for the door. "Let me go! Please let me out of here!"

"It was all arranged. Those pearls were turned over to Packy Daskas. You unhooked them yourself and in the crowd you moved so that it would be easy for him to receive them. Get back!"

He gripped her by both arms and his big, scowling face was close to hers. "Remember," he gritted, "that an old friend of mine was killed. Remember that."

She looked cold white. Her broken voice said: "You're stronger than I am.

You can break my arms—do anything. But I had nothing to do with killing your friend."

"Then tell me what you know."

"I can't."

"You will!"

'I can't! I can't! Let—let me go!"

SHE tussled with him. She heaved and squirmed and he stood rock-still on his feet, holding her with both hands until she should become exhausted. But suddenly she went limp and with a little, hopeless cry she slumped. He let her down to the floor and saw how white her face was. He grimaced. He looked angry and chagrined and bewildered and for a moment he did nothing but stand there and look down at her.

Then he bent down, lifted her in his arms and moved toward the bed. The door opened and a voice said: "All right, lay her down and then watch your hands."

He did not drop her. He looked over his shoulder and saw the haggard man kick the door shut. There was a gun in his hand. Cardigan laid Lily Kemmerich on the bed, straightened and turned to face the man.

"Watch those hands, you!"

"You watch 'em," Cardigan muttered.

"What the hell are you doing here?"

"What the hell do you think?"

"I wouldn't get fresh, funny face."

"Nuts for you."

"And pretty soon a load of lead in the belly for you. How do you like that?"

"No more than my friend Fogarty did."

The man was running sweat. He looked at the bed and snapped, "She brought you here, *huhn?*"

"I find my own way about."

"That's crap. Nobody knew about this but Lily. She brought you here, the two-timing slob."

"She never looked like a slob to me. Was she out of her mind when she married you?"

"Oh, she told you that, too!" His mustache twitched and his dark eyes burned across the room. "Well, it isn't going to do you any good. She married me when I was in the jack. When I traveled the ocean liners and the P. & O. boats taking suckers for a ride on the spotted pasteboards. The first jam I got in she lammed on me, the bum. I was a big shot in those days—"

"I don't give a damn what you were. Right now you're a small-time punk. Get down to business. If you'll let me, I'll put some water in her face."

"To hell with her! Don't you move or I'll let you have it!"

Cardigan grunted. He slid a glance down at the unconscious woman and a shadow passed across his face as though suddenly he regretted having been so harsh with her.

"Just stand there," the man said, as he flung a quick glance at his strap watch.

Fifteen minutes later the door opened and Packy Daskas came in. He stopped, took a few drags at a cigarette while running quick eyes over the scene.

He clipped: "What's this—a rehearsal?"

"It's her," the haggard man said, "and another one of those private dicks. She came here with him to fan the place."

Packy had better nerves than the other. He relaxed, tossed his butt to the floor and stamped it out. "This ain't the berries," he said. "Something's got to be done about it." He was flippant, cold as an icicle.

The haggard man's voice shook. "How about that other thing?"

Packy glared at him. "Clean. Do I have to keep telling you all the time?" He took off his hat and ran a hand over his lacquered dark hair, nodded toward Cardigan and spoke to the haggard man in a matter of fact tone. "This egg knows too much. It's no good. Something's got to be done about it. When it gets dark."

"And her too?"

"Sure."

Cardigan said: "She came here alone. I came here first, you saps. I crashed the place and after a while she came in. There's no hook-up."

Lily came to, turned her head from side to side. Finally her eyes settled on the haggard man and she said, weakly, "Harry."

"To hell with you!" the haggard man said.

"Harry. I—please—"

"To hell with you!"

CHAPTER FOUR

The Crimson Necklace

MAYBE it was the sight of Lily, so beautiful, that gushed fresh rage through Harry's body. He talked as if things had been pent up for a long time—while Packy Daskas stood slim and cold, his gun now in his hand and leveled toward Cardigan. Harry struck the brass rail of the bed with his fists, and his lips became wet and red with frenzy.

"Lammed on me," he cried, "when I got in that jam in Algiers! Bailed out! Left me flat! And now you come here with this dick to my room! And what did you find? Nothing!"

She said, subdued: "I came here alone, to plead with you."

The hushed tranquility of her voice seemed to enrage him. He came around the bed and slapped her face and Cardigan, bitter-lipped, kicked him in the back. Harry spun away from the bed, arching his back, crying out in pain, and Packy came closer with a white, icy look in his face and his gun closer to Cardigan's stomach.

But he spoke to Harry— "Lay off, Harry. Keep your head. We've got to keep our heads. Lay off now and don't go meshuga over a dame. It's the bunk."

"He kicked me," Harry panted.

Cardigan said: "I'd like to put my foot down your throat," without emphasis, in a voice hard and brittle.

It was getting dark. Daylight was fading rapidly beyond the chintz curtains.

Lily sat up. "I must go home."

Harry laughed hysterically. "You're never going home, Lily!"

Packy was matter of fact again. "Never, Lily. You brought this dick here and neither you or him are ever going home. Take that and try to like it."

"She didn't bring me here," Cardigan said, bluntly.

Her eyes widened as though now for the first time she was becoming aware of her predicament. Her hand moved up to her breast and beyond to her throat. The men in the room were becoming vague blurs because of the thickening twilight, but each was made a distinct personality by his voice.

Harry whined: "You left me flat, Lily, and now you brought a dick here to my room."

Her voice was far away—"I didn't leave you, as you say, flat. I met you in Africa and I was young and didn't know men. After a week of it I knew I was all wrong. You changed. Or you didn't change but were your real self and not the man I met on shipboard. When I met you first you acted the part of a world traveler. But I married you and how quickly you showed your real self. And I loathed you. And myself. And then I felt that love was done with me. You left me for six months, and not a word from you, and then I met you in Algiers and took pity on you and then the very next night you were caught. And then I left you."

"Cut this. Cut this," Packy said coldly. Then his voice hardened with finality. "Harry, we've got to lam. We can't hang around here all night. The car's gassed

and all set and we've got to blow while the blowin's good. Turn on the lights."

Harry turned on the lights and these made the room more drab and bare and Harry's face looked more haggard, more sallow and haunted. Ghosts were in his fevered eyes but Packy remained cold and hard and certain.

He said: "The gas."

"*Huhn?*" Harry said.

"The gas—for both of them. Take this guy."

Cardigan moved—got his broad back against the wall. "I tell you, she came here alone."

Harry yammered: "Being brave, hey? Spare the gal and—"

"I'm not being brave, louse. I'm trying to tell you something."

"Take him, Harry," came Packy's crisp, cold voice.

Lily was off the bed—on her feet. She cried passionately: "If I've done anything —anything—my life's yours to do with as you please. Everything is ruined. This will ruin everything. I'm done for. I tried to begin all over again, but there was no use. But I've done nothing wrong —nothing."

HARRY struck Cardigan. The black-jack came miraculously from somewhere, in his clothes and Cardigan was off guard because his eyes, wondering and curious, were on the woman. The blow sent him sliding along the wall. He reached the washstand and braced an arm against it. He looked stupidly down at the white bowl there. Harry came behind and let him have it again.

The woman moaned and Packy said: "Shut your trap, sister."

Harry, striking Cardigan, cried in a hoarse whisper: "I'll give you the same as I gave your partner! He got in here too! He found those pearls and he was taking them out but I got him! And you the same—I'll get you!"

Cardigan muttered: "So it was you got poor old Fogarty—"

Rage must have suddenly overcame him. His foot swung and hit Harry and Harry reeled across the room and landed on the bed. Packy jumped and slammed his gun against Cardigan's stomach.

"One more crack like that, guy, and you get it quick!"

Lily sprang to the door and got it open and cried, "Help!"

Packy choked and spun and Cardigan, drunk with pain and half blind, made a pass at him but only succeeded in getting him off balance.

"Help! Help!" Lily screamed in the hallway.

Harry, off the bed, made a vicious lunge for Lily, but suddenly there was a new tangle in the doorway and out of it Pat came. There was a small Colt automatic in her hand. Harry stopped against its muzzle.

She said: "Stop, you!"

But Harry, wild-eyed, struck at her and she reeled away. He plunged through the door. That scream of Lily's had turned matters. There seemed in Harry's actions only a frantic desire to get out of the room.

Packy, white as death, heard the blast of a police whistle somewhere below. He moved like something shot from a spring. As he reached the hall there was a blinding flash. He ducked. But the flash had nothing to do with him. Lily was falling and Harry was backing away, his gun smoking, his mouth wide open in dumb awe.

Packy still had nerves. "Scram!"

Harry whipped toward the stairway but Packy snapped: "We can't make it that way, dope! Up—the roof!"

Pat choked in the doorway: "I should

have got him, chief. I couldn't. I couldn't—kill anybody."

"You did enough, little wonderful," he muttered. "See about Lily Kemmerich—"

Plunging into the hallway, he saw Lily settling on the floor, her face stricken and her head shaking from side to side as though she were saying: "This didn't happen—this didn't happen."

His lips tightened and a raw oath ripped from his throat. He slammed his way along the hallway and looking upward saw the heels of Packy disappearing through the door to the roof. The door slammed. In a split minute Cardigan was up at it. He almost carried it from its hinges. Then he was in starlight and the cool summer night, among the chimney pots.

Red flame split the shadows of the next roof. Lead tore through a rusty ventilator against which Cardigan's arm brushed. He dropped and then heaved to one side and then shot forward around a chimney and his gun banged. The echoes walloped across the roof, and commingled with them was a short cry. But the two shapes were still running, dodging, scaling the dividing walls between the roofs.

But one began to lag during the next minute. He half turned and fired but he was wide of the mark and wrecked a skylight. Glass exploded and fell with a harsh, rasping noise. Cardigan's gun boomed for the second time and the one lagged, stumbled forward, turned all the way around. But he was late. A third shot slammed him down and his gun bounced six feet across the roof.

It was Packy, panting: "Don't finish me—"

"Now where's your ice-cold nerve?"

"Don't! Here—" Out of his pocket came a pearl necklace. "Take it, but don't—"

Cardigan snatched it from his hand and thrust it into his pocket. He jumped over

Packy and slipped down along the front of the roof. He heard a roof door bang. He plunged past a chimney, reached the door, listened. Heels were clattering down a stairway. Cardigan yanked the door open and a gun belched from the bottom of the stairway. He fired off balance, missed. Harry ducked. Cardigan lunged downward and only when he reached the bottom of the staircase did he realize that his face ached. His cheek had been burned open by the bullet. Blood was flowing.

A FAT woman opened a door, saw his bloody face, screamed and banged the door shut. Harry was down the next flight. Doors were banging all over the house, and women were screaming. Harry went through a door, knocking a woman clear across the room. Cardigan reached the door as Harry crashed into a coal range. The stove pipe broke loose from the wall and coal dust showered downward. Harry fired blindly and his shot smashed crockery on a shelf above Cardigan's head.

Cardigan snapped: "Drop it, Harry!"

But Harry was too far gone to reason things out. Cardigan had to let him have it. The shot pinned Harry against the wall behind the stove for a brief second, and then he sank, slack-jawed.

Cardigan walked across the room, reached down and with little effort took the gun from Harry's hand. The old woman was sitting on the floor, rocking from side to side and moaning. Cardigan lifted her, piloted her to a rocking chair and eased her into it.

"You're all right," he said. "Just be calm."

He turned and saw a cop standing in the doorway holding a gun. "Lift 'em, fella," the cop said.

"I'm O. K.," Cardigan said. "I'm Cardigan, of the Cosmos Agency."

"Who's this?"

"His name's Harry. There's a guy named Packy Daskas on the roof."

"No he ain't."

"*Huhn?*"

"He pitched to the sidewalk. We been looking for him. Him and another guy stuck up a pawnshop on Eighth Avenue this afternoon. We sure been looking for him. The owner was killed."

Cardigan's left hand was tight on the pearls in his pocket. He headed for the door and the cop stepped aside and Cardigan went down into the street. He walked to the red brick house. The riot squad was there. He recognized Flamm, a precinct dick. Then an ambulance pulled up.

"Did you get Packy?" Flamm said.

"I guess so."

"Some guys get all the breaks."

"Oh, you think so?"

Pat came down out of the hall door. She held a handkerchief to her face and Cardigan pushed through the crowd and took hold of her arm.

"Hurt, kid?" he said.

"No. Just"—she grimaced—"sick. She died. They won't need the ambulance. Poor thing—poor thing."

"Chin up, Pat."

"I know, I know."

Cardigan turned to Flamm. "This is Miss Seaward, one of our operatives. I'll get her out of this and then come back."

"Sure—sure thing," Flamm said.

More cops were arriving. Windows were open and hall doors were jammed with wide-eyed people. Traffic was being diverted from this block. Cardigan walked Pat to the next corner and found a cab. They got in.

"Still sick, kid?"

"It was terrible, chief. She was so beautiful."

The taxi gathered speed.

Cardigan said: "She say anything?"

"Yes. She said Harry Pritchard was

her husband, once. She got a divorce and only two months ago he turned up, after nine years. He used to be a gambler. He was down and out and he threatened to tell of her former marriage if she didn't help him. She pawned that necklace, got a paste one to match it and wore that and her husband never knew. He was proud of the necklace. There'd been bits in the paper about it.

"Then this jewel expert Van Damm was coming. She got panicky. She hadn't the money to get the real one out of hock and she knew Van Damm would know the one she wore was a fake. She went to Harry and told him. She was desperate. She had to lose that necklace, have it stolen. All that was arranged. But she wouldn't tell him where she had pawned the real one.

"He was hooked up with Packy. She let Packy steal the fake. Then Packy and her former husband decided to get the real one. How? Well, she had the pawn ticket. Packy crashed the apartment and got it and that's why she said nothing had been stolen. The pawn ticket showed them where she'd pawned the necklace. They destroyed the fake one."

Cardigan said: "And they had to bump Feitelberg off to get the real one."

She lay back in the cab, closed her eyes. "She was a good girl, chief. You've got to believe that. She did her best. She could never have stood it if Van Damm had seen the necklace she wore was paste."

He drew the pearls from his pocket. They were stained crimson. They had got that way from Packy's hand.

The Hunched Horror

by
Westmoreland Gray

Author of "The Beast in Black," etc.

No shoppers swarmed about the counters of Bryant's Store; no eager clerks stood waiting there to serve. But along the aisles a hideous hunchback killer crept. Death was the only bargain he sought there, a bray of horrid banshee laughter his only mark of sale.

Margo scuttled for the elevator.

CHAPTER ONE

Petals of Mystery

JIMMIE BOLTON came into Collin Windsor's den and stood there before the wall mirror to twine his silver-gray muffler about his neck. He was a walking exponent of what the young man will wear, and had a small carnation in his coat lapel. But there was something in his face that did not jibe with carnations and sartorial perfection. Collin Windsor took one look at him, then deliberately laid aside the pipe he was smoking and the book he was reading. He stood to his slippered feet.

Jimmie was donning his long black overcoat and whistling with forced gaiety. Collin grabbed him by the shoulder, spun him around and yanked the small automatic from the boy's overcoat pocket. He pitched the gun carelessly on the bed and shoved Jimmie into a chair.

"Now!" he ordered. "Spit it out! Don't be a fool."

Jimmie's face worked with a spasm of

emotion. That primitive passion verged on the comical in Jimmie Bolton. He was rather chubby, with a round and innocent face, this young reporter, and that face mirrored resentment rather grotesquely.

"If Herndon Bryant or Bob McNeal try to interfere with me tonight," Jimmie said huskily, clenching his fists, "I'll kill them—either one!"

"And if you don't talk sense I'll bat you a couple," Collin Windsor said quietly. Jimmie was Collin's protegé, shared his bungalow and his companionship. Collin could talk to him that way.

"Well—you'd feel the same if someone was keeping you from seeing Ruth."

"Maybe. But I don't think I'd start in by killing him."

"Bryant can't see within a mile of me because of my poverty. He's money mad. Wants Rose to marry millions, I guess. He's forbidden me to enter his house."

Collin calmly picked up his pipe, relit it. "Tell me," he said.

"It's Herndon Bryant and that damn nephew of his, McNeal. They both hate each other, but they both hate me worse. They've got dollars on the brain. McNeal wants to marry Rose so he'll come into the Bryant money eventually, so he's glad Bryant objects to me. He keeps stirring up the old man against me. And Bryant's got nothing against me except that he hates a poor man's guts."

"Let's see. Is Rose Herndon Bryant's own daughter?"

"His step-daughter. Took Bryant's name. But the old devil is crazy about her—loves her as much as he loves anything except money. She'll be his heir—"

"Heiress."

"Heiress, then—and Bob McNeal knows it. McNeal's rotten and always has been and Herndon Bryant knows that. But I'd like to see 'em try to keep me from seeing Rose."

"So?"

"I've got a date to meet Rose at her office in the store this evening—you know, she handles all the store's advertising. Does a damn good job of it too. I've got a perfectly legitimate reason for meeting her there. The Times-Herald's assigned me to write a big publicity article on Bryant's, Incorporated. I'm going to see Rose about that. Bob McNeal's found it out and sent me word to stay away. Let him try to make me!"

Collin chuckled. He slapped Jimmie on the back. "You've got it that bad, huh? Well, go ahead and see your Rose and write your publicity article. But don't be a fool and start out gunning. I don't suppose either McNeal or Bryant is liable to resort to violence against you."

Jimmie shrugged his shoulders and started toward the door. "Wanta use the roadster?" Collin offered.

Jimmie shook his head. "Thanks. I've called a taxi."

Collin said, "Luck," and dropped back into his easy chair. Jimmie went out and Collin's brow knitted in a slight frown. He didn't like the set-up. Jimmie was certainly in love with Rose Bryant, had fallen for her hard. And apparently Rose felt the same way about Jimmie. This had drawn opposition from McNeal, whom Collin knew for a dissolute and reckless fellow about thirty, a man of unsavory reputation in Dalshire; and also from the girl's step-father, Herndon Bryant, owner of the great Bryant's Department Store. Collin knew little of Herndon Bryant personally, but he knew Robert McNeal for an underhanded schemer, who'd be glad to do Jimmie dirt if he could. Collin frowned deeper and settled back with his pipe.

JIMMIE BOLTON got out of his cab a block from where the twelve-story Bryant Building stood. He paid his fare and headed down the block. It was ten o'clock but the street was rather quiet— that hour when most of the crowds were at the shows. Jimmie raised his hand in greeting to the patrolman on the corner, waited for the red light to turn green, then crossed to where the display windows of Bryant's, Incorporated, glittered with dazzling radiance. He turned down Ackman Street and made for the side entrance.

The entrance-way was dark. Rose had told him to ring the night bell there and the night watchman would admit him and take him up to her office on the fifth floor. Jimmie hoped that Robert McNeal would be nowhere around. He was anxious to see Rose alone—to talk to her about something besides store publicity.

He rang the bell and waited. Nobody answered and Jimmie's nerves became tense. He was gnawed by a vague fear. He rang again, then continuously for a long time. He could hear the alarm sounding through the dark cavernous main floor.

He swore under his breath. Involuntarily his hand tried the door. It was unlocked and opened at his shove. Jimmie debated a moment, then committed a fatal indiscretion. He entered the store.

He knew the way to Rose's office. If the elevator were working, he could run himself up.

Just inside the doorway his foot struck something that skittered along the tiled floor and jingled metallically. Jimmie struck a match and searched for it. He found it. A huge key-ring with innumerable keys on it—the watchman's key-ring.

Maybe Jimmie was forewarned a little then—but he blundered on. If something was wrong in the store, then he wanted to know. Rose Bryant was in there; he had to know that she was safe.

The darkened store with its single dim light at the elevator bank was tomb-like. Counter displays and shelves were shrouded in white muslin covers. Heel taps echoed eerily and the mezzanine floor to his right was a cavern of black gloom.

Feeling his way along, Jimmie headed toward the elevators. His way entwined between counters and he had to traverse a long aisle. Midway of this he stopped with a sharp intake of breath, and stared in front of him. There was a splash of dull light on the tiled floor. It came from an electric torch that had fallen and rolled against a counter. Beyond the torch was a huddled, half-sprawled form.

Jimmie knelt over the figure. It was a man in drab clothes—neat denim trousers, a shirt with black sateen sleeve protectors and black suspenders. His cap lay on the floor beside his head.

Jimmie Bolton grasped the flashlight and sent its glow on the figure. He saw an old man, with lined and wrinkled face and sparse gray hair. There was a swollen welt on his forehead and a tiny stream of blood trickled from it.

Jimmie turned the man over and confirmed what he had already guessed. The light shone on a night-watchman's badge, and also on the intricate watchman's timepiece strapped at the man's waist. Jimmie felt his pulse and was reassured. At least the man wasn't dead. But he'd had a bad blow and needed immediate medical care.

Jimmie stood up. He would make his way to Rose's office, and call a doctor from there. Unlighted flashlight in hand, he started swiftly along a dark aisle which was the nearest cut to the elevators.

He stumbled and fell sprawling. A queer shiver ran through his body as he groped for the dropped light and got to his feet. A shiver with a touch of horror in it. The thing that had tripped him was soft and yielding!

Jimmie swung the light around. It shone on the handsome dissipated face of Robert McNeal. McNeal lay on his back in the aisle. There was a great red stain on McNeal's dress-shirt front, and a spreading pool of red beside him. Jimmie knew from the half-open, set, staring, unseeing eyes that McNeal was dead.

JIMMIE'S courage did not desert him entirely, though he was momentarily inert, dumbfounded. He was staring down at the white death-mask of an enemy. He had entered the store illegally, almost furtively. It was known that he had threatened violence to McNeal. His left hand was stained red; there were traces of blood on the edges of his shoe soles. Jimmie shuddered.

His first impulse was to flee the place, first obliterating all signs of his presence. But cooler judgment advised against this. Flight was tantamount to confession in police circles. Then the policeman on the beat had seen him approach the store. Rose had expected him. Collin Windsor had known he was coming here. No doubt McNeal had advised Herndon Bryant of Jimmie's planned tryst with Rose here at the store. All this must come out in any investigation, no matter how reluctant Rose and Collin would be to divulge their knowledge. Jimmie shook his head. Flight was not his solution.

He swung the light slowly about him. He gave a grim, hollow laugh. Already he had left signs of his presence. An alabaster column was defiled with a dark-stained handprint which he had made in getting up from his fall. There were heelprints on the tile and, no doubt, numerous fingerprints. To try to erase them all, here in the dark, was out of the question. Jimmie turned the flashlight back on the grisly thing on the floor.

Something on McNeal's shirt front caught his eye. He stooped and peered closely. A small flower lay on the dead man's chest. A delicate flower it was,

a thing of soft, hood-like petals, now ugly and sinister with its stain of blood. It was an exotic blossom, foreign to Jimmie's knowledge, and bending closer he saw that it was artificial, cunningly fashioned of silk so as to appear real except under close scrutiny.

He did not touch it, but set his head buzzing with questions. What did it mean; why was it there? Was it some emblem of the murderer? Jimmie thought so. It appeared to have been placed there on McNeal's chest, rather than to have fallen there.

Jimmie moved. He must go to Rose, let her know what had happened and notify the police. He must face the music. He was innocent. Somehow he could prove it, possibly help to apprehend the murderer.

He found one of the elevators open. He stepped in, closed it, turned the crank and the elevator moved up. He stopped the machine, got out on the fifth floor. It was quiet as a tomb up there, and the place was entirely dark. The cages of the general offices stretched away into gloomy, shadowy realms, an expanse of mahogany panels and frosted glass and grill work. In the daytime a seething hive of activity, now as deserted as a graveyard.

Apprehensive, Jimmie stood before the door of the advertising office—Rose Bryant's sanctum in that huge department store. The girl had deliberately chosen a business career in preference to one of social activity. She supervised—and brilliantly—the entire publicity program of the store. Jimmie was proud of her for that.

He turned the knob, pushed open the door. The office was a black pit. He felt along the casement, snapped the light switch. Illumination as brilliant as daylight flooded the place.

Jimmie stepped back with a cry of dismay. The place was in turmoil. A chair and a wastebasket overturned, papers, mats, trays scattered on the floor and trampled. There had been a desperate struggle in this room—and Rose was gone!

SHE had been there. Jimmie knew it. The faintest trace of her delicate perfume struck Jimmie, poignantly familiar. A filmy handkerchief was trampled on the floor. Her white-gold compact lay on the typewriter stand, beside her desk.

Half in a daze Jimmie stared about him. For a long time his mind refused to take in this new fact, this new horror. His eyes sought something, some proof that this was not real. That it was the figment of some awful nightmare.

And then his gaze came to rest on her desk. There was a flower there. An exotic, delicate, hooded flower—exactly like the one on McNeal's dead breast!

Jimmie choked back a cry. He lifted up the thing, examined it with a tingling sense of horror and revulsion. Finally he laid it down, half turned away.

He stopped. That white-gold compact there. It seemed mutely to beckon him, to say that Rose had so lately sat there at that typewriter. It seemed crying out to tell him something. He peered closely. He saw that a white edge of paper stuck up from the typewriter platen.

Maybe it was clairvoyance, maybe it was sixth sense. Jimmie's fingers twisted the roller, turning the paper farther up. Typed lines came into view.

> Dear Jimmie: I'm horribly afraid here all alone. There's something in this store. Something brutal, sinister. It has followed me, I feel it hovering close. Oh—it's coming in—an ugly hunch—

The writing stopped short. Plucky Rose! To have the courage and wit to turn back the machine, hide the message, when she saw danger coming. The portent of the message filled Jimmie with dread. What was this hunched or hunch-backed thing that had lurked in the store, struck down the watchman, murdered McNeal and carried away Rose?

Jimmie steeled himself against sheer terror. He reached for the telephone on Rose's desk. He'd have the police on her trail. His own position did not matter now. Rose's safety was the only thing that counted.

Immediately he knew that the phone was dead. No doubt the wires were cut. He slammed it viciously back on its rack, turned, darted out of the office and raced back to the elevator.

The echo of the clanging door had hardly died out, before Jimmie was getting out on the main floor. Then he stopped short. Sturdy blue-coated figures were in the store's side entranceway, figures outlined in the gloom by the reflected light of the street outside. The policeman in the lead was calling, shouting questions.

Courage deserted him. Instead of going to the police, telling his story, bringing them here, they were to catch him lurking here, red-handed, with a murdered man who was his hated enemy! The thought of it put Jimmie to rout. He felt the mark and brand of a hunted, cornered man.

He leaped back into the elevator and sent it rocketing skyward.

The appearance of police in numbers at the Bryant Department Store was no mere coincidence. The store was equipped with a modern alarm system. Twice every hour the night watchman was supposed to check in, turning a key at some certain point in the building. His failure to do so had turned in an alarm at the nearest police station, and brought the bluecoats to investigate. They found plenty to interest them.

Jimmie Bolton felt some hope in the few minutes lead he had on them. It would take awhile for them to light up the main floor, find the bodies, and get over their surprise. Then they'd discover the missing elevator and start their chase.

He rode to the top floor and got out. He crept up the stairway to the roof. For a long time he crouched against the wall of the long, narrow concrete room that housed the elevator motors and pulleys. They were silent now and the room was dark. From far below came the muffled, ghostly, night din of the city.

Quick, unnerving, came a sudden sound close by. It was a whir that shattered the quiet so dramatically that Jimmie started violently, his nerves on edge. Then he understood it. It was the noise of a pulley motor. An elevator had started upward.

It paused, then started again. Listening, with quickened heartbeats, Jimmie heard it pause—start—pause—start. And he knew what it meant. It was the police combing the building for the fugitive who had taken that first elevator up. A pair of men to each floor—lighting the dark corridors, searching among the racks and counters and cases, peering up the enclosed stairways. Floor by floor, thorough, relentless, they were coming toward him. And he could go no farther skyward.

JIMMIE moved to the door of the elevator room. He tried it, and swore with disappointment. There was a tiny dew of sweat on his forehead. New apprehension dismayed him as another motor whirred. More police coming up. Soon he'd be trapped—trapped like some animal.

He left the door, made for the other side of the motor house. From here he could see the city spread below, its flashing, dazzling lights like sparkling, colored gems in black velvet. But Jimmie did not pause to contemplate their beauty. There was only an eighteen-inch space between the wall of the room and the parapet of

the building's edge. Jimmie squeezed between these until he was under a high window.

He climbed up on the parapet and leaned across to the cement wall of the room. Poised there in space he was smitten with an instant of dizziness. It passed and his fingers sought the window sill. He gave a brief sigh of thanks. The window was open.

With a show of acrobatics of which he'd hardly have been capable under less stress, he drew himself up, scrambled through the window and dropped inside the dark room. He fell to his hands and knees on the concrete floor. He remained thus an instant staring toward the dark forms of the motors. Two of them were going at the moment, their armature brushes spraying blue-and-red sparks of light. Jimmie threw off his overcoat and advanced cautiously toward one of the silent motors.

He felt for the gang plank with a tentative foot—found it. He stood on it then, and stared down into the horrible well of blackness that was the elevator shaft. It seemed miles to the reflected half-radiance of the main floor lights below. But how near it was to those two approaching cars!

Only desperation could have driven Jimmie to it. But escape he must. Behind bars how could he search for Rose— the thought of whose possible plight turned him to shivering with dread?

Feeling his way around the motors, he encountered the twin cables stretching away and away below. Jimmie grasped them. He forced his body between them, wedging it. Then he kicked his feet clear of the gang plank and hung suspended in space!

He entwined a leg around each cable, and began to slide. Nausea gripped his vitals and he felt weak, but he clung with every muscle, every fibre of his body. The thick, gummy grease on the cables balled up in his palms, smeared his clothes hideously, and then filled his nostrils with its sticky smell.

His speed accelerated. Floors went by, marked by the elevator doorways and dim corridor night lights. Blackness below rose to meet him. It seemed interminable, that sliding fall, and he clung with every vestige of will and muscle power. To release was death.

He stopped with a sickening jolt on top of the elevator cage. He sat there, clinging, gasping for breath. His eyes were just on the level with the main floor, for the elevator was on the basement level. He saw the lights and moving figures of officers in the aisles. He barely heard the mumble of their voices.

He ducked and slid to the edge of the cage. He climbed down the grill work of the empty shaft next to him, and opened its door. He stepped out into the cool darkness of the basement.

This space below was deserted still. It was closely packed, for economy's sake, with counters and glass cases and shelves, all now shrouded in their ghostly white muslin. Jimmie moved among the maze, groping, ready to duck and hide at the first alarm.

He knew there was a sidewalk entrance to this basement at the east end of Bryant's, which fronted on a lesser street. If—

Like a wraith he crept the long, mysterious length of the basement and finally came to that east doorway. His grease-stained hand felt over it. His heart gave a bound of joy. It was bolted and locked, but both could be manipulated from the inside.

He lifted the bolt, threw the lock, opened the door a crack. He peered out and up the stair-well to the sidewalk. This side of the street was almost deserted. Only a pedestrian or two. The other side was crowded. Throngs before the garishly lighted front of a second-rate movie house.

Briefly Jimmie lurked there in the stairwell. He guessed that not enough time had elapsed for a cordon to have been thrown around the building. Jimmie watched his chance and climbed to the sidewalk, unnoticed, he hoped. He straightened his clothes and walked to the first cross street. Avoiding passersby as much as possible he made quickly for the nearest darkened thoroughfare. He turned north on this and broke into an excited run.

CHAPTER TWO

The Banshee Laugh

JIMMIE BOLTON was no more than halfway to town after leaving his and Collin Windsor's bungalow, when Collin's perusal of his book was interrupted by the ringing of the telephone. Indolently, deliberately, Windsor got up and lifted the instrument from its hook.

"Yes?"

"Collin Windsor?" The voice was brusque, businesslike. But there was another note in it, something for the moment Collin could not classify.

"Speaking."

"This is Herndon Bryant." Collin jerked to attention, all signs of indolence gone. Then the voice again. "You are a detective?"

"I prefer to call myself an investigator."

"So much the better. Can you come by my house, say in thirty minutes. I'm troubled by a matter."

"You wouldn't suggest its nature over the phone?"

"Well—I— Hang it, man! I'm in deadly fear. I've been threatened, that is, my daughter—my step-daughter—has. She doesn't know it. She's gone out.

Someone called me on the phone only a minute or two ago. Said that she—she would disappear!"

Bryant was speaking under great stress and with reluctance. Collin sensed that, even over the wire. Collin looked at his wrist watch.

"I'll be over in thirty minutes," he said briefly and hung up.

Before he went to his bedroom, Collin snapped on his short-wave radio set, an instrument which kept him in touch with nearly all the city's criminal doings. He kept it tuned in on the police broadcasting station which sent out a continuous stream of orders to the department's cruising radio cars. Among these might be something relevant to Bryant's case. Almost immediately came the voice of the sergeant announcer.

Collin listened a moment but none of the items interested him. He turned toward his bedroom door, opened it, then halted on the threshold. He turned and strode quickly back to the radio.

"Warning, warning, all cars," said the voice. "Keep lookout for young man of low height and plump build. Wears neat dark suit and possibly gray muffler. Probably hatless, no overcoat, and clothes grease-stained. Maybe prowling or hiding out in dark areas. Watch taxis. Name, James Bolton. Sought for murder of Robert McNeal at Bryant's Department Store. Arrest."

Before Collin could get over his shock and absorb this his telephone rang again, jangling, imperative. Collin snatched the receiver. "Windsor speaking."

"Hello, Mr. Windsor," A suave, stilted voice. "Mr. Bryant's valet speaking. You are not to come to see Mr. Bryant, sir. He is forced to break his appointment because of another, more serious matter."

Collin grunted and slammed the receiver on the hook. Jimmie in trouble!

McNeal murdered! What did it mean? Collin dressed with the dispatch of a fireman. Even as he slammed out the back door and ran for his garage, his thoughts were racing ahead of him.

He opened the wide doors and groped in his pocket for the ignition keys. A voice spoke to him from the shadows beside the garage.

"Collin!"

In two strides Collin was facing Jimmie there in the gloom. He saw that the boy was hatless, frenzied, and his clothes were a wreck, smeared with grease. "Jimmie! What fool thing have you done? I took one gun from you—"

"I didn't do it, Collin. He was dead when I got there."

"Why did you run, you imbecile? It looks—"

"To hell with that. To hell with me and my affairs. Listen, Collin, Rose has disappeared!"

"Disappeared?"

"Been kidnaped. Collin, I had to get away, to do something about her. You've got to help me!"

Collin saw that the boy was on the verge of mental and emotional exhaustion. He put a hand on his shoulder and spoke soothingly. "Let's get in the car and sit down. Try to calm yourself, Jimmie."

Seated in the dark in the roadster, Collin said: "Now tell me all and tell it fast. The place will be lousy with cops as soon as they check up on our address."

"I'm not going back," Jimmie said defiantly. "They won't lock me up when heaven knows what has happened to Rose!"

"Have it your way, but I think you're crazy."

Jimmie told Collin his story, rapidly but in detail. Collin was particularly interested in the two small flowers at the scene of each crime.

"Sounds like wolf-bane," he said. "More commonly known as monk's-hood. They grow rather freely among the rocks in certain sections of our Western deserts. Their roots are poisonous, containing aconite. These flowers have some sinister meaning, some bearing on this case, Jimmie."

In the end Collin was forced to become an accomplice in Jimmie's flight. He went into the bungalow and brought out another suit, clean linen and shoes for him. Then he hid him in the rear compartment of the roadster and drove away. Halfway downtown he stopped at an unlighted corner and let the boy out.

"Get out of town, Jimmie," he advised. "And leave everything to me. I'll do all I can to find Rose. I'll try to get word to you some way."

Collin felt a deep pang as he drove away and Jimmie was swallowed by the shadows. He refused to put Jimmie's tale to the test of cold logic. It sounded too fantastic, too unreal and far-fetched.

And Jimmie had only that night declared he'd kill McNeal if McNeal tried to come between him and Rose Bryant!

LIEUTENANT RINEHART was speaking, and his voice showed that he considered the case in the bag. "It amounts to this. Bolton has smeared himself all over with incriminating facts. That's usually the case when an amateur commits a crime of passion. Watts, the traffic cop at the corner, saw Bolton approach the store and turn toward the side entrance. He wore a long dark overcoat and gray silk muffler and a soft, light-colored hat. We found the overcoat in the bottom of the elevator shaft and the hat here on the main floor. We found the east sidewalk entrance unbarred, where Bolton evidently escaped through the basement—after we arrived. There are fingerprints

here that we'll be able to check up on soon."

Collin nodded grimly. He looked around at the little crowd there. A doctor was administering to Mintlow, the slugged store watchman, who was on a small cot from the store's first-aid room. Besides Rinehart there were two other detectives, several uniformed men who were guarding doors, and still others searching the building. Jamieson, the fingerprint man, was there and the police photographer, all busy as bees in a hive. A host of reporters hovered outside the entrance, refused admittance. Lastly there was Herndon Bryant, the store owner. Collin studied Bryant covertly. His face was normally carved in immobile, blocky lines. But now it was drawn and haggard. Collin decided that if he'd ever seen a man who was distinctly uncomfortable and ridden by dread, it was Bryant.

Collin turned back to Rinehart. "How do you reconstruct the crime, Rinehart?"

"Jimmie Bolton was in love with Miss Bryant. Bryant says he objected to Bolton strenuously, considered him impudent in his poverty for aspiring to the favor of this wealthy girl. Also McNeal had voiced objection, and Bolton hated McNeal also, because he was a rival. Jimmie had a date to meet Miss Rose here at the store tonight. McNeal found it out and told Jimmie not to show up or there'd be trouble. Also McNeal informed Mr. Bryant of the tryst. McNeal came down to prevent it, and, according to my theory, told Mintlow the watchman not to admit Jimmie."

"Yes." Collin spoke softly. He was scanning the scene around him on the now lighted main floor. He could see McNeal's body with the photographer hovering over it.

"Jimmie rang the bell. Mintlow unlocked the door, but refused to let him in. Jimmie flew off the handle and struck him down. Either that or he found the door open, entered and struck Mintlow from behind. We'll check that with Mintlow's story when he's able to talk. But—no sooner does he turn from the watchman than he faces McNeal, in a rage, within the store. He shoots on impulse."

"Jimmie didn't have his gun," Collin said. "I happen to know it's at home."

"There's hundreds of guns. Anyway this gat must have had a silencer or someone would have heard the shot from the outside."

"What then?" Collin's tone was edged with slight irony.

"Jimmie went to the girl's office. He told her what he'd done and they ran away together, making the scene give an impression of forcible abduction."

There was an interruption then from an unexpected source. It was Herndon Bryant. "I tell you," he cried, "my stepdaughter didn't run away with young Bolton! She was kidnaped and is now in deadly danger!"

The depth of conviction in Bryant's voice gave Collin a little start, as did also the man's attitude. Knowing how little the capitalist cared for Jimmie, Collin was surprised that Bryant was unwilling to believe the worst of him.

"It all fits, Mr. Bryant," Rinehart said defensively. "Can you point out something that contradicts this theory?"

Bryant opened his mouth as if to voice objection. He seemed to think better of it however, and fell silent. His eyes turned to Collin. Collin decided that this man was troubled nearly to the breaking point. And this, too, was puzzling.

"What about the two little hooded flowers?" Collin asked. "And the message in the typewriter? Where do they come in?"

"Props," Rinehart said with a gesture of dismissal. "Pitiful attempts of Bolton's to camouflage. Probably typed that mess-age himself. Flowers might have come from the millinery department."

"Those flowers are copies of a rare thing that blooms in the desert," Collin said evenly. "They have a meaning in this business, Rinehart."

RINEHART shrugged his shoulders and turned to direct the search for further clues. Just then the doctor who was attending Mintlow stood up and turned toward the group around Rinehart.

"You can talk to him now," the doctor said. "No fracture and no serious concussion I believe. Shock from the blow caused insensibility. The hypo brought him round."

Mintlow, lined and pinched of face, lay back on his cot and stared up with dull eyes. He said: "Miss Rose told me to unlock the side door so Mr. Bolton could come in. Then Mr. McNeal came along and ordered me not to let Mr. Bolton in. I had unlocked the door and was talking to McNeal when I heard somebody here at the side entrance. I took my flash and started this way. But whoever it was had already got in and hid in the dark by that case yonder. As I passed it something struck me and I remember going down. That's all."

"What did I say?" Rinehart demanded triumphantly. "Knowing there'd be difficulty, Bolton slipped in, hid and slugged Mintlow. Then he shot McNeal when he confronted him."

"You caught no glimpse of the man?" Collin asked. "You couldn't say whether it was Jimmie Bolton?"

"No, Mr. Windsor," the watchman said frankly. "I just saw a blur. But if it was young Bolton he was stooping low and had to come up to tiptoes to strike. I kinda got an idea it was deformed man, a—"

"A hunchback?" Collin asked quickly.

"Yes." Mintlow mumbled.

A faint groan broke the little silence that followed this. It came from Herndon Bryant. All eyes swung on him. There were beads of sweat on his face and a tortured stare in his eyes.

"Gentlemen," he said in a strained, hollow voice, "there's something I ought to say. There's a third man in this. A man from my—"

Bryant stopped, as if just realizing what he was saying. Men hung on his next words, intent in a dead, weighted silence. But the next words did not come. Instead a startling, unearthly and blood-chilling shriek sounded across the store. It was mocking, that shriek, mocking and maniacal, and it ended in a raucous and nerve-racking laugh, like the jeering bray of a donkey. It was unnerving, a frenzied sound, and seemed to come from the pitch-dark mezzanine floor. Its wild, eerie notes hung in the air for torturing seconds. And then followed a silence as dramatic and unrelieved as the sound itself.

"My God!" Herndon Bryant cried. Collin saw his hand go to his heart. The man's face was the color of dead ashes. His eyes were glued, unseeing, on the gloom above. Then Herndon Bryant sank limply and sagged across the display counter beside him, knocking shrouded racks of beads and novelties helter-skelter.

The doctor leaped to Bryant's side. He turned quickly from his cursory examination and said: "It's his heart. That noise gave him a scare that made it go blooey. He's all right—I'll bring him round. Go catch that laughing fiend!"

Collin, with Rinehart and two other officers, bounded toward the wide stairs that led up to the dark mezzanine floor. Guns were out and the excitement of a chase flamed in men's faces. It was ominously silent up there now and gloomy shadows shrouded the place with mystery and a sense of deadliness.

CHAPTER THREE

Madman's Vengeance

ALL the lights were turned on on the mezzanine, which was a horseshoe-shaped balcony that ran around three walls of the main floor. Under the beating glare of that radiance the glitter of mahogany, the reflection of plate glass, the dull sheen of velvet carpeting made the place one of magnificence.

But no furtive figure lurked there, though they prodded behind every case and counter and searched into the rest rooms on each side. In disappointment Rinehart looked at Collin.

"He got away! Did you see anything?"

Collin shook his head. "Not a trace. But I'm not so sure the sound came from up here. It seemed to, but then again it seemed to fill the store, to come from everywhere."

"We'll rake the whole building through —including the basement," Rinehart said stoutly. "Maybe there's something to what Bryant said about an unknown man."

"A hunchback. Remember what Mintlow said—and you surely don't think that Jimmie Bolton made that noise!"

"It didn't sound human." Rinehart's voice was a little shaky.

"Rinehart," Collin said, "there's an unknown something in this affair. Bryant knows it and hinted at it. Mintlow got a faint flicker of it. The flowers are signs of it. It's one time that doesn't mark the spot but equals the unknown quantity."

They went back down the stairway to the street level and Rinehart gave quick, efficient orders to his assistants to set his corps of policemen searching the whole store again. The building was twelve stories high, entirely occupied by various departments of the great store. When the bluecoats had gone scurrying about their hunt, Collin drew Rinehart aside.

"This sounds fantastic, Rinehart, but some things seem to indicate it. Suppose some madman were living in the Bryant Building, with a hideout in some vacant office or in the basement or the elevator room, coming out by night to wreak death and terror!"

"But why?"

"Maybe just the prank of a deceased or insane mind. But maybe—and more likely —some enemy of Bryant's terrorizing him and his family in revenge for some real or fancied wrong of the past."

"Say!" Rinehart exclaimed. "That's the bunk. Don't suggest such stuff to me."

Collin caught Rinehart's coat lapel. "I'm serious. Listen. Where did Bryant first make his big money—the stake that gave him his big start?"

Rinehart considered. "Let me see. I've heard. He made a strike in the gold fields, didn't he?"

Collin nodded. "In the desert country, if I'm not mistaken. What does that mean to you? Think! Those hooded flowers are a product of the desert— monk's-hood or wolf-bane, they're called. They allude to something in Bryant's past, don't you see? Something he fears to tell but has already hinted at. And that laughing scream! It startled us but it didn't give us heart failure as it did Bryant. That has a meaning for him that it hasn't for us."

"Come on," Rinehart said suddenly. "The doctor's brought Bryant round. Let's talk to him."

BRYANT was fully conscious but hollow-eyed and haunted looking. He was jumpy and unnerved, and the doctor watched with an anxious eye as Rinehart and Collin Windsor approached the store owner, now seated on a settee that had been drawn up for him.

"I hope you'll pardon my display of weakness, gentlemen. My heart's a little unreliable and that noise sent it haywire."

"Mr. Bryant," Collin said gently, "you've heard that screaming laugh before, haven't you?"

Bryant's eyes hardened and his lips compressed. For a moment Collin thought he would refuse to answer. Finally Bryant said: "Twice before. Each time it preceded or followed some awful misfortune in my life."

"You—you are superstitious then?"

Deep distress was in Bryant's eyes as he looked up at Collin. "I don't know. Hardly—though that shrieking, fiendish laugh seems to mock me in my grief. I heard it first when my wife died a year ago. It interrupted her funeral—sounded over her grave as the casket was being lowered. Then it came again when a fire broke out in the basement of the store during a Christmas rush—and several customers were badly mangled in the awful stampede."

"I remember the fire," Rinehart confirmed.

"We kept that jeering scream and most of the story out of the papers," Bryant said. "I tell you it's uncanny—it's hellish."

"Mr. Bryant," Rinehart said carefully, "does that noise or those two hooded flowers have no meaning to you? You have no idea who or what could cause them? Or why?"

Bryant hesitated. His nervous hands caressed each other in what was almost a wringing gesture. His voice was low when he answered. "I haven't the least idea, Mr. Rinehart."

Collin said: "You mentioned another— a third man, you called him, Mr. Bryant. Is there someone in your life who'd wish to cause you harm—or would profit in some way by your misfortune?"

Fear seemed to clutch the man. "No one!" he said vehemently.

"Then," Collin said slowly, "do you

know anything of a hunchback? Has one ever crossed your path in the past?"

Bryant cried: "No, no!" half rising from his seat. He sank back and mopped sweat from his face.

"Please," the doctor cut in. "Don't ask him any more questions. He mustn't be excited again, in his condition."

Collin felt that Bryant had lied. Disappointedly he turned away. Henderson, one of Rinehart's assistants, came up.

"We've raked the place from bottom to roof, chief," he said. "We couldn't find nobody nor any place where anybody coulda got out."

"No one could have got by our lines outside anyhow. We've got the building surrounded. But something or somebody made that sound and we've got to find 'em. Now, listen, Henderson," Rinehart said briskly. "Get headquarters on the phone—" the phone wires had been repaired by now— "and tell 'em to put out the dragnet for all hunchbacks—every shady one in town, see. Then tell them to put every man they can on the hunt for Rose Bryant."

"And Jimmie Bolton?" Henderson suggested.

"And Jimmie Bolton."

When the man was gone Rinehart passed a hand across his eyes. "Somebody made that noise. He ain't in the building and he couldn't have got away. Bah! It's impossible."

"Rinehart," Collin stated with conviction, "somebody's hiding in this store and mocking us with his ability to evade us."

"Nice and cheerful, you are," Rinehart said wearily. "Well, I'm going to take this damn building apart, piece by piece. What a job! There's thirteen floors if you count the basement. We'll poke into all of 'em again. But in spite of all the trimmings I still believe Jimmie Bolton killed Bob McNeal and Miss Bryant ran away

with him. That warrant for Bolton's arrest still stands."

COLLIN reached his bungalow at four in the morning, surfeited with macabre thrills. It seemed that he had only turned in and got to sleep when his telephone rang brazenly. But sunlight was streaming in through his window and his watch said eight o'clock. Rinehart's voice came over the wire.

"Just a little bad news for you," Rinehart said cheerfully. "We checked up on the fingerprints around the scene of the murder—on that alabaster column, and other places. They're Jimmie Bolton's, no doubt about that. We got plenty of his prints from things about his desk at The Times-Herald — and compared 'em. They're identical."

"Oh, the devil!" Collin exclaimed testily. "What does that prove? Nobody contends that Jimmie wasn't there. But being there doesn't make him a murderer. Have you got that bullet out of McNeal yet?"

"Yep. Thirty-eight calibre—flattened a little against a rib at the back. Haven't found any gun so far. I'm saying it'll be an automatic with a muffler when we find it."

"Any news of Rose Bryant?"
"None."
"Nor Jimmie?"
"Nope. But the police are working on clues—"

"And expect to make an arrest any moment," Collin jeered and hung up the receiver.

The Bryant Department Store opened for business as usual that morning. All traces of the night's two tragedies—the murder and the kidnaping—were gone, but the place was mobbed with morbidly curious crowds that milled about the main floor and plied the poor clerks to distraction with impossible questions. The saleswomen and floorwalkers had been drilled. Their invariable answers were: "We've no news to give out so far madam; we've no news to give out so far, sir."

Reporters thronged the place, too, eager for each gruesome morsel of information. But, attesting to Bryant's standing and influence as a large advertiser, carefully censored accounts of the affair appeared in the morning papers. The sensational evening sheet plastered the streets with extras playing up every tiny scrap of knowledge it could glean from any source.

But the business had to go on. Customers shopped and clerks waited upon them. And, unknowingly, the patrons elbowed plainclothes detectives with which the place was honeycombed. On every floor search and examination went ahead. But so far it had netted nothing.

At noon Collin drove his roadster down Ackman street and parked it a block and a half from the Bryant Building. As he stepped from it, the siren of an ambulance wailed and the hurtling machine roared around the corner on two wheels. Came another then, from a different direction, and still a third shrieked in the distance, rushing rapidly nearer. A police riot car howled up, loaded with bluecoats. They all converged at the side entrance of the Bryant Building!

On the run Collin headed that way. A great milling noonday crowd was massed about the place. The police had already thrown a line around the entrance, holding the throng back across the street and down the curbs from it. Traffic was stopped by the congestion of machines and pedestrians; people stood on their tiptoes; questions buzzed, and alarm showed in men's faces. Cops threatened the wavering, pushing line with their night-sticks. The din and clamor was almost deafening.

Collin did not add his voice to that of the querying mob. He saw white-garbed stretcher bearers carrying their burdens from the entrance across the curb to the waiting ambulances.

A pimply-faced youth erupted from the smother of forms at the entranceway spreading the news with unholy joy, excitement blazing from his face. "A escalator collapsed!" the youth howled hoarsely. "Killed about forty people, I guess, and injured about a hundred!"

A police car nosed its way through the milling crowd, horn going raucously. Collin saw Lieutenant Rinehart get out, harried of face and quick of step, and lead a trio of his men into the store.

"Smart Rinehart," Collin soliloquized. "He knows this has got something to do with his case."

COLLIN turned and walked away from the scene. Nothing to be learned in that bedlam. An hour later he entered Rinehart's office. The detective had a flushed and worried frown on his face. On the desk before him were three flowers, identical with the two that had been found the night before. They were soiled and trampled.

Rhinehart indicated the flowers with a gesture. "Souvenirs of murder," he said, grimacing. "Found on the floor near the escalator. God, it's got me, Windsor!" Rinehart loosened his collar which seemed to be choking him and went on: "I'm damn glad you showed up. I need somebody to share my troubles. I tried to phone you at your home. Windsor, the supports of that escalator had been tampered with!"

"I'd guessed as much," Collin replied, loading his pipe and lighting it. He dropped into a chair across from the detective. "Just how?"

"Concrete was chipped away and replaced with flimsy plaster. Two steel braces were sawed nearly in two. All that was needed was a load like that crowd today to make it come crashing down. God, man, it was a mess!"

"Anybody killed?"

"One woman and child may die. Half a dozen were badly injured and as many not so severely."

Collin fixed Rinehart with an accusing eye. "And you," he said, "think chubby, happy-go-lucky Jimmie Bolton is behind all this!"

Rinehart squirmed. "Hell, don't rub it in. Anyway this looks like sabotage. May not be connected at all with the McNeal case," he hedged weakly.

"It's not sabotage," Collin said decisively. "It's a madman's vengeance on Herndon Bryant."

"And that's not all," Rinehart said uncomfortably. "Bryant admitted he heard that banshee laugh shortly after the tragedy—as he was making his way from his office down to the main floor. It sounded down the elevator shaft."

Collin sat forward tensely. "Was there a search?"

"Of course. But what could you find in that bawling mess?"

Collin got up and paced about the room. He whirled and fronted Rinehart again. "I checked up in Bryant's life this morning. He's had loads of publicity you know, and I borrowed the newspaper files on him. He made his first fortune out of a gold strike, following a desert prospecting trip. Rinehart, I'm going up to Bryant's office and sweat him. By God, he's withholding information that may cause other deaths! He's got to talk."

Collin caught up his hat and started for the door. He turned on his heel and came back. "Oh, yes! What about the hunchback line-up this morning?"

Rinehart drummed his fingers on his desk. "Our men brought in about a dozen. A sad looking lot. Several were snowbirds. We coundn't prove that any of them would know Herndon Bryant or

Robert McNeal on sight—except one. This fellow was named Shapiro and had worked at Bryant's as a wrapper. He was fired, store records show, by Bryant personally, a little over a year ago. No reason given. He's a tough bird in spite of his twisted spine. I'm detaining him, though he's got a kind of alibi."

"May or may not mean anything," Collin said. "Bryant is deathly afraid of some hunchback, mark my words. He might have fired Shapiro simply because of that fear. Well, so long. I'm going up to beard Bryant in his den."

CHAPTER FOUR

Margo—The Hunchback

COLLIN found Bryant in his carefully guarded private office on the fifth floor of the store building. There was a mob in the anteroom, mostly reporters, but Collin was admitted immediately on presentation of his card.

Bryant's secretary was a tall, extremely smart and intelligent-looking young woman. Bryant sent her from the office and he and Collin were alone.

"I've been wanting to see you, Windsor." Bryant's face showed marks of his last night's harrowing experiences. His cheeks were hollow and seamed and his eyes dull, lackluster.

"About what, Mr. Bryant?"

"I want you to take up the search for my daughter. Don't let fee stand in the way—"

Collin waved that aside with a gesture. "But the police are doing everything."

"Damn the police. They move like snails. Besides—but never mind. It seems to me not enough's being done. I know my daughter is in fearful distress and great danger. I want her back!" Bryant's voice grew vehement.

Collin stood up, placed his palms on the glass-topped mahogany desk and pinned the merchant with his stare. "Mr. Bryant," he said grimly. "There's only one condition on which I'd take the case."

"And that?"

"That you'll be absolutely frank with me."

Bryant lowered his gaze to his long-fingered, trembling hands. "I am frank with you."

"Like hell!" Collin blazed. "You know something your're not telling. Who and what is this hunchback that you fear? Who is the man that is hounding the life out of you—and why? To what thing in your past do these monk's-hood flowers refer? And what thing does that braying laugh recall?"

"I don't know what you mean, Windsor."

"You're lying, Bryant! You're afraid to tell!"

Bryant flushed angrily, half rose from his chair. But he sank back, resentment going out of his face.

"You!" Collin cried with indignation. "You'd let Rose Bryant suffer in kidnaper's hands, let innocent Jimmie Bolton be hunted and hounded for this murder when you know the guilty man! You're a coward—you're yellow, damn you."

"But I tell you I don't know the man —wouldn't know him if I saw him."

Collin crowded in on his advantage. "Is he a hunchback?"

Bryant nodded.

"Was he ever in the employ of the store?"

Bryant hesitated. "Not that I know of."

Collin sat down facing the other man. "Mr. Bryant, was that hunchback at your wife's funeral when you heard that banshee cry the first time?"

"I didn't see him. If he was, he was hidden."

"And on the occasion of the fire in the basement?"

"The same in that case, too."

"Mr. Bryant, won't you tell me what you know—what happened out in the desert when you found gold? Tell me so I can clear Jimmie Bolton and find Rose Bryant."

Grief was in Bryant's face. He squirmed miserably. "Give me time to think, Windsor. I dare not speak now. Come back tonight. I'll—I'll meet you here in my office at nine."

And that was all Collin could get from him. The investigator left, disappointed, and went back to Rinehart's office. He didn't tell the lieutenant about Bryant's promise. He felt that if the police were dragged in again, Bryant would close up and refuse to speak.

But Rinehart had news for him. He opened his desk drawer, took a small object from it, and passed it across to Collin. It was a tiny gold fountain pen and was daintily engraved with the inscription: "Rose Bryant."

"Where did it come from?" Collin demanded.

"A fellow brought it in."

"When? From where? Hell, speak up man!"

RINEHART grinned. "Interested, hey? It was a nicely dressed young fellow named Smith—Ben Smith. About twenty-five. He was scared and nervous. Said he found this in the rumble seat of his roadster—and didn't know how it got there! Fancy that!"

Collin shook his head. "How do you figure it?"

"Like this. This Smith boy helped Jimmie Bolton to run away with Rose Bryant and the girl lost the pen in Smith's car. Then Smith learned about the murder and found the pen. He was scared the dicks might find it and connect him up somehow and yet he didn't dare not to report it. So he just brought it in and

said he didn't know how it got there."
Rinehart laughed loudly.

"What did you do with the Smith chap?"

"Turned him loose and put a man on his tail."

'Good! Where does he work?"

"At the Western Paper Company, a wholesale house on Minerva Street. Hey! Where you going?"

"To see Smith."

But Ben Smith could add little to what he had told Lieutenant Rinehart. Collin found him to be a frank young fellow of pleasant manners, and apparently willing to help all he could in the mystery. At Collin's suggestion he described to the best of his memory, his itinerary in the car during the day.

"Mostly my car was parked out there in front of our office," Smith said. "I used it to call on some customers. Once out on Whitaker Street, and twice down on Elm. I drove down Ackman a couple of times, passed by Bryant's an hour or so after the escalator accident. I don't know how in the world that gold pen got in my car."

That was the upshot of the whole thing. Collin spent the afternoon trying to puzzle it out. Somewhere in his mind a tiny voice, it seemed, kept trying to tell him the vast and important meaning of that pen. But it could not make him understand. He went home to think things over, but dark came and still he had not fathomed the thing.

It was eight-thirty, and after Collin had eaten dinner, when a thought struck him like a thunderbolt. He leaped to his telephone, snatched up the instrument, and dialed the number Smith had given him. A long minute and Smith's voice came over the wire.

"Listen, Smith! Windsor speaking. When you drove down Ackman Street, was the rumble seat of your car open?"

"Yes. Keep it open most of the time. Fellows often ride with me, you know."

"And you stopped for a signal light, there by Bryant's?"

"Yes. I was back of a line of cars—traffic was kinda heavy then. My car was about midway along the block, right beside the Bryant Building."

Collin hung up the receiver, stood staring into space. "My God! What a fool I've been. There it all was waiting for me. I just couldn't see it!"

He glanced at his watch. There was no time to take action on the clue now, however. Only a few minutes to get downtown and meet Bryant—an appointment he certainly couldn't afford to miss.

And when he left the bungalow Collin wore under his coat a skeleton underarm holster, supporting his automatic with a full clip. Precaution had whispered a vague warning in his ear.

ON Ackman Street, there beside the Bryant Building, Collin stood and stared up at the long, converging lines of blank windows. He could see an edge of the small elevator house on the roof. He shook his head. Suppose the hunchback terror of Bryant's, Incorporated, lived and hid by day up there among the cables, and roamed the store by night! There were a thousand shadowy places to hide.

Old Mintlow answered the night bell promptly as Collin rang it. There was a bandage on his head, but otherwise he showed no ill effects of the night before.

"Mr. Bryant told me he was expectin' you and to show you right up, Mr. Windsor," Mintlow said in a kind voice.

"Thanks, Mintlow."

Mintlow, with his flashlight, led the way through the dark aisles to the elevators.

"The office with the light on," Mintlow said, as he led Collin off on the fifth floor. "Mr. Bryant's waitin' for you."

Collin wanted to surprise Bryant, catch

him off guard. He moved silently to the door of his office and opened it quickly without knocking.

Herndon Bryant, seated at his desk, whirled quickly in his chair, as if caught in some covert act. He had been staring down at something on his desk. He made a gesture as if to hide it in a half-open drawer. Collin stepped swiftly across and caught Bryant's hand.

"Just a minute, Bryant," he said. "Let's play fair. You want to know about Miss Rose. I want certain information to clear Bolton and solve this murder mystery. Don't cheat."

Utter resignation came over Bryant. He wilted visibly as, for a long minute, Collin stood over him. Finally he handed Collin the thing he had been studying on his desk.

It was a small, cheap photograph. A horrible photograph—the picture of a man bent almost double, so twisted was his body, and a great ugly hump was on his back. The man's face was covered with wild, gray-streaked whiskers, but his eyes showed bitter and fanatical. There was an inscription below the picture.

Here's what you made of me, Bryant. I'm not dead as you thought—only half dead, after years in hospitals. Remember the burro that brayed when you shoved me off the cliff? Remember the monks-hood among the rocks? You'll hear that laugh again, Bryant. You'll see those flowers again. You'll know what it is to suffer before I kill you!

Margo.

A little shiver ran through Collin's frame. From the gruesome message in his hand he raised his eyes to Bryant, whose head was sunk on his chest. "Margo was your prospecting partner in the gold fields?"

Bryant nodded. Collin waited for him to speak. Finally the man's voice came, little more than a croak. "It was twenty-five years ago. All along I've thought he was dead. A little over a year ago I got this message from him."

"Will you tell me the whole story?"

Bryant took a grip on himself. Collin sensed words of refusal coming to the man's lips. He checked them. "Let's bargain," the investigator said. "I'll tell you first. Your step-daughter is in this building."

Bryant leaped to his feet. "Where? Where?"

Collin pushed him back into the chair. "At least she was at about two o'clock this afternoon. On one of the upper floors —I think in the elevator room—though I'm not sure. We can search in a minute or two. But first tell me about—about Margo, so we can catch *him.*"

Bryant clenched his hands and beat the glass desk top with his knuckles. "He's been an actor——"

"A ventriloquist?"

"I think so."

"That explains that banshee laugh."

"But he'd got in some kind of trouble so he had to quit the stage. I ran across him in a gold camp out west. He was at loose ends then—a fugitive, I imagine. He always wore a heavy beard, I think as a sort of disguise—I really never knew what his face looked like. He put in with me and we went prospecting in partnership. We made a rich find—struck it big. But coming back to the town where we could record our claims we got lost in the desert. We were both tenderfeet, you know. Food and water got low, barely enough to bring one of us through. I read treachery in his eyes—he meant to kill me, Windsor, kill me and take the whole claim for himself.

"We camped on the edge of a cliff. Those sinister flowers grow all around there in the rocks. Margo was surly and quarrelsome, trying to start a fight, find an excuse to kill me. We watched each other like a cat and a canary. I saw my chance and shoved him over the cliff. I saw his body slide and roll and tumble down that cliffside, then lie still at the bottom of it. At that moment our burro brayed unnervingly."

BRYANT had great drops of perspiration on his face. "He—he meant to kill me, Windsor. I tell you I saw it in his eyes. That's why I did it."

Collin wasn't convinced. Herndon Bryant had always loved money, had a fatal ambition for wealth, he guessed. Collin felt that greed had prompted him to do away with his partner.

"I thought he was dead," Bryant went on. "Years went by. I built this great business. I felt secure. Then I got this awful message. Someone must have found him out there in the desert—and rescued him."

Confession was not good for Bryant's soul. He seemed to melt within himself. He was a craven and he would not raise his eyes to face Collin.

"Robert McNeal was a snoop. He found that picture and message from Margo. Wanted me to let him investigate it, hunt the man down. I ordered him to keep out of my affairs. I think Margo has been hovering around Dalshire. He may have killed Robert for what Robert had learned. But so far as I know I've never seen Margo since that fatal day in the desert."

"Thank you, Bryant. Brace up. What you've told me will help clean up things. It's my theory that Margo lives in this store building, hiding out somewhere. We'll hunt till we find him. Now we'll go and see if my guess about Rose Bryant is right."

Collin caught the shaken man by the shoulder. Bryant stood up, staggering a little. The store building was ominously silent. Came the sudden sense of a nearby, utterly evil presence. A premonition gripped Collin.

Then the silence was shredded to tatters by an awful sound. It was that fearful, ear-splitting shriek which ended in the jeering, raucous, braying laugh. It rooted both men motionless for a second by the indescribable horror of it.

Then a small side door to Bryant's office flew open. Beyond it was darkness, gloom. That darkness was pierced with a stab of flame, accompanied by the puff of a silenced pistol. Bryant, under the glare of the light over his desk, recoiled with the impact of a bullet. An expression of ludicrous surprise crossed his face. Red stained his shirt front. He collapsed on the deep-piled carpet.

Instantly Collin's gun came from its underarm holster. He fired three times through the doorway. A jeering laugh mocked him from the darkness. Then Collin darted through the door in pursuit.

CHAPTER FIVE

Behind the Mask

THERE ensued several exciting minutes of the most baffling chase in which Collin Windsor had ever taken part. First he heard the jeering laugh above, seemingly on the stairway that led to the sixth floor. He sprinted across the tile corridor and rushed halfway up the stairs, then heard the laugh below him, apparently near the elevator. He plunged down and the laugh taunted him from above again. Not until then did Collin remember he was chasing a man who was a ventriloquist—and that the man was not where the sound seemed to come from. The fiend might run Collin to exhaustion with his vocal tricks and never move out of one hiding place!

Collin groped along the wall until he found the switch panel for the lights. His finger was on the switch to flood the place with radiance, when there came a step behind him.

Collin's body twisted about with the whiplike speed of a cat. His gun came up, finger on the trigger. "Steady!" he called hoarsely.

The blurred figure in the gloom stopped. "Collin!" came a low voice.

Collin's gun went down. "Where in hell did you come from, Jimmie?"

"I couldn't stand it," Jimmie said in a strained voice. "I couldn't stay away and not know about Rose! I read in the evening paper about that gold pen. I figured she threw it from one of the upper windows trying to get attention and it fell into that Smith fellow's car."

"You figured right, I believe, Jimmie."

"That means she's somewhere in the Bryant Building!"

"Yes. Bryant and I were going to look for her when someone shot Bryant down from the dark and fled."

Jimmie, wordless, passed a hand across his eyes.

Collin had turned on the lights. The pair stood there in the glaring illumination, staring at each other. Jimmie's face was unbelievably haggard and drawn, revealing something of what he must have suffered in the last twenty-four hours.

"How did you get in?" Collin asked.

"I've learned to be wary since I've been on the dodge," Jimmie answered. "I managed to get by the surveillance of the police and came in the side entrance. The door was unlocked. Didn't see the watchman."

Collin turned to the elevator and put his finger on the down button. "We've got to find Rose Bryant, before that murdering fiend can get back to her!" Collin cried. "Now that he knows we're on his trail no telling what he'll do!"

They heard the elevator start from the main floor. Presently it stopped and old Mintlow opened the cage door.

"To the top—and snappy, Mintlow!" Collin ordered bruskly.

Jimmie said, as the cage shot skyward: "Where is she, Collin?"

"I'm sure she's hidden in the elevator cable room," Collin answered. "Last night she must have been on one of the upper floors—for the elevator room was searched then. But—he moved her about to avoid discovery. Before morning he must have taken her back up to the elevator room, for every floor was searched thoroughly today."

Jimmie's horror and concern was reflected in his face.

They stopped on the top floor and Mintlow slid open the door with a muffled clang. "Shall I go up with you, Mr. Windsor?" the old man asked.

"No—there may be violence. You wait here. Just tell me where the cable-room light switch is."

"On the left, just inside the door."

Collin ran up the stairs to the roof, his gun still in his hand. Jimmie Bolton was but a space behind him. They came out on the flat expanse, under the stars. The square block of the elevator house was silhouetted dully against the night sky.

Collin did not pause at the door. He turned the knob, pushed viciously. The door flung open and Collin leaped in to twist aside and press his back against the wall. He half expected a shot, or some challenge. But none came. There was only silence. Collin's fingers touched the light button.

Illuminated, the place lost its mystery. There was no one there. It was vacant except for the bulky forms of the elevator motors.

IN ONE corner was a small supply closet, with its door closed, locked. Collin tried the knob, hefted against the door with his shoulder. The door held but in the silence that followed his effort a small sound stirred within the closet. The scraping of a foot on the floor!

"Jimmie!" Collin cried exultantly.

'Jimmie! She's in the closet!"

"But—but why doesn't she call?"

"Gagged, probably."

Jimmie was desperate, crazy. "Rose!" he shouted. "We've come for you!" He backed off and ran toward the door. He made a headlong dive and literally pitched his chunky body against it. There was a splintering of wood, the rending of metal, and the door flew inward.

Rose Bryant was in there, her wrists handcuffed, feet bound, and a cruelly tight gag in her mouth.

Minutes later, after she was freed, Jimmie held her in his arms, consoling her, talking to her, trying to soothe that reflection of horror from her eyes.

Collin touched him on the shoulder. "We must go, Jimmie. Herndon Bryant, you know—and the murderer."

Jimmie carried her in his arms. They went down the stairway and on to the elevators. They stopped there and stared. Mintlow was gone!

The door to the elevator that had brought them up was closed, but the one beside it was open. As they stood, puzzled, grouped before it, a stealthy, slithering footstep sounded behind them and Rose Bryant screamed.

Jimmie and Collin turned about. Coming toward them was the most hideous, misshapen creature any of the trio had ever seen.

"The hunchback!" Rose cried hysterically.

The face was a bearded, grotesque, all-covering mask. The man was so bent as to be walking almost on all-fours, and a great hump protruded up between his shoulders. He advanced with an awkward, waddling slide; and there was a gun in his hand, pointing toward them. It was an automatic with a silencer.

"Get in folks and take your ride down," said a rattly, reedy voice behind the bearded mask. "But first, Mr. Windsor, drop that gun on the floor."

Collin's arm flexed, his wrist twisted, his gun came up and he jerked the trigger. But the hunchback had already fired. Collin's gun was whipped from his fingers and his hand was numbed to the wrist.

"Get in! Get in!" the hunchback screamed in a snarling voice. Spellbound, dismayed, the trio backed into the elevator.

A fiendish laugh came from behind the whiskered mask. "Now ride to your death, fools! I've sawed the cables to this car so nearly through that when the brake's released it drops to hell! And you three with it!"

Margo laughed his screeching laugh again. "I had it fixed for a crowd tomorrow—but you three will get the death ride instead!"

A lean, knotty hand reached out to twist the brake handle, while the right held the gun covering the three in the elevator. Maniacal eyes glittered from the whiskered mask.

And then Jimmie Bolton became the hero. Unmindful of that gun bore staring at him, he moved. Straight into the maw of it he dived, lunging at Margo the misshapen beast of a man! This surprise move seemed to bewilder Margo. Instead of firing he cursed fiercely and leaped backward trying to dodge the impact of Jimmie's flying body. It jolted him but he whirled to flee. Jimmie tackled him at the knees. The man kicked him venomously. Jimmie rolled over, groaning.

By now Collin had leaped from the elevator. Margo was running toward the stairs to the roof. Collin snatched up his gun and sprinted after him. Jimmie and Rose joined the pursuit. Halfway up the stairs Margo caught the bannister and leaped over. He struck the floor running. Collin fired, but in the half-light he missed. He fired again as he and Jimmie and the girl turned about to follow the maddened Margo. Margo stumbled with that last shot but dragged on. Again Collin fired and the man came heavily down to all-fours, still scuttling on.

He was up before they could get to him, diving into the door of the elevator. He stood up, inside the cage facing them. He was bleeding from his shoulder and an arm.

That raucous, jeering banshee laugh that had been the terror of the Bryants rang out from the wounded madman's lips.

"Thought you had me!" He laughed again, shrilly. 'You can never get me! Here goes Margo the Hunchback!"

He twisted the brake handle. The horrified trio heard the rending of metal as the sawed cables parted, saw the cage swoop downward, lightning-like whisk from view. They heard the screech of the cage-guides as they scorched the rails. But above all they heard the insane laugh of Margo, until it died in the weird silence that preceded the detonating crash which announced that the hunchback was at the end of his ride.

Rose Bryant gave a little whimper as she hid her face in her hands.

"My God!" was all Jimmie could say for a long moment. Then: "Let's hustle and find old Mintlow, Collin. We've got to see about Mr. Bryant."

"No use to hunt Mintlow," Collin answered. "I didn't guess it until a minute ago, but—old Mintlow is Margo the Hunchback!"

HERNDON BRYANT wasn't dead. Collin's phone call brought an ambulance and Bryant was carried away to the hospital where it was learned an hour later that he would live. Rinehart came on the heels of the ambulance and, with Collin and Jimmie, he went down to the bottom of the elevator shaft, where amid the twisted steel and splintered wood of

the fallen cage they found the crushed body of Margo the Hunchback.

And behind that whiskered mask they found the wrinkled, kind-seeming face of old Mintlow. And under that false hump on the shoulders and the make-up clothes of Margo was the thin, slender, wiry body of Mintlow.

"Margo was never a hunchback," Collin explained. "No doubt he was for years an invalid from his fall from the cliff. His suffering made him fanatical for revenge. Being an actor and mountebank, he conceived the idea of sending Bryant that photo of himself made up as a miserable, twisted hunchback. This, so that when he did appear on the scene—as Mintlow the watchman—to avenge and terrorize Bryant no one would be looking for such a person as that."

"Mintlow!" Rinehart exclaimed incredulously. "How could he have killed McNeal when he'd been knocked out—unconscious?"

"He wasn't knocked out—until after he'd killed McNeal. Here's what happened last night. Margo was all set for his big revenge coup. He phoned Bryant he was going to kidnap Rose. He did so, disguised as Margo—and leaving that flower. Then he went down—became Mintlow again—to wait for Jimmie's arrival. And McNeal came in! McNeal had been digging into Bryant's past—maybe to blackmail him, or force himself into Bryant's will. He learned enough to suspect Mintlow—and probably last night accused Mintlow. Mintlow shot him down. Then expecting Jimmie any minute he bashed his own head against a heavy column— to knock himself out.

"Naturally, finding Mintlow slugged and McNeal murdered, and hearing Mintlow's story, the police concluded that Jimmie—or some third person—had done both—first slugging the watchman to gain entrance, then waiting to kill McNeal

Later Mintlow gives that screaming laugh to frighten Bryant out of confessing the desert episode. Tonight he shot Bryant, mainly because he feared Bryant's story might turn investigation his way. I'm sure the fiend wasn't ready for his kill. He intended to terrorize Bryant more before murdering him."

"Well, Windsor," Rinehart said generously. "I'm proud to withdraw that warrant that's out for *Jimmie Bolton's arrest.* You did good work tonight!"

"Me?" said Collin. "What I did was nothing compared to Jimmie Bolton's deed. His tackling Margo in the face of that automatic was the bravest thing I ever saw!"

"Huh!" Jimmie Bolton grunted. "That wasn't bravery. It was brains. I know gats with heavy silencers won't cock from recoil. You have to handcock 'em. Margo had just fired at you, Collin—so I knew there wasn't any cartridge under the firing pin!"

When Collin and Jimmie were back on the main floor, Jimmie said: "I'm borrowing your roadster, Collin."

"How come?"

"*Going* to the hospital and see if I can drag Rose away from Bryant's side for a little while. Want to talk to her."

"About store publicity?"

Jimmie grinned sheepishly. "Yeah. They'll need a lot of good publicity now to offset this unfavorable notoriety they've been getting!"

Eyes of the Dead

A Horatio Humberton Mystery

By

J. Paul Suter

Author of "The Angel of the Damned," etc.

"The little bird is gone from the nest!" That was the crazy phrase the half-witted Blake girl kept muttering to the priceless painting on the wall. What could her words mean? Why should that simple statement mark her for murder—turn the Rance mansion into a flaming horror trap?

CHAPTER ONE

The Singular Mr. Smith

TED SPANG, senior hearse driver and general assistant in the funeral parlors of Mr. Horatio Humberton, waited jauntily just within his employer's book-cluttered office, and behind him, his harsh outlines softened by the green shade of the lamp on Humberton's table, a huge giant of a man stood and also waited, with surly impatience.

Spang's employer was sitting at the table. For quite five minutes he did not look up. His high forehead, surmounted by a chrysanthemum-like bloom of yellow hair, was wrinkled in contemplation of a curiously misshapen skull, which he slowly

revolved on the table for examination. Suddenly, he smiled. His thick spectacles lifted, and he saw Ted.

"A suggestive specimen, Ted," he remarked, briskly. "The people at the museum were kind enough to lend it to me. It was dug up near Verdun, in some very old strata. The more I study these prehistoric crania, the more convinced I am that crime is a throw-back, the reversion to an ancient type, for which the criminal is hardly responsible."

Spang accepted the statement without argument. "Now, this Smith, Mr. Humberton—" he began, confidently.

"What Smith?" Humberton's tone was sharp. He sensed an interruption.

"This man we've had working around

"We can't make it," the necrologist gasped.

the parlors. You remember, you let me hire him for a while when I fell downstairs a week ago and sprained my arm? He's been fixing the roof this afternoon, and now—"

The huge man in the shadows cut in. His deep voice quavered with an unpleasant quality, midway between a snarl and a whine. "And now I'm quitting, guvnor," he said. "Quitting cold on your blasted job, and I'd thank ye to give me my money."

"Give it to him." Humberton cut the words off short, and returned to the examination of the skull.

Spang grinned, and scratched his red head. "I could have paid him off without worrying you," he explained, easily. "But you're interested in queer things, Mr. Humberton. I thought maybe you'd like to pop a question or two at him. He says he keeps seeing a dead woman."

TED SPANG'S judgment of what appealed to his employer was accurate. The tall necrologist placed his prehistoric specimen carefully on the table, pushed back his chair, and stood up. That gave him a better view of the man Spang had brought in. He saw a big, heavy-featured face with pendulous lower lip and eyes which were red and bleary. It was the face of a drunkard.

"He's a good carpenter," the driver put in.

Humberton nodded, and stepped around the table to confront the man.

"Now, what did you see?" he demanded.

"A dead woman, guvnor, looking at me from the back of the big house on the next street."

"How could a dead woman look at you?"

Smith pushed back a dirty cloth cap, which he had not bothered to remove, and scratched his head. "This one did."

Through his thick glasses, Humberton studied the massive, dull-witted face. Nothing was to be gained from impatience. The man was defiant and in haste to be gone. Given his money, he would not have waited for questioning.

"Where were you when you saw this?" the necrologist pursued.

"On your roof."

"And the dead woman was on another roof?"

The giant shook his head with a surly growl. "Gimme my money!" he demanded. "I've told ye where she was. In the big house on the next street."

"The rear attic window of the old Rance house on Clifton Avenue," Spang volunteered. "You can see it from the roof. Smith says the dead woman wasn't there all the time. She came and went. Sometimes when he went up he wouldn't see her at all. Then again she'd follow him, when I had him working around the yard."

"I didn't say she followed," the giant snarled. "I said I could see her. She was still in that house."

"You can't see the Rance house from the yard," Spang objected.

"I don't care. I saw her. Look here, guvnor—" The heavy eyebrows lowered threateningly. "I ain't always done odd jobs of carpenter work. I was head man in a quarry, once. Played with dynamite the way you're playing with that crazy skull. I ain't no man to fool with. If you know what's good for you, you'll give me my money—and you won't argue!"

Humberton smiled at his red-haired assistant.

"Give it to him, Ted. Who knows? He might blow us up if we keep him waiting. I fear, though, he is troubled with delusions produced by alcoholism. Did you go up on the roof yourself and look at the window he refers to?"

"I did, sir. Couldn't see a thing."

"No doubt because there was nothing

to see. By the way, Smith, how did you know the woman was dead?"

The carpenter had just received his money from Spang. He glanced at it, slipped it into a pocket in his greasy trousers, and looked up again with a sneering grin. "Can't you tell a dead woman when you see one, guvnor?" he inquired.

HUMBERTON returned to his table, and the examination of the skull. The office door slammed—the door to the long, narrow hall of the establishment, on the rubber matting of which the heavy, shuffling footsteps of the man Smith were audible as they receded toward the street.

"Sorry to keep on bothering you, Mr. Humberton—"

"I thought you were gone, Ted." Humberton looked up, with no trace of his former impatience. The singular case of Smith, carpenter, quarry man, and seer of dead women, had been worth the interruption. "Do you wish to see me about something else?"

"There's another queer bird out there." Spang's already ample mouth widened in a grin. "He's waiting in the reception room. Poor devil, he's one of the lamest birds I ever saw. Takes about six motions to every step. He says he wants to talk to you about a funeral."

Humberton sighed. After all, he was a funeral director by profession. Engagements of this sort could not be declined. His hobby of crime detection, aided and indulged by his friend, Detective Clyde of the Cleveland Police, absorbed him to such an extent that he was prone to forget his legitimate calling. Funerals thrust it back upon him.

"Show him in, Ted," he said.

There was quite an appreciable wait. Humberton had time to use a pair of calipers on the skull, to note down several dimensions, and to forget all about the impending interruption. When Spang's

brisk tread became audible in the hall, followed by a curiously dragging sound, the necrologist therefore looked up with freshened annoyance.

"Mr. Pokemoff," announced Spang, holding the door wide so that a tall but pitifully bent young man, leaning on a cane, could enter.

The young man smiled, easily. "The name is Vladimir Pobedoff," he corrected, in a surprisingly pleasant, low-pitched voice. "Our Russian names are difficult. I am speaking to Mr. Horatio Humberton?"

Humberton nodded. His visitor's unusual countenance interested him. It was not a handsome face, but there was high intelligence in the broad dark forehead and black eyes. Possibilities of humor flickered in the subtle turn of the mouth, beneath a small, precisely trimmed mustache. But the expression at this moment was very grave.

Spang left the office. The lame man took the chair Humberton indicated. Resting both hands—long, slender hands—on the head of his cane, he looked keenly across them at the necrologist.

"Mr. Humberton," he said, slowly, "I come to you to arrange for a funeral. Am I correct in assuming that you still discharge such duties personally?"

Humberton nodded again.

"That is well. My friend would be greatly disappointed if you should refuse."

"Who is your friend?" the necrologist demanded.

"Mr. Bartholomew Rance."

HUMBERTON'S interest, which had been entirely in his visitor and not at all in his visitor's mission, suddenly quickened a little. If this was a coincidence, it was an odd one. Perhaps the man Smith actually had seen a dead woman in the Rance mansion.

"Do you mean Bartholomew Rance, the art collector?" he asked.

"The art collector," Pobedoff confirmed. "He has also been a noted explorer, I believe. His house is directly back of yours, on Clifton Avenue."

Humberton recalled that Rance was reputed to live alone. "Who is dead—one of the servants?" he inquired.

The lame man shook his head. "Mr. Rance is my friend. It grieves me greatly to tell you this. You are asked to conduct his funeral."

The necrologist leaned both elbows on his desk and scrutinized his visitor's calm, grave face. He was thoroughly interested now. "When did Rance die?"

"Ah—that I cannot tell you. Half an hour ago he was alive and well. He assured me of that, over the telephone. Quite well, in body and in mind, he put it—but bored of this life and curious about the life to come. You see? He intended to kill himself. He wished you to conduct his funeral. So he called me, his friend. 'Wait one moment, and you will hear the shot,' he said. But I did not wait."

Slowly Horatio Humberton rose to his feet. His mouth was set in a thin, accusing line. His voice was deliberate and cold. "You are a lame man," he said. "No doubt you could not personally prevent this suicide. But you have a telephone. I am waiting to hear how you used it."

"I used it to call the police." A faint smile curled on Pobedoff's grave mouth. "Surely I would not neglect so obvious a duty. Even though I am but a tobacconist now, there were days—old days, in Russia—when I was considered intelligent. I have come to you with the tardiness of a lame man, and have spoken calmly, because all I could do has been done. When one has done that, he can take his time."

Humberton sat down again and slid a telephone directory from the table drawer.

He had just begun to search in it when an idea struck him. "Do you know Rance's telephone number?"

Pobedoff shook his head. "I seldom had occasion to call him up. I became acquainted with him because he dropped in to buy cigars. Later he would come in the evening, after closing hours."

"Did he ever talk of suicide?"

The lame man gazed dreamily, speculatively into the shadowy corners of the office. "How does one talk of suicide?" he said, softly. "If you mean the physical act—the gun to the temple—he did not talk of that. But I have heard him say that he had seen all of the world that interested him. At last, he said, even art lost its capacity to charm. Would there be art in the next world—glorified art, relieved of our narrow sense limitations? He often wondered as to that, Mr. Humberton."

Humberton had found the number he wanted—that of the Rance house. He called it. A familiar voice answered—a voice which even tragedy could not rob of its naturally cheerful timber.

"Clyde!" The necrologist's own voice expressed his satisfaction. "I understand Bartholomew Rance intended to commit suicide. Were you in time to prevent him?"

"Can you come over, Ho?" the voice at the other end countered.

To no one else among his circle of friends was the dignified necrologist known as "Ho" but coming from Clyde's lips the familiar term implied not the least lack of respect. Humberton expected it. Any other name—from Clyde, and Clyde only—would have been hardly short of unfriendly.

"I'll come if you want me," Humberton replied.

"I want you, all right." The detective's short laugh had an edge of excitement to it. "Something has broken here that will make every front page in the country.

Come right over, if you can. You'll find the door open."

"Then it is suicide?" Humberton inquired.

"Suicide?" Clyde laughed, again. "Not on your life! It's murder!"

CHAPTER TWO

The Third Bullet

SOMEWHERE in the back of his mind Horatio Humberton cherished a conviction that the well-rounded man should be interested in everything. His career had been modeled on this theory. He had taken up criminology as a hobby and it had developed into a passion. Without having made a study of architecture, he had a smattering of that, too; enough to know that the old Rance mansion, before which his sedan drew up, was late Georgian, and to appreciate some of its minor structural features.

His sedan was driven by Spang. On the way they had dropped Vladimir Pobedoff at his little cigar store, which was less than a square from the Rance place. As the necrologist stepped rather gingerly to the curb, the front door of the house opened, and Detective Clyde's large figure appeared on the top step. Three other figures appeared from the darkness outside with a smooth promptitude which threatened an attack on the police, but he brushed them gruffly aside and came down the steps two at a time, his substantial shadow dancing before him. In spite of the blackness of the street, he evidently recognized the sedan and its occupants.

"I forgot to ask you, Ho," he cried, when he had reached the sidewalk; "how did you know about this affair?"

The tall necrologist favored him with an unhurried smile, which was lost on the darkness. With equal deliberation, he stood and looked up at the house. The second story windows were alight, the remainder dark.

"The answer to that is very simple," he returned, at length. "I was informed by the same man who telephoned you. Tell me something—isn't this the place from which a servant girl disappeared some months ago?"

"Have a heart, Mr. Clyde!" interrupted one of the three men who were following as Humberton and Clyde went up the steps.

"Listen, you fellows!" Clyde stood on the top step again, and addressed them curtly. "Up to now, you know just as much about this thing as I do. When something else breaks, I may let you know—if I can without gumming up the investigation. You're not coming into the house yet—get that?"

"Care to make a statement, Mr. Humberton?" The youngest of the three started forward, hopefully.

The necrologist shook his head and followed his friend into the hall. "You seem rather short with the newspapers, Clyde," he observed, dryly.

"Why wouldn't I be short with them? Haven't they been riding me for a fare thee well?" Clyde's tone was bitter. "Gang murders have hit this town, just as they have every other big city in the country. Only here the police are the goats. And the papers have elected me chief goat. If it keeps on, they'll have the citizens helping me out of town on a rail. I'm glad this one isn't a gang murder!" He stopped, abruptly. "You asked about the servant girl, Ho. This is the place, all right. She disappeared from here. You weren't in on that case. I hardly thought you'd recall anything about it."

HUMBERTON stopped just within the entrance hall, nodded to the policeman on duty, and looked past him to the broad staircase directly in front of them. He sized up two paintings, one on each side wall, and turned to Clyde. "As

I remember, Rance was writing a book," he remarked. "Something about Assyrian art."

Clyde grunted assent. "And he had an odd little trick of giving the servants a few days holiday when he wanted to concentrate. Remember that, Ho? This girl—her name was Minnie Blake—went on one of those vacations and never came back. We couldn't get a trace of her—not a smell. Odd, too. She wasn't very bright—not much more than half-witted. Such people are generally easy to trace. Rance was pretty well cut up about it. Offered a reward. No good. It's astonishing how many disappear each year in a city the size of this. Come upstairs, Ho."

He started up, but Humberton laid a detaining hand on his arm. "One minute. I wish to get my thoughts straight. There was another odd circumstance about the girl's disappearance. I noticed it in one of the news accounts at the time, but paid no particular attention to it. It was something about a bird."

"About a bird?" Clyde's ruddy face was blank. "I don't seem to recall that, Ho. Suppose we go up to the library now, and when Lurdle, the butler, happens around, I'll ask him. He ought to remember. He's been here for years. And of course he knew the girl."

The scene in the library—one of the lighted rooms in the front of the house—was of a kind very familiar to Humberton. The body of a man lay on his back on the floor. He had a high, narrow forehead, a large nose which seemed incongruously assertive in death, a gray Van Dyke beard. A very diminutive man, so small as to be almost a dwarf, knelt beside the body, making an examination with quick, nervous movements of his pudgy hands. As they entered, this man rose to his feet.

"Very good, Clyde," he said sharply. "Cause of death, shooting. Wound is at base of the brain. There are two bullet wounds in the body, also, but neither of them would have been fatal. In my opinion, those two were made after death. Have the body taken to the morgue, where I will extract the bullets and tag them to show from which wounds they emanate. Good evening, Clyde. Good evening, Mr. Humberton."

Coroner McNamara walked out, radiating importance as he went; and almost colliding, just outside the door, with Ted Spang, who was coming in. The driver's small eyes were twinkling.

"Well?" demanded his employer.

"I was just thinking that these little men haven't got any more dignity than the rest of us, after all. They just have to spread it thicker to get it all on. The bull downstairs said you were looking for Lurdle, the butler."

"I shall want him presently."

"Well, he came around the corner of the house to talk to me in the machine. He's in the butler's pantry now."

"Bring him to me in a quarter of an hour, Ted."

AS THE driver departed, Humberton looked inquiringly at a revolver which lay near the body.

"That's just where it was when we came in, Ho," Clyde volunteered. "I lifted it with a handkerchief, looked into the cylinder, and put it back. I did that because what I saw in the cylinder made me feel, right then, that I'd like you in on this. If you had been two minutes later telephoning me, I'd have called you. You heard what the coroner said. He's a pompous little duffer, but thorough. This man Rance had three bullets in his body —three."

Humberton nodded, absently. He was looking about the room—which really was entitled to be called a picture gallery rather than a library. There was one section of an inner wall, hidden from floor to ceiling with comfortably filled book shelves, but the remaining wall space, though most of it was likewise covered, owed its concealment to row after row of paintings in oil and water color. Clyde hesitated a moment, then seeing that his friend's attention was still concentrated on art, sprang his bomb.

"Three bullet holes in the body, Ho," he said, impressively. "But only two discharged shells in the gun! Get that? If there's any other gun in this room, I haven't found it, after a careful search. I'm asking you—where did the third bullet hole come from?"

Humberton's retort was curious. He stepped up to a small landscape, hung at about the height of his head on the wall by the hall door, and examined it carefully.

"A Murphy," was his verdict. "A sterling artist whose work will grow more valuable with age. Suppose you stand where I did a moment ago, Clyde. The light there falls just right. What do you see?"

"It isn't—" The detective pushed his cap back and ran fingers through his dark hair, as he came closer. "It isn't a bullet hole in the canvas, is it, Ho?"

"I believe it is." Humberton crooked his head critically to one side. "It has been very neatly repaired, and but for the accident of light reflection from where I stood, it would not have been apparent at all. I wonder—" He grasped the frame firmly with both hands and after a little manipulation took the picture down. "No, the hole in the wall is still there. Would you call it a new hole, Clyde?"

From a side coat pocket Clyde produced a flashlight. "Lucky thing this hole is in the paneling—we can tell more about it," he remarked. "The wood is thin. The bullet went right through it into the plaster. See that brown dust, Ho? That didn't settle in an hour or two. I don't believe that bullet was fired

this month or last or the month before."

"Suppose you dig it out and add it to the collection McNamara gives you," Humberton suggested. "I am going to talk with Lurdle."

Ted Spang was a highly satisfactory assistant. He had a way of obeying orders with imagination and speed. Humberton's remark was sufficient now to bring him in with a very large and very fat man behind him—a man whose pendulous cheeks fell almost comically at sight of the pathetic figure on the floor.

"James Lurdle, the butler," was Spang's introduction.

The butler achieved a complicated movement, made up of a bow and a dive into the coat-tail pocket of his dress coat, from which he exhumed a handkerchief. He dabbed each eye separately and blew his nose, then held the handkerchief ready for further need.

"Suppose you take me through the house," Humberton suggested.

"Very good, sir," was the reply, in a deep and liquid bass. "Will you begin with the top or the bottom, sir?"

"With the attic."

"If you're through with the body, Ho, I'll call up and have it taken away," Clyde put in. "McNamara might as well be taking out the bullets, then we can go right ahead with getting them examined, to see which came from this gun. I'll tell the boys to step on it. We ought to hear the dope before we leave here."

CHAPTER THREE

The Titian Doge

CLYDE was a fast worker. Humberton followed the butler's deliberate lead through the picture-hung upper hall to a narrow attic staircase, but they had no more than reached the top of this before the big detective was after them, two stairs at a time.

"Taking the grand tour with you, if

you don't mind, Ho," he announced, cheerfully. "I haven't been through the place yet, myself. Ted is in charge of the body."

The necrologist received this information with a non-committal grunt. "Lurdle, are you the only servant?" he asked the solemn and puffing butler.

"Oh, no, sir." Lurdle mopped his forehead, then, with an evident after-thought, dabbed his eyes again. "There's a little Russian girl, Sonia Hansky. She took the place of the girl that disappeared, sir."

"I haven't seen her around here," Clyde interjected.

"You wouldn't till day after tomorrow, sir. This afternoon, Mr. Rance gave us a little vacation. He did that occasionally, sir. When he reached certain points in the book he was working on, he preferred to be entirely alone in the house."

"Then how did you happen back?" Clyde demanded. "You know, Ho, he walked in on us just after we got here."

"In a way, sir, that was chance." Lurdle elevated his eyebrows and turned an earnest gaze upon the inquiring detective. "In another way, it was not. Of late months—perhaps I should say for nearly a year—the master has been acting rather peculiarly. Nothing important, sir—little things. I have been worried. I really feared for what he might do when all alone in the house. So I have made a practice of walking past occasionally when I was supposed to be absent, and keeping an eye on the place. Of course, when I glanced in and saw a policeman in the hall—"

"What were some of the little things you noticed?" Clyde demanded. Humberton, meanwhile, walked about from one attic room to another, all of them dimly but partially lighted by the beams from an ancient chandelier hung midway of a broad, uncarpeted hall. He kept within earshot, nevertheless, and after each ex-

cursion into a room stood a moment at the threshold with his eyes fixed thoughtfully on Lurdle.

"They were so very little, sir," the fat butler was explaining, "that folks who didn't know the master as I did wouldn't hardly have noticed them. Take the way he used to stop and look behind him." The butler shook his head, sadly. "He used to be the kind of man, sir, that didn't care for god nor devil. Yet I've seen him again and again, these last few months, stop short and glance behind him—for all the world as if something was following him up, treading on his heels. He'd be walking down the hall. All of a sudden, that's what he'd do."

"In the daylight?" Humberton queried, from the doorway of the third room he had explored.

THE butler scratched his closely cropped gray head. "Mostly at night, sir. Sometimes in daylight, but it was on dull, dark days, when the house was in a kind of twilight, as you might say, sir."

"What other little things?" Clyde inquired.

"Well, he'd groan and talk to himself, sir. I don't like a man to do that. It gives you the creeps. He never used to do it. And he'd got a lot sharper lately—almost bad-tempered, though I say it with proper respect. Little things again, sir. Just the other day, I was going down cellar to bring up a bottle of wine for his dinner—we have an excellent cellar, sir, all pre-war stuff—and he said to me, 'Where are you going, Lurdle?' When I told him, he flew at me like—like a tiger, sir. 'I'll have you understand that I am not a drunkard,' he said. 'I resent your taking it for granted that I require liquor. Hereafter, you will go into the wine cellar only on my orders.'"

"Was he a heavy drinker?" the detective asked.

"Not at all, sir. For weeks at a time he would take nothing. I have brought the same bottle up a dozen times and returned it to the cellar, without having had to draw the cork."

"Any other little thing?"

"Nothing that occurs to me at present, sir," was the staid reply.

"Then if you've seen all you want to, Ho, suppose we go down a story. There ought to be more to look at on the lower floors."

"First, come into this room at the rear," requested the necrologist. "Bring your flashlight—and bring Lurdle."

"Now, Lurdle," he went on when they were assembled in the bare, narrow room. "I wish you to look through this window. You will see a house with a mansard roof, facing on the next street."

The butler bent his tall figure, obediently. "Your own establishment, if I am not mistaken, sir," he suggested.

Humberton nodded. "Is there any other window from which you can see it?" he inquired.

"I believe not, sir. This is the only window on the north side of the third floor. The second-story windows would not be high enough."

"Lurdle, so far as you know, has any dead body been in this room recently?"

The fat butler's start was real. His pendulous cheeks sagged. For a moment his jaw seemed to drop. "A dead body, sir?" he repeated. "No, indeed, sir!"

"Very well. That is all I wish to ask."

They descended to the second floor accompanied by the puzzled butler, and here Humberton became an art connoisseur, passing rapidly from picture to picture hung along the hallway, and applying to Lurdle for confirmation of his views.

"Where is the Titian, Lurdle," he inquired; "the one Sir Michael Denton commented on last year?"

The fat butler's expression became cherubic. "I am glad to hear you inquire about that, sir," he said, cordially. "So many gentlemen don't know art. And this is an art treasure. Mr. Rance always used to say so, sir. We keep it in a room by itself, with electric lights which were installed especially for it. It's the next room to the library. This way, sir."

In his eagerness he almost hurried to the room, opened the door with a benevolent sweep of his arm, and stood back expectantly. Humberton, however, first glanced into the library. The body of Rance was gone. Spang sat reading in a Turkish rocker. His chief turned without speaking, and followed by Clyde, stepped into the next room.

"The 'Portrait of Doge Gilberto', sir," intoned the butler.

"How much is it worth?" Clyde demanded, looking without emotion at the painting of a white-bearded old man perusing a scroll in the shade of a tree.

The butler replied in a reverent whisper: "At least a hundred and fifty thousand dollars, sir! I know, because a gentleman from Australia was here less than a month after Sir Michael. He offered that amount, but Mr. Rance refused to sell."

"Is it insured?"

"Yes, indeed, sir."

LURDLE had turned on the electric lights above the painting. They brought out the luminous depth of the shadows and made the seamed yet benignant face of the old man startlingly lifelike. Even the straw-and-twig structure of a bird's nest, tucked into an angle of the limbs near the top of the tree, stood out distinctly on the side nearest the trunk, though on the other it blended with the soft Italian background.

The detective shook his head with a sigh. "A hundred and fifty thousand berries—and he refused it! And only two servants in the house! What a pipe for a high-class crook! Of course, you and I know, Ho, that paintings like this aren't stolen once in a generation—they're too hard to dispose of without detection—but think of the opportunity if a man was willing to take a chance!"

"The sight of that bird's nest reminds me," Humberton put in. "What was the name of the girl who disappeared?"

"Minnie Blake, sir," the butler volunteered.

"Something about a bird was connected with that case. I'm sure of it!"

The butler bowed. "Your recollection is entirely correct, sir. It was not a real bird, however. You may recall that Minnie Blake was weak-minded—poor girl! Well, she seemed to get it into her head one day that there had been a bird in that nest in the picture——that painted nest, sir—and that it had flown away. I might tell you that she was particularly fond of the Titian. Odd, is it not, sir, that a girl of low mentality should show such good taste? I have known her to spend an hour before it, just gazing. But after this odd notion struck her, she used to go about the house crying to herself and saying, over and over, 'The little bird is gone from the nest! The little bird is gone from the nest!' It was most annoying, sir. It got on Mr. Rance's nerves terribly, though he was too kind-hearted to give her the sack."

Humberton nodded, with satisfaction. "That's it. I recall perfectly now. The point was brought out in one of the newspapers at the time of her disappearance. I suppose you never learned what she meant, Lurdle?"

"I don't believe she meant anything, sir. That was the master's view. As he said to me, 'There's the picture and there's the nest. If any birds are in it they are not visible. So how can one of them have flown away?' And anyway, as he used to say, painted birds don't fly. It was just her poor mind, sir."

"When did she get this notion?" the necrologist pursued. "Was it before Sir Michael passed on the picture?"

"After that, I think, sir."

"Before the Australian made his offer?"

Lurdle's fat chin creased into two double chins in his effort to recollect. "After that, too, sir, I believe—but not very long after."

"Oh, well." Humberton shrugged his shoulders. "Unless you have further business on this floor, Clyde, we may as well go downstairs. I am particularly anxious to look at the wine cellar."

Clyde was an easy man for Humberton to work with. On investigations of this sort he always yielded to his friend's eccentric and sometimes sketchy methods, even though he might return later to make a more thorough examination on his own account.

"The cellar, Lurdle," he directed.

"Very good, sir. The steps go down from here."

CLYDE had unlimbered his flashlight, but he soon put it back. It was not needed. Lurdle touched a switch when they reached the extensive cellar, and it blazed with light. Humberton stood on the lowest step, blocking the way for the genial detective, and regarded this phenomenon with interest.

"Why so much light, Lurdle?"

"Mr. Rance's wishes, sir. He installed this system within the past year. I remember he told me that a cellar ought to be the most brightly illuminated part of the house, because everything else was built upon it."

Clyde snorted. "What in hell did he mean by that?" he demanded.

"I haven't the least idea, sir. As I have said, the master was just a little odd lately. One didn't like to ask him to explain himself, sir."

Humberton's interest in the cellar, now

that he was there, seemed perfunctory. He walked about the extensive cement floor, glanced at the furnace, and at a neatly piled supply of wood beyond it, favored the stationary washtubs with a slightly closer examination, and at length pulled vigorously at a locked door at the nearer end.

"I forgot to mention, sir," the butler put in, hastily; "only last week, Mr. Rance made me give him the key to the wine cellar. To tell the truth, sir, I felt rather hurt."

"Then you have no key?"

"No, sir."

"I can fix that in a hurry, Ho," Clyde suggested. "Probably the key is on Rance, but this'll be quicker."

He picked up the heavy furnace shaker, eyed the lock for a moment, and struck it one well-placed, shattering blow.

"There are no lights in the wine cellar, sir," volunteered the butler. "We used to have two in there, but Mr. Rance transferred them to the main part of the cellar when he had this other change made. He said wine kept better in the dark."

"That's all right." Clyde tugged at the door, and the split lock parted. "What have we got flashlights for, eh, Ho? Well, I'll be—"

The necrologist pushed in behind him. Clyde's first inquiring sweep of the light had caught the most significant feature of the fragrant basement room.

"He's been digging in here!" was the detective's amazed comment.

"Let me have the light." Humberton directed it first at the long narrow excavation, with a pile of yellow soil beyond it, at one side of the wine cellar; then at the rows of bottles looking down at them from shelves which climbed higher than their heads; then at the dark dirt floor. Finally, he walked up to the hole in the ground and shot the brilliant beam into it. "A grave," was his verdict; "an

open, unoccupied grave. You can bandage up your wounded feelings, Lurdle. This is why he took the key from you."

The butler's deep voice broke in a heavy sob. "Then he must have killed himself, sir. He was digging his own grave!"

The tall necrologist smiled. "You think so? Well—everyone to his own theories! Tomorrow I shall try to find the little painted bird!"

CHAPTER FOUR

The Little Bird is Gone

DETECTIVE CLYDE pushed his cap back from his forehead, and his normally humane face assumed an almost vindictive expression. He stood across Humberton's office table from his friend, who remained seated, busily writing on a telegraph blank.

"I suppose you've seen the morning papers, Ho?" he inquired.

The necrologist shook his head.

"Well, it seems this is another gang murder—another one the police are going to muff. The Clarion suggests that if I don't get on the job pretty soon I mustn't be surprised if respectable citizens take matters into their own hands. But what amuses me is this—" Clyde grinned without relaxing his tone of indignation, "I've picked up Pobedoff so quietly that not one of them has tumbled yet to his arrest. That's one on them. You haven't put them wise, I suppose?"

"I have declined to talk to reporters."

"That's that! Now let me tell you something. I don't pretend to be infallible. I've made enough mistakes myself, and seen enough of them made, to be as modest as anyone. But when I come across a man with a Russian name, who looks and talks like a college professor, yet keeps a cigar store—"

"You feel that he must be a murderer."

Humberton pulled the telephone toward himself over the smooth surface of his work table, and murmured a number into the transmitter.

"Well, not exactly that." Clyde grinned again. He could not remain ill-tempered for long at a time. "You haven't heard the half of it yet, Ho. Suppose I tell you that two of the bullets in Rance's body came from that gun which we found on the floor beside him, and that Pobedoff's finger prints are on the gun?"

"And the crime—has be confessed to that?" The necrologist finished his message, read it over slowly, and enclosed the blank in an envelope.

"He will. Take that as a prophecy, if you like, and remember it when I report to you a few hours from now. He's weakening fast. We're going to get this whole thing from him. By the way, Ho, did he tell you anything about his business relations with Rance?"

"Only that he sold him cigars."

"He told me that, too. I saw Lurdle early this morning, and learned that Rance smoked nothing but cigarettes. Just a little slip, which Master Pobedoff will have difficulty in explaining! Now I'm off again. Found your little bird yet?"

"I am cabling to Australia about the little bird," Humberton returned. "The name of the Australian who visited Rance some time ago is Patrick Trigal, and he lives in Melbourne. Newspapers are excellent institutions, Clyde. The Plain Dealer dug this information up for me, and promised to keep my asking for it a secret, for the present. By the way, can I get into the Rance house?"

"There's a policeman in charge. He'll let you in. I am detaining Lurdle at headquarters as a material witness. When the maid shows up we'll make a house guest of her, too."

Humberton nodded. "No doubt I shall drop in there this afternoon. My morning will be taken up with visits to art stores, and possibly to the public library. I expect to get track of my little bird in that way, and then I must visit the Rance house again."

"Righto! See you later, Ho." Clyde left, shutting the courtyard door briskly behind him, but immediately looked in again, with a grin. "If you don't find it in the art stores or library, why not try a bird store?" he suggested.

HUMBERTON did not trouble to reply. He had relapsed into meditation from which Clyde's second shutting of the door failed to rouse him. He merely glanced up when the messenger boy entered, some minutes later, and pushed the envelope toward him mechanically.

"To be sent by your fastest way and reply rushed to me," he directed. "If no one is here, get in touch with Detective Clyde, and he will find me."

For ten minutes longer he remained motionless with closed eyes. Then his finger slid down the telephone dial again.

"Clyde? Has your man confessed?"

"Not quite, Ho, but—"

"Where was the pool of blood in Rance's study?"

"By his head. You don't think—"

"I saw none from the body wounds. Did you?"

The detective's voice was hesitant. "No-o-o—" he began.

"I advise you to have a talk with the coroner. And when you have had it—"

"Yes?" Cyde's tone was thoughtful and distinctly respectful.

"Try the effect of asking Pobedoff why he fired two bullets into a man who was already dead."

Humberton replaced the receiver, put on his hat and walked down the hall of the funeral parlors. He found Spang eating a belated breakfast in a spare room at the rear, which was used for a kitchen.

"Any more visits from reporters, Ted?" he inquired.

The senior hearse driver juggled half a fried egg into his mouth, by dexterous manipulation of a table knife, and looked up with a grin. "The reception room is alive with them. Are you going out, sir?"

"I am likely to be out all morning—on a walking tour. Tell the reporters I have nothing to give them, as yet."

But his mission took more than the morning. By the middle of the afternoon he had exhausted the pubic library's resources and had worked through the principal art stores to their more obscure competitors, without finding what he sought. It was nearly closing time when, from a grimy little uptown shop, he telephoned Clyde.

The big detective's voice was exuberant. "See the papers, Ho?" he demanded.

Humberton returned a rather curt negative.

"Then you're missing a real thrill. Pobedoff has confessed! Not only that, but it is a gang killing, after all. For once, the papers took a wild shot and hit the bull's eye. Rance was put on the spot."

"You have the gun that killed him—the one which fired a bullet into his brain?"

"Pobedoff threw it into the river. He told me where, and I'm having the river dragged. You remember that bullet which went through the picture into the wall? Well, he had a run-in with Rance once before. Rance took a pot-shot at him and missed. Pobedoff got Rance's gun away from him then, so he had two guns when he actually put the old man on the spot. He became excited and dropped one of them. They always slip somewhere, Ho—darned if they don't! Going to call it off now, I suppose?"

"I have not yet found the little bird," the necrologist returned, enigmatically.

"Unless I do find it soon I shall be obliged to leave for New York tonight. What reason does Pobedoff give for firing two bullets into a dead man?"

A shade of hesitation was noticeable in Clyde's reply. "To tell you the truth—I forgot that point when I questioned Pobedoff," he admitted.

The old man——a dried husk of an old man with an ear trumpet—who ran the little shop, was hovering at the necrologist's elbow, waiting for the telephoning to be done.

"It was Titian you said you were interested in, sir? I have some portfolios here. Quite old. Portfolios of old masters have their vogue, like everything else. These are sadly out of the vogue, I fear—you are not likely to find them at all in the bigger shops. Still, it might be worth your while—"

The light was poor—a single dangling carbon bulb in the dark back room of the little shop. Humberton was about to bring the portfolios to the light of the street window when he discovered that there no longer was anything of the sort. Evening of a cloudy day was at hand. He returned to the ineffectual bulb and began a search through the pictures.

There were three portfolios. The fifth picture in the second one was that of Doge Gilberto.

SOME hours later—having supped meanwhile—Humberton and his versatile hearse driver drew up in the big sedan before the Rance place.

The avenue on which the old mansion fronted was dark, except for occasional street lights. It was a thick evening, however; a light mist already had begun to drift in from the winding Cuyahoga, and stronger lights than those would have had little authority. Humberton walked up the steps, Ted Spang just behind him. He expected to find a policeman in charge. Yet the sudden appearance of the latter, who seemed to separate himself from the darkness at the top of the steps, took the necrologist slightly by surprise.

"Beg your pardon, sir. Didn't know you till you near ran into me. I'm Kennedy. You want to go in, I suppose?"

"Why have you no lights in the house, Kennedy?"

The policeman's hoarse voice dropped to a confidential growl. "There's someone about, sir."

Kennedy had unlocked the front door and pushed it open. Humberton stopped at the threshold. "What do you mean?" he demanded.

"I've seen him twice. Better come inside where we won't be spied on. He's trying to get into the house. You know, sir, there's a sort of walk on both sides of the place, and a little yard behind it. I saw him once in that yard. The second time he was here in front just as I come around the side, and that time I heard his footsteps but I can't rightly say I saw him. You see, there's more light in back than here, because of the way one of the lamps on the next street shines into the yard. That's all, sir, but I'm keeping a mighty close watch."

"Did you challenge him?" the necrologist inquired.

"I did not, sir. I thought maybe, I might have a chance to get him by the heels a little later on."

"Quite right. If you catch him I should like to be notified. You can find me through Clyde, if I am gone from here."

"Very good, sir."

"Ted and I will carry on our investigations- by flashlight, so the house will still be dark."

Humberton had Ted's flashlight in his right hand, the print of "Doge Gilberto" in his left. He led the way up the broad staircase.

"The room next to the one where the body was found, Ted," his chief announced. He noticed suddenly that the

driver had stopped halfway up the stairs. "You are not nervous?"

Spang came on. "Just fancied I heard something moving, sir. Rats, likely enough. You never know what you'll hear in an old house like this."

Humberton was about to grunt an impatient reply to this reflection, as he continued down the hall, when he too stopped abruptly. "I must telephone Clyde," he said. "Suppose you hold the light, Ted, while I do so."

THE phone was in the library—in which Rance's body had been found. Clyde was a glutton for long hours. His friend expected to find him at headquarters, and so he was.

"Heard the latest, Ho? The papers have a new song now. Since Pobedoff confessed himself a gangster, they're beginning to ride the courts. You know the racket—'An Outraged Citizenry Demand Justice, Not Mercy.' It's O. K. with me. I can stand to see them ride somebody else for a change."

"Has the girl come back?" Humberton interrupted.

"The crazy girl?"

"The servant who was given leave of absence and who is due back today, according to Lurdle."

Clyde laughed. "Beg pardon, Ho. I'd forgotten her for the minute. But we've been on the lookout. She hasn't come to the house and we have no track of her yet. I suppose she reads the papers."

The necrologist hung up, thoughtfully took the flashlight from Spang again, and walked slowly to the room next the library, where the Titian reigned supreme. He pulled the chains which controlled the picture's special illumination. The figure of the old man reading beneath the tree, with the Italian landscape in the distance, was flooded with light. Elsewhere, the room remained in darkness.

"Pull down the blind, Ted. We must

not interfere with Kenedy's trap. He may stumble on to something."

With little regard for the sanctity of antiques, Humberton mounted an upholstered chair and held his microscope close to the painting. He unrolled the print he had bought, and examined that, too, with the aid of the powerful electric bulbs above the Titian.

"Your eyes are good, Ted. Look without the aid of this glass at the spot I indicate on the painting—the nest in the tree."

"I see is very clearly, sir."

"Now take the microscope and examine the same place on the print."

Spang obeyed. He referred again to the painting, then held the lens once more above the print. Presently he looked up, with a grin.

"Now that's an odd thing. As sure as I live there's a bird in the nest on the print. You can see her wing. But if that nest in the painting on the wall ain't empty, I'll eat it. What do you make of it, Mr. Humberton?"

"The print is old. It was taken from the original painting," his employer returned.

Spang stared a moment, and his lips slowly puckered into a long-drawn whistle. "Are you telling me that the painting on the wall is a fake?" he inquired.

" 'The little bird is gone from the nest!' " Humberton quoted, enigmatically. "Gone because a superb imitation, precise in every detail except for that one curious slip, was substituted for the original! The half-witted girl knew the painting perfectly because she loved it. She noticed the change in the nest—but never understood the reason. I begin to think we are nearing the end of the case, Ted, though perhaps I am mistaken. After all, it is not much more than a hunch. I shall take a minute to instruct Policeman Kennedy—who seems intelligent—to let his visitor

effect an entrance and not to arrest him too soon; then we will go to see Pobedoff, in his cell."

CHAPTER FIVE

Lynch Law

THEY had reached the main hall again when upstairs the telephone began ringing. Humberton halted within a few steps of the street door.

"Get it, Ted," he said, tersely.

Spang was up the stairs, two at a time. The circle of his flashlight zigzagged before him. In a moment his rather high-pitched voice floated down. "Western Union for you, Mr. Humberton."

As the necrologist hastened upward, helped by Spang's light from above, he offered a brief but caustic commentary on second-floor telephones not equipped with ground-floor extensions. Once actually at the receiver, however, and listening to the gradually unfolded message, his vexation gave way to amazed delight.

"Ted!" he cried, excitedly, hanging up. "The newspapers! They have done what I couldn't possibly have done! I have just listened to a day letter from a man in Chicago. He saw the news account of Rance's death. He wires to say that he was on the point of closing a deal with Rance for 'Doge Gilberto'."

Spang whistled. "The fake painting, sir?"

"I was expecting a cable from Australia. But I did not expect this telegram. If the Australian cable contains what I believe—"

The telephone interrupted.

"I'll take it, Ted." In the yellow circle of the flashlight, Spang saw his master smiling broadly. "If this is the cable, it will be a coincidence. Yet not so much so. There has been time—"

He picked up the receiver. Spang kept the light on him and waited breathlessly.

Again he saw an unwonted smile broaden on his chief's face. At length Humberton leaned back in his chair at the telephone table, as the receiver clicked on its hook, and indulged in a silent laugh.

"It was from Australia." Humberton's laugh became audible. To the driver, accustomed to his employer's almost invariable reserve, there was something uncanny about it. "Mr. Patrick Trigal, of Melbourne, bought the Titian for a hundred and fifty thousand dollars. He has it now in his private gallery. A confidential condition of the sale was that he should keep the purchase secret for ten years."

"Why should he do that?" Spang inquired, out of the dark.

"No doubt he is a genuine collector. There are such, Ted. There are men to whom the joy of possession is everything. I think I understand Mr. Trigal. And I understand Rance's reason for the request. Ten years is a long time. Australia is on the other side of the world. If he could sell his excellent copy of the 'Doge' as an original he could make double money, and his chances of escaping any ultimate penalty would be quite good."

"But it's a fake. The Chicago man—"

"No doubt he was relying on Sir Michael Denton's word—which applied to the original painting. The purchaser would be quite unlikely to observe for himself—that 'the little bird had flown from the nest'." Rance had an excellent reason for getting the half-witted girl out of the way. What she was saying as she went about the house was dangerous to him. She stood between him and a fortune. You see that?"

"Yes, but—"

"There was an old bullet in the wall. It might have been fired about the time she disappeared. Rance was killed by a bullet from the same gun. Pobedoff says he shot Rance and threw the gun into the river, but if so why did he pump two bullets, from another gun, into Rance's body some time after Rance had died? You are following?"

"Y-e-s, sir," the driver maintained, manfully.

"You saw the grave down cellar—the open grave. Is it very deep?"

Before there could be a reply to this last question, a confused noise came from the street. Spang rushed to the window. "Mr. Humberton! Quick!"

TWO cars had drawn up to the curb. Both were filled with men. A man in the tonneau of the front car stood up. It was an open touring type, with the top down. As he rose, someone else opened the door, and a light was switched on; not a strong light, but strong enough to show the pale countenance of a man with a rope around his neck, who was being forced to his feet.

A deep, powerful voice, hoarse with excitement, carried clearly even through the closed window behind which Humberton and Spang watched.

"Have a look! We can't hang you here. Some fool would come along and cut you down. Have a look at the place where you did it! Then you're going for a ride, you dirty gangster, the way you've taken plenty of others."

"Come on, Ted!"

"It's Pobedoff. They've got him out of jail to lynch him!"

Humberton bumped into the telephone table and upset both table and phone. The echoes of the crash followed him into the hall. Going down the stairs, the driver passed him. Yet they were almost neck and neck when Spang wrenched open the broad front door.

A revolver barked outside. One of the men in the rear car brought his flashlight beam across the face of Policeman Kennedy, rushing forward across the sidewalk, his gun still smoking. Humberton and Ted Spang were on the top step when they saw this. They had not reached the bottom one before Kennedy was garroted from behind, and forced, kicking and swearing, into the second machine. With a snort and a vomit of pungent exhaust smoke it lurched forward to follow the first car, already roaring up the street.

"We must follow them, Ted!"

Spang seemed to open the door and slide behind the wheel all in one move. His chief tripped, getting in at his side. Ted's hand gripped his collar and almost lifted him in, with the car in motion.

"They mustn't lose us!" Humberton gasped.

"They won't, sir."

The two cars ahead were driven not merely with wild speed but with skill. At the first crossing they crashed a red light. The opposing traffic was heavy, yet they both got through. The second won clear only by jumping the curb and rounding a telephone pole.

"Shall I crash the light, too?" Spang shouted.

"Yes," his employer returned, grimly.

But the light changed at the critical moment.

They gained a little in the next block when both cars slowed suddenly, with screaming brakes, to avoid a machine which came composedly out of an alley. Spang had time to swerve without cutting speed. At the next street—a quieter thoroughfare without traffic lights—the cars turned right. A siren shrilled, somewhere in the distance.

"Police cars," the necrologist diagnosed.

"Running by on another street," Spang agreed. "Now if they should look this way when they cross—"

But the two cars jack-knifed to the left after one short block. Spang gave the wheel a mighty wrench and followed.

"They're clever boys," he muttered. "They gave the police the slip that time. We've got new tires, but they won't stand too many twists like that. I wonder—"

He was interrupted by a sharp report from the second of the two cars ahead. Humberton instinctively ducked. But his driver chuckled. When the car involved plunged violently to the right and smashed to the curb as they passed, he laughed aloud.

"That's what I was wondering, whether their tires were good. We've got just one to trail now. That's the car they forced the policeman into."

HUMBERTON looked around, with his arm on the back of the seat. The occupants of the wrecked car were piling out. He was turning frontward again, when something touched him lightly on the arm. He glanced back with a jerk. It was a human hand.

"Please! Pardon, please!"

Not ten times in as many years had the tall necrologist lost his poise. He lost it now, for an instant. His startled cry so astounded Spang that the car lurched, ominously. Then Humberton recovered himself.

"Don't slow down!" he directed, sharply. "Our business is to be with that car when it stops. There is a woman in our back seat."

The machine lurched again.

"Keep the car straight and give it all the gas it will take. I will attend to this matter. No doubt she crawled in and hid when we were parked in front of the Rance house." He turned again, and addressed the dim figure in the darkness of the tonneau. "What do you mean by this? Who are you?"

"Sonia Pobedoff," was the faltering response.

"Pobedoff's wife!" The words thundered even above the roar of the speeding car.

"Yes." Her voice was high-pitched yet tuneful. It carried without the necessity for being loud. "I am—maid—Mr. Rance," it explained.

Humberton glanced at the tail-light of the machine ahead. If it was no nearer, neither had it widened the distance between them.

"Give it everything, Ted," he directed.

"Her tail's on the floor board now."

Then Humberton turned his attention again to the tonneau. Conversation was difficult. Yet there was something in the agonized crouch of the figure behind in the darkness which impelled him to learn more of her.

"Where have you been?" he demanded.

"In the house. I came back. I have a key."

"How did you get into this car?"

"I jumped in—when you started. I ran out of the house after you. Please—please—"

"What?" The entreaty in her voice grated on his nerves. He shot the word at her harshly.

"You must save him. Please! See, I am kneeling to you! I love him!"

"Do you hear that, Ted?"

The driver replied with a grunt. They were making a sharp right turn, and all his attention was required at the wheel. At once they were off the city streets. A rough macadam merged into a rougher dirt road. The machine ahead bumped on, but seemed to be slowing.

"They are stopping. Oh, they are going to kill him! They must not! He did not do it! I tell you, he did not!"

The other machine, pulled suddenly into the ditch, stopped with a grind of brakes, and its occupants leaped out. They were dragging their prisoner with them. Several flashlights in the party illuminated their way toward a wooded ravine at the farther side of a field.

Spang came to a noiseless stop, a few feet behind the other car.

"Soft pedal it, sister," he advised, gruffly, toward the back seat. "They're thinking we're shook off. If they don't

know we're tailing them, maybe we'll have a chance to save your boy friend's life."

"I will be quiet." The words came with a sob, but in a voice that was barely audible. She dropped lightly to the footpath, just behind the necrologist. Usually, he walked with dignified deliberation, but now he started across the field at a rapid, jeerky pace rather too fast for the others. Spang flashed his light just often enough to show them the ground.

"They've reached the trees. Got a gun, Mr. Humberton?"

"I have not. One gun would be useless, anyway."

"And we haven't even got that. Come on, sir! Let's run for it. They're throwing the rope over a limb!"

"Shout!" his chief commanded, tersely.

CHAPTER SIX

Fire!

THEY raised a stentorian halloo. It echoed from some night-enshrouded height and came back almost as loudly as its original. In the circle of light from their lanterns, the group turned sharply; all except one who was tying the hands of the man with a rope about his neck. A tall member of the party spat out a hurried order. Instantly, everyone slipped on a mask. Some of the masks were mere bits of cloth. Most were black dominos. The tall man had donned a red domino. It might have been a Hallowe'en revel. He stepped forward—not excitedly, but with a quiet air of determination.

"Sorry, friends, but you'll have to stay where you are. Don't try to go back till we say the word. We are doing a little clean-up job." He motioned to his companions. "All right, boys. Get it over with!"

"Just a minute." Humberton had continued to walk forward. He spoke slowly

—almost casually. The man in the red domino laughed. "Oh, hello, Mr. Humberton. Hope you don't know me with this mask on. We'd rather not be known. You see, we've stolen this fine bird from the police, and we intend to make an example of him for the benefit of other gangsters. If the officers of the law can't clean this town up, we will."

"By hanging an innocent man?"

"Innocent?" Three men had begun to pull on the rope. It was tightening. The girl, just behind Humberton, was sobbing quietly, but she had not spoken. Rather, she was listening desperately to the exchange between him and the man in the red domino. Red Domino laughed again. "Just a minute, boys. I guess the police won't be on us right away. Now, Pobedoff—you've confessed already, do it again. Tell Mr. Humberton—did you kill Rance?"

"No, no! He did not! I tell you he did not. I know who did!"

It was the girl. She had run forward. Her arms were around the prisoner. "You must not hang him without hearing what I have to say!" she cried.

Humberton spoke—still very quietly. "Isn't that fair?" He looked about the masked circle. "I don't know what she wants to tell. I haven't heard her story—yet. But I should like to hear it. What if Pobedoff has confessed? Perhaps he did it to save this girl."

The girl involuntarily stepped back from the lame prisoner. "Vladimir! You think I did it?"

For the first time the tobacconist spoke. "Silence, Sonia!" he commanded, sternly. "I am the guilty one."

"But, no! You were not there! You—"

THE necrologist laid his hand on her shoulder. In the converging circle of the electric lanterns, he now shared the stage with the two of them. The masked company in the shadows were frozen into sudden immobility. The men at the rope had relaxed their grip. Only Spang shifted his position a little, to a spot where he could operate to better advantage if his chief gave the word for an attack. But his chief did not. Instead, he smiled about him at the lynching party.

"I'm sure we wish to hear this girl's story, gentlemen," he said confidently. "Of course we must hear it before, rather than after the painful ordeal you have in mind. Mr. Rance gave you a little vacation yesterday, did he not, Sonia?"

She nodded. The matter-of-fact question evidently steadied her. "I was to finish the lunch dishes, then go," she said. "Go—and not come back till this afternoon. I went to a movie." She smiled at the prisoner, who was watching her with compressed lips and tense eyes. "Poor Vladimir, he would be busy all day, so I had to go alone!"

"Vladimir and Rance were close friends?" asked Humberton.

"Friends? They did not know each other. They never knew each other."

The necrologist nodded. "I suspected that. And after the movie—"

"It was dark. I had supper—all by myself, at a little restaurant. I was going to Vladimir's then, but I had forgotten my vanity case. It was in my room. I should not have gone back." She shook her head, so vigorously that the dark hair fell over her low, straight forehead and had to be tossed upward out of her eyes. "Never should I have gone back. Mr. Rance did not permit that, when he gave us vacations. But I had my key. If I went in quietly, and right out again, would that be wrong? How should I know they would be fighting in the library?"

She stopped, with her hand to her throat.

"Careful!" Humberton noted with satisfaction that the masked circle had drawn in closer. "We want to know exactly what you saw."

"I did not see. How should I see with the door shut? But Mr. Rance was talking, and a great, a terrible voice was shouting back at him. I can not tell you what Mr. Rance said. I do not remember. But the other man was swearing at him, and saying, 'You want to kill me? You want to kill me? Well, I'll kill you!'"

"You are sure?" In his eagerness, Humberton shot the question at her in what was almost a whisper. "You are sure that is what was said? And it was not Rance speaking—it was the other man?"

"It was the other man. And I shall not forget what he said." She shuddered. Her dark eyes had lost their fear of the menacing faces around her. They were filled instead with the memory of a past terror. "I wanted to run in and save Mr. Rance. But what could I do? I am not strong enough to fight a man who could shout like that. Then I remember that Vladimir has a gun in the drawer under his counter. I ran to him. Oh, how I ran! He was alone. I think he asked me why I wanted the gun. I said, 'Mr. Rance!' I ran back again. Poor Vladimir, I knew he could not run."

"Wait!" The prisoner's pale face was blazing with emotion. "I asked you whom you were going to shoot!"

"How should I know what you said? I knew I must run back, to give the gun to Mr. Rance. The front door was open—wide open. I ran up the stairs. The library door was open—it was shut when I heard the man with the terrible voice. I went in." She stopped again. Her breath came in short, sharp gasps. "He was lying on the floor. He was dead!"

"And then?" Humberton prompted.

"I ran out of the house. I was crazy. I think I must have run about the streets. But at last I went to the house of my aunt. I was afraid. I did not even want to see Vladimir."

THE lame man's hands could not have been securely tied. He freed them suddenly, and, grasping the girl by the shoulders, turned her so that she faced him. His dark, cleanly chiseled features were working convulsively.

"Sonia! My little Sonia!" His thought was for her alone. At this moment the blaze of lantern light in which he stood, the pressing darkness without the circle, the variously masked lynching party, did not exist for him. "Sonia!" he said again, hoarsely. "You did not kill him? After all, you did not kill him?"

She met his imploring gaze wonderingly. "Why of course not, Vladimir!"

"I should have known it! But after what you said, I thought— I thought—" His face relaxed into a smile; but still it was a scene between the two of them only, with the rest of the world non-existent. "Listen to me, little Sonia. Then you will see how cunning I have been. And what a fool! I could not keep up with you. You are lithe and graceful and fleet, like a gazelle. I followed on these twisted legs of mine. As soon as they would take me there, I was in Rance's library—the only lighted room in the house. I found him there. My gun was beside him. You dropped it, I suppose?"

She nodded, mutely.

"I picked it up. He was dead. Because I thought you had killed him, I put two more bullets into his body—so that I should take the blame. I left my fingerprints on the gun. You see, Sonia?"

"Vladimir!"

"Do you know why I chose Mr. Humberton, Sonia? Or do you even know that I went to him? It was because he is an undertaker and also a detective. I could not confess at once. That would excite suspicion. The police would discover that I was shielding someone. But if I went to him to arrange a funeral for my friend Rance who was about to commit suicide —you see. Sonia—that would start everything—the investigation—the discovery of my gun—my finger prints. Then afterward I said I was a gangster, to make it surer. Then—"

Suddenly, Humberton spoke. His voice overbore Pobedoff's, with quiet authority. "Am I to understand that you do not know who killed Rance?"

"I do not!" the lame man said, calmly.

"And you, Sonia?"

"But, no."

The tall necrologist whirled abruptly upon the red-masked leader of the lynchers. "You have heard this man's story—and this girl's. I can add to what they said my profound conviction that they are telling the truth. Are you satisfied that you have made a mistake?"

"We are!" the man in the red domino declared, heartily. There was a general nodding of heads.

"What you have done is serious. You are all amenable to the law. You will maintain, I suppose, that you are good citizens, and that you have taken this way to stamp out lawlessness. Well—consider where the way you took led you. I shall expect you to drop these two within a short distance of police headquarters. That is the least you can do. After that, your getaway is your own affair. You, Pobedoff, will tell whoever is on duty that I have gone back to the Rance house to search for the killer, and that I should like official help. Come, Ted! We have lost too much time, already!"

AS SPANG whirled the car around, with reckless disregard for the elementary principles of safety on a dirt road with a deep ditch at one side, his chief issued a terse command. "We must develop real speed this time, Ted!"

"O. K., sir!" His turning maneuver complete, Spang stamped on the brakes with a tooth-loosening jolt, shifted gears in the same split second, and threw his weight on the accelerator. The rear wheels skidded clear of the ground. They gripped the uneven road surface, and the big machine leapt forward with a roar. The hearse driver permitted himself a joyous chuckle. "Do we crash all lights, Mr. Humberton?" he inquired respectfully.

"Yes."

"Then hold tight. This isn't going to be a funeral procession."

The necrologist leaned forward tensely. The speed at which they were traveling affected him not at all. His thoughts were racing ahead to the solution of the odd problem of the Rance killing.

"You remember what Kennedy said, Ted—about the prowler around the Rance house?" he asked.

Spang's answer was exactly what it would have been had he occupied one of this wonted spots in the morgue, instead of the driver's seat in a seventy-mile-an-hour car. "Was that the same one I heard in the house do you think?" he countered, thoughtfully.

"I think not. No doubt it was Sonia, the maid, whom you heard. But remember Kennedy is gone now. The prowler may try to carry out his plans—whatever they are."

The car lurched into higher speed. Humberton involuntarily gripped the seat for a moment. Spang leaned across his steering wheel, peered alertly to right and left at the intersections, once or twice glanced at his impassive companion.

"This is the street," he said, surprisingly soon; then— "Hey, Mr. Humberton—what's that? There's a—"

But the keen edge of another sense had made up for the necrologist's near sightedness. He leaned forward in his seat, sniffing the air, and interrupted his assistant's exclamation with a curt— "The house is on fire! Faster, Ted!"

There was still another cross street. Ted crashed the red light squarely. The big car veered sharply to the right, slowed down, bringing Ted's chief off the seat and abruptly to his knees, and stopped within an inch of the curb.

"That's as near as we'd better go, sir. The fire department will need the ring-side seats."

It was quite near enough—not more than two lots away. The sullen old house stood lurid and transfigured. Fire spouted out of its front windows. Humberton raced forward, hesitated an instant, and plunged around the side. "Find a way in, Ted!" he shouted. "We must save him. We can't wait for the firemen—they'd be too late!"

The hearse driver's sense of obedience was too well disciplined to permit a question at that moment. He followed, out of the glare, into the comparative darkness at the side. His roving eye caught the dull black of an open window.

"Here we are!" he announced, briskly. "The fire's in front. This'll be a furnace before the firemen get here, but we ought to have a minute to spare. You stay here, sir. Tell me where to look for him and I'll get him—whoever he is."

CHAPTER SEVEN

Murder Will Speak

HUMBERTON placed his hands deliberately on the window sill. Great height has its advantages. He raised himself easily on the sill, and squirmed over it into the room. But youth and agility have their points, too. He had hardly found his feet when the active Ted Spang was behind him. Ted had gathered himself like a cat, and vaulted over the sill. Since he was not permitted to take all the danger upon himself he was at least sharing it.

"The cellar, Ted!"

"This way, sir." The smoke was suffocating, but Spang put his head down and

ran infallibly in the right direction. Talents which might have made him a distinguished burglar had been sacrificed when he took up hearse driving. The tall necrologist followed, thankful for his expert guidance.

The cellar door was off the kitchen. Reaching it and finding it shut, Ted seized the knob, but Humberton's large hand was laid on his shoulder.

"One minute, Ted," he gasped. He braced his foot against the door, and very slowly opened it an inch. There was no pressure, so he pulled it wide.

With the opening of the door, the dull roar of the flames had deepened, yet the air seemed a little clearer. There was a flickering glow from the wide cellar, but no fire to be seen. Spang descended swiftly and very cautiously.

"No fire down here," he diagnosed quietly, at the foot of the steps. "Wait a minute, though — it's breaking through at the front end. See there—right above the wood pile? That's where the flicker and smoke come from. Once it reaches that dry wood—*pouff!*"

"The wine cellar," his chief said, briefly. "That's where our man is."

"Right you are, sir—I see a light in it."

"I see nothing," the necrologist whispered.

"Bend down a little. Stand where I'm standing. The door's shut, and it fits good and tight. See?"

Humberton did as directed. At first his near-sighted eyes still perceived nothing but darkness in that direction. Then he became aware of a slender strand of light, threaded into the darkness.

"Want me to open the door?" Spang demanded, eagerly. "We'll have to work fast. After that fire reaches the wood pile and starts shooting across, we're trapped!"

But Humberton declined to be hurried. "The man in there is not afraid of death," he replied. "I think he wants to die. He will defend his right to do so. Open the door very gradually. See whether he is armed."

"Keep right behind me, then," the driver whispered. "You'd better be where you can see just as quick as I do." He listened, his head cocked to one side. "There's a queer noise there, and it ain't the noise of the fire. Hear it?"

Humberton did not reply. Spang crept forward alertly. He reached the door—his chief just behind him—fumbled a moment, and slowly pushed. The thread of light broadened. The door swung inward, and they were able to look into the wine cellar.

THE inexplicable sound they had heard became clear. It was a queer, muffled sobbing—the sobbing of a man. He knelt beside the open grave at the farther end of the fragrant room, and an electric lantern, so placed that it shone into the excavation, emphasized at once the deep furrows and ignoble puffiness of his face.

They need not have been cautious about rousing him. His thought was only for what lay in the grave; except when he straightened a moment, groped dully in the shadows beyond his huge torso, and tilted his head back while he pulled at a bottle he found there.

Humberton stepped into the wine cellar. "Smith!" he said, sternly.

The man by the grave slowly turned his head, with something of the wavering irresolution of a gigantic measuring worm. He remained posed uncertainly upon his knees, one hand behind him, until he found the bottle again. He did not lift it to his mouth, but its presence seemed to reassure him, as he struggled to his feet.

"No!" he said, thickly. "Not Smith! Blake!"

"Blake?" The crackle of flames from the front of the cellar became a little louder, but, for the moment, Humberton had forgotten them. He walked over to the man by the open grave and looked into his face. "You called yourself 'Smith' when you worked for me. The girl who disappeared from this house was named 'Minnie Blake.'"

The big shoulders heaved. Though the man was half drunk, there was something profoundly tragic in his attitude which lent him dignity. He pointed with his right hand, still keeping the left behind him.

"Look down there. She was my sister. Buried her in lime he did, and I guess that's what preserved her. She was a good girl. She had better things coming to her than to die at the hand of a dirty hound like him. Look for yourself!"

Humberton glanced into the open grave; merely glanced, and averted his face.

"Chief!" Spang was urging tensely, just behind him. "Get him out of here! Get him out, quick! The fire's almost on us!"

The sodden man heard. No one would have credited him with keenness of ear—with keeness of any kind—but he heard. His left hand came slowly from behind him. It held no gun. He seemed to be struggling to say something, but a strident voice cut in from the main cellar: "Hey, you folks! Want to get burned to death? Out with you! Out!"

It was Detective Clyde. His red face appeared in the doorway of the wine cellar, just behind Ted Spang.

The man Blake looked at him deliberately, and smiled: "Wait a minute, mister!" he said.

His bleared eyes had cleared for the moment, purged by profound emotion. His left hand, in front of him now, held one end of a copper wire, which glistened for a few brief inches in the light then wriggled into the shadows behind the lantern.

Clyde's deep voice muttered something inarticulate. It sounded like an exclamation of horror. Blake answered, as if it had been spoken words.

"Think you're going away?" he demanded, heavily. "You're staying with me." His right forefinger stabbed toward each of them, in turn. "You—and you— and you!"

Clyde's red face had turned white. "Drop that wire!" he snarled.

BLAKE'S hand slowly lifted, palm outward. It held a small, boxlike contrivance, attached to the end of the wire. The hand twisted a little, and a round, white push button became visible.

"Drop it, you fool!" Clyde screamed the command. All he accomplished was to bring another smile to the sodden face.

"You must know what it is, mister! Maybe you used to work in a quarry, too? Maybe you was in charge of the blasts, like I was?" He laughed, discordantly. "Maybe you can figure what's at the other end of this wire—eh? Dynamite!" His voice rose to a scream. "You hear that? Dynamite! Think you're going to get out of here? Think because I killed that dog it pays for her death? She was worth a lot more than him. She was worth more'n all of us. We're all going to pay for it— here, by her grave!"

Clyde's reply was magnificently foolish. He leapt for the mocking, tragic giant. But Humberton's long arm shot across his body like a bar, and sternly pushed him back. The voice of the flames had jumped an octave higher. It had become a ravenous snarl, rather than a roar. As the tall necrologist began to speak, soothingly, a hot wave from the cellar caught him by the throat, and he faltered. But he went on, slowly, evenly, as if talking to a child.

"Don't press the button for a minute, Blake. Detective Clyde thinks Rance didn't kill your sister. We don't want anyone to think that, do we? You and I

know he did it. Do you know what Clyde says?"

As he spoke, he was inching forward, without lifting his feet from the clay floor. But Blake's eyes blinked with the cunning of madness. He laughed at the necrologist, and retreated a good twelve inches.

"Playing for time, ain't you? Trying to bluff me! It won't do you no good. See that little button? Watch me press it! Watch, now! Wa—"

A high, soaring laugh interrupted. Ted Spang, his voice ripping through the roar of the flames behind him, screamed ecstatically: "I've cut the wire! I've cut the wire! Look! Look!"

For an instant—only for an instant— Blake's eyes shifted, to where the driver's gesticulating finger pointed. In that instant, Spang's hand flicked past him, with the short, quick chop of a basket-ball player. The little box in which the fatal button was set spun from Blake's grasp. It had hardly reached the earthen floor when Clyde, leaping across the open grave, smashed his blackjack down upon the giant's head.

"Great work, Spang!" he shouted. "Grab his feet, Humberton. I'll take his head. You lead the way, Spang!"

"We can't make it," the necrologist gasped.

"We've got to make it! If Spang could cut that wire—"

"I didn't cut it. I was bluffing. Come on! We're going—out!"

"Don't stand there like that, Humberton!" The big detective was almost weeping with excitement. "Don't you understand? We've got to get out! Before the fire reaches the dynamite!"

But Humberton stubbornly shook his head. "We can't," he repeated.

Before either of them could stop him, he ran back toward the interior of the wine room. He blinked a moment at the copper wire, dully reflecting the glare of the flames. Then, with a curious chuckle of satisfaction, he followed the wire half a dozen steps into the shadow, and returned staggering under the weight of a box.

Suddenly, Clyde understood. He jumped into the grave. Humberton handed him the box. In a moment, the detective was out again, and the three of them were pushing the pile of earth over the brink until it covered the dynamite a foot deep.

They had forgotten the unconscious Blake. Now they were recalled by a stentorian laugh. He was on his feet, facing them. A wall of flame, blocking the entrance to the main cellar, reflected from his eyes. He turned and looked at it without blinking, then, with a hoarse shout, deliberately ran into the heart of the fire.

"After him!" yelled Clyde. "Crawl along the floor, where the air is. It's our only chance!"

Humberton sank to his knees, in an effort to obey. He was aware that Ted Spang, looking as if framed in fire, had caught his hand. Then he pitched forward.

HORATIO HUMBERTON had come very close to requiring the services of his own funeral parlors; but he lay instead between the clean sheets of a bed in one of the sunny wards of St. Luke's Hospital. The ward really amounted to a commodious private room, which he was sharing with Detective Clyde, who filled another bed at his right, and—resting easily at his left—with that dauntless spirit, Hearse Driver Ted Spang.

Nothing much was the matter with Humberton. His luck had held magnificently. The firemen had dragged him out suffering merely from shock. In the language of the attending physician, he was being held "for observation." Ted Spang, unfortunately, had broken an arm, be-

sides receiving minor burns. He could account for the burns, but not for the break—yet there it was. As for Clyde, he was burned somewhat more severely, thought not dangerously, and in the part of his body where a large man might expect to be burned if crawling on hands and knees on the floor, with the fire above him.

It was the afternoon of the day following the fire. The detective had decided that his friend in the middle bed had been silent long enough. Humberton was awake, as he could see, and beyond doubt there was much the necrologist could say which would be of interest. So why should not Humberton talk?

"It was a grand way to die, at that," ventured Clyde, by way of opening the subject. "I suppose it's pretty clear that he set fire to the house and planted the dynamite, isn't it, Ho? That way, he'd go up in a funeral pyre, along with his sister's body. Would you say I was dumb, Ho, if I asked you why Rance killed her?"

Humberton turned his head and smiled at Ted Spang, who was listening, bright-eyed and attentive, to this catechism.

"I trust that I should not be so discourteous Clyde," he replied, gravely. "He killed her because she knew too much—about the little bird that was 'gone from the nest.' He had to silence her in one way or another—and what other way was there to silence a half-witted girl?"

"That's it, sir!" Ted Spang, eager and enormously interested by the turn of the discussion, broke into it. "I can see that he must have killed her, all right. But what I can't see is how this drunken bum, this brother of hers who used 'Smith' for an alias, got wise." His voice sank. "Do you remember how he said there was a dead woman looking out of the Rance house? He must have known it even then!"

" 'Known' is too definite a word, Ted. Suppose we say 'suspected.' Did you ever read 'Hamlet'?"

Ted Spang shook his head.

"I've heard of it," Clyde contributed.

"You might look it up some time." He was speaking to both of them now. "It contains a curious statement, to the effect that murder, though it have no tongue, will speak with most miraculous organ.' That seems to me to cover the present case very accurately. This 'drunken bum,' as you call him, Ted, became more and more suspicious. At length, he actually began to have hallucinations—at least, so I surmise. From that point, it was only a step to his vengeance. He chose a spectacular finish for himself—and us—but since we escaped I think we can afford to be charitable and credit that to his dra-matic instinct." He glanced at the big detective, who lay awkwardly on his stomach. "Life, Clyde," he observed to the latter, "is a queer business."

"I've often thought so," was Clyde's rejoinder.

"An artist whose name I do not know, and who probably lived many years since, was careless," the necrologist went on. "He left the wing of a dove out of his copy of a famous painting. Because of that—solely because of that slight omission—a fraud is prevented, and two human beings are dead with violence."

"At that, it might have been worse," Ted Spang observed, philosophically.

And his chief, thinking back to a circle of masked figures near a country road, and a man in their midst with a rope around his neck, silently nodded where he lay.

The red-hot bar swooped toward the girl's eyes.

House of Fiends

by
Paul Ellsworth
Triem

White-hot lightning lashed the sky and driving rain whipped eerily about that silent mysterious house. And inside, floating face up in a subterranean cistern, was a ghastly corpse. What human fiends had been at work? What bloody hands had more than equalled the fury of the storm?

WITH the crash of a world torn in twain, lightning hurled another challenge at the deluged earth. The two men, splashing and slipping along the timber road, neither spoke to each other nor tried to look ahead. But every time the green radiance flashed out, the driving rain showed milky white, with great black trees throwing themselves sidewise, like souls tormented, on both sides of the highway.

They were slowly climbing. The road here ran over a series of ridges, each higher than the one before. Of a sudden, they came out on one of these giant steps, and the younger of the pair—a tall, yellow-haired man of twenty-five or thereabouts—twisted his glistening face up and stared ahead. At this moment the lightning again lashed out, like a white-hot whip, a mile long. The weird radiance threw the trees and the hills into startling relief; and he saw, on the final ridge of the series, a big white building, high above a somber valley. Then the night in a breath turned dead black, with only the roar of the wind and the rattle of rain on oak and maple leaves to indicate that the end of the world had not come.

"There's some kind of a joint up there, Mike!" the young fellow said, turning his face sidewise, so that the rain wouldn't fill his mouth. "A big stucco house!"

Mike, the lightning revealed, was a wizened little old man, with a gaunt, haunted face. He mumbled something which his companion couldn't hear.

They plunged on. Eventually the house was close before them, and then they were tumbling up wide front steps. In the shelter of a deep porch, the two fugitives from the night stood breathing hard, and wiping rain from their faces and necks.

Old Mike peeped stealthily in at one of the front windows. There were no lights, anywhere. Not the faintest whisper of sound reached them from inside the building.

"Dese guys must go to bed wid de chickens!" the old man muttered. "Shall we give dem a ring, kid? Maybe dey'll let us in—fer sweet charity's sake!"

His voice was unsteady, and it was more than the storm that had made it so. He had the mark on him of a man who had spent his life in hobo jungles and in cheap city flops. And he looked, tonight, as if a long course of drinking smoke and canned heat had about done for him. Every flash of the lightning showed that haunted glare in his eyes. He seemed unable to stand still, in spite of his weariness, but kept jigging about, first on one foot, then on the other.

Jim glanced down at his companion with faint, contemptuous pity. Jim was no bum. He might be a hobo, an itinerant, who would work when the mood hit him, but he looked powerful, clean-cut. And his young face was masklike, in repose.

"Probably there is no one here," he said, in a deep, easy voice. "Even a bunch of home guards wouldn't lie in bed, in a storm like this!"

He strode to the door and pounded. Inside, the hollow reverberation sounded like the echo in a burial vault. There was no answer, and Jim knocked again, and then tried the latch. The door was locked.

Old Mike had jigged his way to a window, and at this moment his chattering voice again sounded above the steady roar of the storm. "Shall we bust in, kid? This winder is easy—see, I take it wid dis!"

He drew from under his coat a curved iron, sharp at one edge, like a chisel, but with a heavy shaft. Mike was something of a box-car thief, when the drink was not too heavily on him, and this was one of the tools of his profession.

He slid the edge of the jimmy under the window, and applied cautious pressure. Above the roar of the wind and rain came the crackle of the window latch. Then the sash slid up.

The house, apparently, was deserted. The room they first entered was long and deep, with a fireplace at the farther side. But the two fugitives from the wrath of the night didn't tarry long here. It was contrary to the nature of old Mike to linger in the open, when there were crannies to hide in. So he shuffled away, along a hall and into the kitchen wing.

THE big house seemed to have been long deserted. Jim had produced a flashlight, and the shifting blade of white light showed dust, everywhere. Then Mike found a door, opening upon cellar stairs. He started down, and Jim, after a moment of silent scrutiny, followed. He closed the door, and the two men went prowling down into a great basement, with many rooms, which seemed to extend under the entire length and breadth of the house.

The roar of the storm was muted, but they could feel the vibration of it in the walls about them. They came, at last, into a damp, mildewy laundry room. There was a rusted stove and a box filled with firewood, in one corner. Soon Mike had a fire going, and was perched on the edge of an up-ended box, rubbing his bony, purple-veined old hands, and muttering crazily to himself.

It must have been fifteen minutes later that the faint tread of footsteps came to them. Jim had turned off his flashlight, so that only the red glow which shone through the open front draft of the stove eerily lighted the underground apartment. But the steps came tramp, tramp, tramping over their heads, and after a time they could hear, faint and tenuous, the sound of voices.

Jim had been leaning against a wall, immersed in thought. Now he nodded to the old man, who was plainly scared.

"I'll sneak up and see who it is," Jim said.

"Suppose it's de bulls?"

"Out here—in the woods? They don't want you that bad!"

He slid into the hall that ran toward the front of the house. Old Mike cowered beside the stove, still automatically warming his hands.

When Jim came back, his manner had changed. He moved with stealthy precision, and his voice, when he spoke into his companion's ear, was tense and vibrant. "Some more folks come in out of the storm! They'll leave as soon as it stops blowing and raining."

The old tramp seemed irritated by this news. "What dey want to come poking in here for?" he demanded. "We found dis lay first!"

But Jim didn't answer. He had settled back against the wall, and seemed to be listening eagerly to the occasional footsteps overhead. He knew, dimly, that Mike was shuffling and jigging about, looking under boxes and exploring shelves. He moved farther and farther from the stove, which still sent out a grateful heat.

Then, for a time the house was utterly silent. Only the distant wailing of the wind filtered down into the laundry room.

Abruptly, high and terrible above the background of the storm, there came a hoarse scream. It came once, and twice, and ended in clipped silence that was more significant than any sound could be.

Jim swung from the wall. He jerked his flashlight from his side pocket, and swerved the blade of light into the hall.

That cry of agony had seemed to come from the basement floor. He stood for one long moment, poised, squinting along the pathway of light. Dust motes danced in it, and as it swept from side to side, old boxes and barrels sprang into view, only to be swallowed, next moment, into abysmal darkness. But old Mike had vanished.

JIM slid a hand under his coat. When it reappeared, the strong fingers were curled round the square butt of a big automatic pistol. He crept along the hall to the front of the basement.

Above-stairs, a door opened. There came to him, as he stood listening, a man's voice, high and unsteady. "Who is down there?"

"A couple of drifters—come in out of the wind and rain!" Jim called back. "But something has happened to my pal!"

At the head of the stairs, two voices engaged in angry talk. One was heavy and authoritative. It said, "You go down there, Masters, and see what's wrong! We owe something to society. There may be something we can do!"

The other voice—the one Jim had heard first—muttered an unsteady protest. Then came the sound of feet, creeping down the steps, and the light from another electric lantern wavered into the darkness.

Jim saw that the man who was coming down was thin and tall and well dressed. He carried a tubular flashlight in his right hand. His face, dimly revealed, was of the nervous type. He wore heavy-rimmed glasses.

"Look out for that bottom step, sir!" Jim warned him. "It's loose!"

The newcomer seemed to have no relish for his job. He looked with nervous dislike at Jim. "What's the matter?" he demanded. "Where did this partner of yours go?"

"That's what I'm trying to find out. There's a door open, over in that corner. It was closed, I'm pretty sure, when we came down!"

They were standing near the foot of the stairs, in a square, empty chamber. And, in the farther corner, Jim's flashlight revealed the gaping blackness of an open door.

He crossed toward it. He heard the unsteady steps of the other man, Mas-

ters, coming on behind him. They entered a smaller room, with rock walls and a low, slanting ceiling. And just before them was the black circle of a hole in the floor.

Jim held his pistol in his right hand. He kept the flash trained steadily on the hole, and advanced toward it.

Then he was looking down, and the cone of light stabbed through the iron-rimmed opening; and down there, twenty feet below his feet, was black, oily water. Something floated upon it. Something white, with a crimson stain—the white, dead face of old Mike.

Jim said something, under his breath. The death-mask floated sluggishly, sometimes slowly sinking, then as slowly rising to the surface. The old tramp's glassy eyes seemed to be staring upward, with a terrible meaning in them.

The man at Jim's shoulder said nothing, but his teeth began to rattle.

"Stop that!" Jim told him. "We've got to find a rope. Or a ladder. Pull yourself together, and help me!"

He cast one swift glance round the apartment. There was a box, against the rock wall, at the farther side; and above it, just flush with the outer earth, a broken window, two feet high.

"Come, snap out of it!" Jim said to his companion, again.

They both whirled and stood stiffly listening. From the floor above there came a scream—a quavering scream, in a man's voice. It registered both anger and fear.

With his flash held stiffly before him, Jim raced for the door. He went through and was upon the stairs. No sound came from above, now.

He reached the first-floor hall, switched off his lantern, and stood rigid and silent. Still not a whisper of sound.

Masters had followed, driven by fear. As Jim began to grope his way along a hall toward the big living room, he heard the other man creeping at his heels. In this formation, they reached a closed door.

Jim paused, for a couple of heart beats. The roar of the wind came more clearly here than it had down in the basement, but the rattle of rain on windows and roof seemed to have abated. There was no other sound. The house crouched, silent, and ominous, about them.

Jim had dropped his flashlight into his pocket. "Don't show a light till I tell you!" he said to his companion.

His left hand crept out and found the door knob. He slowly twisted. An inch at a time, he pushed the door open.

The lightning came only from far to the east, and the pale flashes were just sufficient to show that the big living room was empty, and that the outer door stood open. Jim stepped quickly across the threshold and slid out his flashlight. He swung the light over the floor. Tracks in the dust—nothing else.

Jim turned upon his companion. "Who was with you?" he demanded. "Talk fast, brother!"

Masters was close to collapse. Jim prodded him with the gun. "Talk!" he snarled.

"It—it was Mr. Griffith—Mr. Sidney Griffith! I am his secretary."

Jim's eyes flashed. "So, that's it!" said he. "How did you come here?"

"We were going up the coast, on a fishing trip. We missed the way. When we got this far, it seemed best to turn in till the storm passed. We found a window open. The door was locked!"

Jim asked just one other question. "Who was driving the car?"

"Hazzard, the chauffeur. He thought he knew the road!"

Jim strode across to the door. The thin young man kept close to him. But when they stood above the wide steps that led to the sodden earth, Masters shrank back.

"Surely, you aren't going out—into all that darkness?" he quavered.

"Where did you leave the car?"

"Why, right in front here—it's gone!"

Jim's flash revealed the tracks of balloon tires. A big machine had driven close to the steps, and afterward had been backed away, skidding a good deal, and had headed into a narrow road which ran into the timber.

"You can come or stay," he said, and went down the steps.

But Mr. Griffith's secretary wasn't ready to be left alone—yet. He came, muttering and protesting, but sticking close to Jim's heels. They were in a wood road, with dripping branches close above their heads. And now there came to them the distant pound of wind-lashed breakers.

The road ran through the woods for about a quarter of a mile. It mounted to a high, cleared space on a bluff, and down below, dimly seen through the sullen darkness that followed the storm, the sea heaved and beat against the rocks.

But the tire tracks went straight on. Mr. Sidney Griffith's limousine had been driven over the cliff, into the sea.

Jim nodded and turned back. His eyes were narrowed, his face intent. When they were again at the foot of the steps leading up to the deep porch, he looked at his companion.

"The nearest town is ten miles from here," he said. "I'm going there—for help. You can do as you please."

It seemed impossible for Masters to decide. He was shaking with cold and dampness and terror. But after a time he shook his head and turned.

As Jim's footsteps went splashing off, down grade toward the highway, the thin young man looked fearfully after him.

"Ten miles—I never could make it! I'll go in here—and hide!"

But the house was a place of crawling terror. He went into the big living room. At first he turned on his flashlight, and the pale, reflected radiance gave him a momentary feeling of relief.

Then he feared that the light would attract to him the same mysterious fate that had overtaken his employer. What had happened to Mr. Griffith? And to Hazzard, the chauffeur?

And then the solitary occupant of the room cried out, for he had just remembered that his employer's daughter, Irene, was sleeping in a corner of the back seat, at the time they drove up to the empty house. They had left her there, covered up with rugs, comfortable and oblivious to the storm.

His thin hands shook as he crept about, looking for a corner to hide in. He thought of the white, blood-splotched face, down in that subterranean cistern. He moaned aloud and turned toward the front door. It wasn't too late, even yet, to overtake the only living creature who seemed to have come alive through that horrible five minutes.

But as he stood irresolute, his dilated eyes fastened on the outer door, something crept swiftly upon him, from behind. Something that had moved like a shadow through the door leading into the rear of the building.

It leaped, with the fierce bound of a panther. A dull thud sounded—and the attenuated figure of the secretary collapsed, without a groan or a whisper.

MASTERS came to, hours or days later. Time was a confused jumble, in his twitching mind. In the first moment, he was conscious of steamy heat. He opened his eyes, and stared.

He was tied hand and foot to a straight-backed wooden chair. In another chair sat his employer, Sidney Griffith, the banker and traction magnate. And beside him Irene, a slim, yellow-haired girl, with eyes which now looked as blue and as cold as the sea, on a winter's day.

Two masked figures stood ominously near a door. Masters saw that the room was a small one, and that a sheet-iron stove glowed, cherry-red, in one corner. Mackinaw coats and other heavy garments were steaming against the wall behind it. The wind still moaned fitfully, outside, but the storm seemed to have passed.

One of the masked men looked, through diamond-shaped slits, at Sidney Griffith. "All right, big man, the time has come for you to make up your mind. Will you write that letter, or won't you?"

Griffith was a heavy-jowled individual with a big middle and thick shoulders, and a masterful nose that stood out like the prow of a battleship. He sat with his hands bound behind, his ankles roped to the front legs of the kitchen chair which held him. There was a skinned place over his right eye, and his mouth was puffy and bleeding. But now he maintained an obstinate silence.

"Not going to talk, I take it?" said the man by the door. "Now, we know how to deal with that situation, Mr. Griffith. I should think a man of your mental ability—your scientific imagination—would see the possibilities of the situation! Of course, we could beat you with a rubber hose, but that would be a little childish. Are you fond of your daughter?"

Griffith moved, sluggishly. His frowning eyes measured first one of his captors, then the other.

"I want to say this," he told them. "I am a rich man, and I can afford to pay the money you demand, for my release. But I have no intention of doing it. If you bother my daughter, in the slightest degree, I shall devote the remainder of my life to tracking you down. There isn't a hole so dark or obscure that I can't dig you out of it, for I will spend one million, five million—as much as is necessary. Stop where you are. I sha'n't pay you a penny. Where is my chauffeur? Did you kill him?"

One of the men beside the door swore, and the other laughed. The one who swore stretched out a thick, dirty hand and grasped his companion's sleeve. He pulled him outside.

Sidney Griffith turned his head and stared through bulging, rage-choked eyes at his secretary. "They think I'll write out an order for one hundred thousand dollars, and let them send you into the city to cash it!" he snarled. "I'll see them —and every one of us—in hell first!"

The girl looked at her father. Her face turned pink. It had been white. "Bully for you, dad!" she said. "Stick to it!"

The men came back into the room. The one who had laughed spoke drawlingly. "Mr. Griffith, your little speech has made a decided impression on my companion. I tell you this just because I know it will interest you as much as it does me. We are both thinkers. The power of words— ah, words are the Lilliputian chains that bind the brute men of this world. You and I know how it is done. But—I won- der if you will go through with it? This little experiment in applied psychology in- terests me immensely! I wonder if you will go through with it!"

He crossed over to the stove and picked up a rusty poker. He removed the round, sheet-iron lid and thrust the rod down into the fire. He stood there, and the dia- mond-shaped slits in his mask showed slowly moving eyes—eyes that seemed to leer and twinkle, first at the man in the chair, then at the blue-eyed girl.

His hand went down. It was a slim, white hand, with daintily manicured nails. It gripped the handle of the poker, and drew it out.

The bar was red-hot, and little red flecks darted from it, as he advanced across the room. But he walked, not to- ward Sidney Griffith, but toward Griffith's daughter.

"I am going," he said, in a voice that was low and light, "to burn my brand on her face! I am going to do that just to teach you not to use words when you are dealing with a thinker. I know just how little they really amount to. Can all your masterful talk—or all your money—re- move the cicatrixes from your daughter's face? Can you undo—this!"

THE red-hot bar swooped toward the girl's eyes. She held them stiffly open, staring at it as if in this way she would fend it off.

In the last moment, her father cried out, in a hoarse, shaking voice.

"No—no—not her—"

But his words were, as the man with the poker had said, futile. Masters closed his eyes and drew his knees up. He cringed, fearing each instant to hear the hiss of the incandescent iron, to smell the bitter scent of burning flesh.

But instead, in the instant when horror seemed to gather itself into a single knot of pain, there came to him the crashing explosion of a gun.

He jerked open his eyes and tried to sit up. The man who had held the poker still held it, but his arm sagged slowly to his side, and as he stood there, his head drooped, his body began to sway. Then he fell heavily to the floor.

The door smashed inward, and a fig- ure appeared in it.

A change had come over Jim. The last trace of the hobo was gone from his face and manner. He held his big pistol in his right hand. He looked down at the figure of the dying kidnaper.

Then he swung the muzzle of the gun till it was pointing at the other masked figure, which crouched against the wall, dirty hands pressing against the unplaned boards.

"The show is over!" Jim snarled. "Get that rag off your face!"

The dirty hands came shaking up, and the mask was stripped away. A wide, flat face, with small, blood-shot eyes and un- steady lips was disclosed.

" 'Snooty' Nolan!" Jim grunted. "I thought so! And the other lad is Ike Hartwell, isn't it? Pull off that mask, Snooty!"

Snooty got down upon his knees and slowly crept toward the huddled body of his partner. The poker had fallen upon the floor. It had charred the boards, but now was cooling rapidly.

As the second mask came away, a slim, arrogant face—a face dominated by a great hooked nose, like an eagle's beak, and a high, narrow forehead—glared with dying hate at the master of ceremonies.

"It's taps for Ike!" Jim said.

He drew out a pair of handcuffs, stooped, and slid one over the wrist of Snooty Nolan. Then he snapped the other over the slim wrist of Nolan's partner.

Snooty cried out, and tried to jerk away. "He's dead!" he chattered. "Galloping Japers, don't fasten me to him!"

Jim untied the girl. He unfastened her father. Last of all, he looked down at the thin young secretary.

"Sorry you got hurt, buddy!" he said. "I was afraid you might—but I had to chance it. I didn't figure on old Mike's getting killed. I picked him up and kept him trailing along for scenery. The state bureau has been working on this snatch racket, the kidnaping of wealthy men for ransom, for the last six months. We finally figured that the outfit at work had their headquarters up in this part of the hills.

"So I came up here, on the tramp, and picked up Mike. Tonight he and I reached this house. I had had my eye on it, but it was just a break, our getting there when we did.

"Nolan and Hartwell were already hidden in that room where we found the old cistern. Poor old Mike blundered onto them, and they croaked him and threw him into the well.

"They slipped out the windows before we got there, and came round in front.

They had keys to the house. While I was looking down at Mike, they put through the job they were planning—right under my nose. And, once out of the house, there was no telling where they had taken Mr. Griffith—and you, miss. So I had to use Masters for bait. I was pretty sure they would come back for him—and they did. Then I trailed along, and was lucky enough to be in at the finish!"

Sidney Griffith stood beside his daughter. He looked steadily down at the two kidnapers—the one dead, the other cringingly alive.

"Did these two men handle the entire business, alone?" he demanded.

Jim shook his head. "Your chauffeur was in on it. He's been waiting his chance for the last six weeks. When you began to talk about going fishing, he told you of this place, up on the coast, where he used to go. Then, when you swallowed the bait, he pretended to lose his way, in the storm, and brought you to the empty house."

"Who are you?" Griffith demanded, with frowning wonder. "You seem to know a lot about it all!"

"I'm Belford, of the State Criminal Bureau. Ought to have introduced myself earlier. Yes, I know all about it. That's what you pay taxes for—so that someone shall know things that ought to be known!"

"And my chauffeur?" Griffith persisted.

"Is out in the woodshed—handcuffed round a beam and with a lump over his head the size of your fist! He tried to get frisky with me, and I was glad of the chance to clout him.

"Now I'll get out Hartwell's car, and drive you to the county seat. I'm sorry to say that your machine was run into the sea—to get it out of sight.

"I'll ask you to hurry. And you, miss. I've got to get back to the empty house, and haul what's left of Mike up out of the cistern!"

It Might Have Been

THOSE are sad words—the four at the top of the page. At least they're supposed to be. The saddest of all of tongue or pen according to somebody. We can't think who that somebody was and don't care very much because we don't happen to agree with the dictum and can spot flaws in it big enough to drive a truck through.

For example—

It might have been that we had listened to all the confirmed pessimists and gloomers who predicted that it was clear beyond the realms of possibility to build and market a detective-story magazine of the quality and caliber we had in mind for only a dime.

But we didn't! We took the bit in our teeth, said it *is* possible, and went ahead.

Then again—

It might have been that finding it a tough job and an expensive one to keep DIME DETECTIVE MAGAZINE on the same high thrill level at which it started we had begun to economize on quality and excellence of material.

But we didn't. Instead of losing stride, slipping back a notch now and then—or even standing still, we kept on forging ahead. Kept on going after and getting better and better writers, greater and more thrilling stories—until it became evident that far from being a dubious venture DIME DETECTIVE MAGAZINE was a sure-fire bet for any mystery-story fan.

And that's the way we're going to keep on. Month after month the thrill fare you will find between these covers is going to increase in popularity and appeal, making new friends and loyal ones. That's a promise!

AND now it's time to introduce another of our yarn concocters, Westmoreland Gray. We'll let him have the floor.

Westmoreland Gray

"It would be hard to say just how long the love of detective and crime stories has been imbedded within me. Probably since the days when I hid "Nick Carter" behind the covers of my Geography —and smuggled "Sherlock Holmes" up to my room, to read in bed at night. As early as the age of fourteen, I think, I wrote a story about a mysterious person who dodged unbidden into opportune houses, but strangely could never be found when his trailer searched said houses. I'm vague as to just how and why this man of mystery did these things. At any rate the story was never published in book form—or any other form— so it is lost to clammering posterity.

Later I realized that quite a bit of knocking around, rubbing against the world and the people I wished to write about, was necessary if I was to write crime stories that might really interest people. So I went into other avenues —advertising, newspaper work, the army, even selling at times, though, I detested it. This took me, over a period of several years and with varied and more than sundry stop-overs, from Mexico to New York City and finally back to Dallas, Texas, which was my home for seven years. This much I'll say about knowing crooks —not all I've met are of the underworld!

I sold my first story in 1927—a detective story. When I found out that editors would actually pay me good money for desecrating virgin white paper with a lot of words, nothing could hold me back. Through the indulgence of editors and the low price of copy paper, I've been at it practically ever since."

IN OCTOBER

THRILLS ! ! !   MYSTERY ! ! !

ACTION ! ! !   DANGER ! ! !

TERROR ! ! !   SUSPENSE ! ! !

You will find them all in

THE TORSO TRAP

by

John Lawrence

Beckett cleared his throat loudly, coughed twice and finally called his host's name. Still there was no answer from the man in the chair. Then Beckett walked around where he could see—

No wonder! The man's head was missing!

And on the floor lay a bloodstained saber—

You'll Find This Great Detective Novelette Complete in

Dime Detective Magazine
for
October

On the Newsstands SEPTEMBER 20th

125

Here is YOUR High School Education

Make up NOW for that education you missed and get your High School Certificate. Let these 15 amazing "Question and Answer" books fill your spare time with pleasure and entertainment as they prepare you easily and quickly in your own home for bigger pay, broader culture, and both social and business success.

You Learn from Fascinating
Questions and Answers!

This new method teaches the High School subjects you *ought* to know: Correct English, American Government, Geography, Ancient and Modern History, Literature, Spelling, Grammar, Plant and Animal Life, Science, Latin, Physics, Physiography, Civics, Economics.

Without a high school education you cannot hope to get far in life. The better positions, the bigger salaries, are barred from you. Why chain yourself to a low-pay, blind-alley job, when a few minutes of pleasant reading a day will open the door to BIG opportunities?

A high school education is the surest way to increase your earning power. It gives you culture, enables you to meet and know educated, worthwhile people.

It's Fun to Learn

this *easy, inexpensive way*—now used in 12,000 High Schools. All you do is read the fascinating questions and answers in your spare time *at home*. A few minutes and a few cents a day will bring you rich rewards. Increase your earning power; improve your social standing; qualify for *your* High School Certificate. This Certificate is invaluable to you in applying for a position or gaining advancement with your present firm.

High School Home Study Bureau
Dept. 3346, 31 Union Square, New York, N.Y.

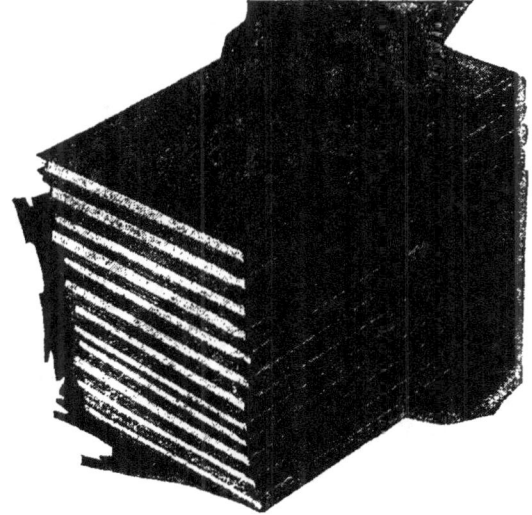

Send No Money !!

Let us put this **Million Dollar High School** in your home **on approval.** Send No Money—Just mail the coupon below. We will send you the complete set of fifteen books at once. When they arrive, simply deposit with the post man the first payment of only $3.85. Examine the books for five days absolutely without obligation. If you are not delighted, mail them back to us at **our expense** and we'll refund your deposit of $3.85 at once, without question or argument. If satisfied after five days examination, pay only $3.00 a month until the amazingly low price of $24.85 has been paid. No risk to you on this "Send no money five days approval offer." No obligation. Mail coupon below today.

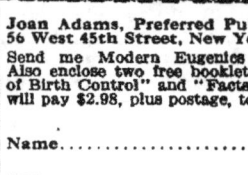
128

www.ingramcontent.com/pod-product-compliance
Lightning Source LLC
Chambersburg PA
CBHW080911020726
47502CB00008B/2420